# DREAMS OF VENGEANCE

£2

## THE THRONE **2** TRILOGY
# DREAMS of VENGEANCE
### Artemis OakGrove

**Lace Publications**
an imprint of Alyson Publications, Inc.

Copyright © 1985 by Artemis OakGrove. All rights reserved.
Cover photograph copyright © 1991 by Jennie Sullivan.

Typeset and printed in the United States of America.

Lace Publications is an imprint of Alyson Publications, Inc.,
40 Plympton St., Boston, Mass. 02118.
Distributed in England by GMP Publishers,
P.O. Box 247, London, N17 9QR, England.

Second edition: June 1991

ISBN 1-55583-306-3

Library of Congress Cataloging-in-Publication Data

OakGrove, Artemis
   Dreams of vengeance.

   (Throne trilogy ; v. 2) (Lady Winston series)
   I. Title. II. Series: OakGrove, Artemis
Throne trilogy ; v. 2. III. Series: Lady Winston series.
PS3565.A4D7   1985        813'.54        85-24241

This book is dedicated to Karen Hays who continues to make all my dreams come true. With all my love.

The author wishes to thank these patient souls for their encouragement, information and instruction:
Lindsay, Tibi, Pat Califia, C. Taylor, Lynn, Mr. Dan Otero, Mr. Neil Woodward and Mr. Nightingale.

# TABLE OF CONTENTS

## Other titles by Artemis OakGrove

The Raging Peace
Volume One of the Throne Trilogy

Throne of Council
Volume Three of the Throne Trilogy

Nighthawk

# Prologue

Three thousand years ago, in a land north of the great channel lived a peerless beauty: the white-eyed Priestess Anara.

Anara, a holy woman in the Pagan faith and ruler of a wealthy, esoteric clan of women in service to her, took to herself a lover, a young maid of ten who was known as Korian. Korian had long black hair like Anara's, but unlike Anara, her eyes were ebony and guileless.

As she grew, Korian returned Anara's love and prospered. She was instructed in the mysteries by her lover and Priestess. As the years went by, Korian successfully completed and survived the Ordeals of Water, Earth and Air under Anara's careful guidance.

In time, the peace and harmony of Korian's apprenticeship gave way to discontent and disillusionment. The fair, young lover opened her eyes and saw evil intent, greed and self-aggrandizement. No longer did she fool herself by believing that compassion or understanding existed in Anara's heart. Truth and the ideals of young love must snuff out this flame of wretchedness.

In the middle of her nineteenth year, she chose to end the misguided life of her Priestess. Thinking herself clever, Korian sought the aid of another to commit this righteous deed. Together with others from the clan, Korian arranged for a youth they knew only as Lizack from the inner city to poison Anara. Lizack agreed quickly to the heinous act, seeing Anara as her sole obstacle to Korian's heart.

All was well for little more than a day after Anara's death. Then, tragedy befell the clan. Anara's faithful handmaiden, Fila, took her own life to join her Priestess. Lizack was stoned to death by an angry mob when they learned of her part in the murder. Finally, three days later, the lovely Korian was slain in her courtyard by one of Anara's faithful.

# 1

. . . . . . . It was shadowless in the cool stone courtyard. The heavy fragrance of flowers settled thickly about Korian's diminutive frame and distracted her. She stared into the stillness of the pool at her feet and tried to forget the mourners' keen ringing in her ears. Her ceremonial headdress mocked her from its resting place on the bench next to her. She fidgeted with the golden tassle of her waistcinch. The memory of Anara's solemn funeral procession haunted her. Yes, she was High Priestess now and had done her duty. None of the townspeople suspected her of being the mastermind behind Anara's death, and she knew they would pay the same respect to her that was once reserved for her predecessor.

The cortege had gratefully toured away from the street where Lizack's bloodied, mangled body lay in a heap. Korian knew that littered about the body would be stones and sharp rocks. The scapegoat. Sacrificial blood taken to ease the loss. Korian wondered to herself if it were truly a loss or a beginning. She remembered her mother's warning about Anara. Counsel of truth.

A musty, sour smell purged her thoughts of the recent events and turned them to the immediate present. Something in the chafing sound of paw pads made her stand and turn toward the sound. She had never learned to feel comfortable around the massive white tigress coming toward her with restless efficiency.

Anara had raised the cat from a tiny cub and it had been loyal to her for many years. It stopped in the entrance of the courtyard, cutting off retreat with purpose and cunning.

A surprise breeze carried Korian's scent to the cat's sensitive nostrils. The air shook from the low rumbling growl of approval sounding in the ribcage of the white feline. She opened her mouth and tasted the fear. Saliva dripped to the stone floor below her giant head.

Korian was paralyzed with fear. In her mind's eye, she could see herself edging backwards along the pool toward the vine-covered wall. Her heartbeat quickened so, that she knew she would die of fright before the cat could act. The deadly, bloodshot stare in the tigress's eyes locked her in a trance, robbing her of her ability to react to the danger. Her body did not move toward the wall, did not scale the vines, did not hurl her over the wall to safety. She couldn't outrun the great cat, nor could she scream for help.

For a horrifying instant they were at a stalemate. In the next shocking breath the tigress leapt upon Korian's frail, helpless body and they both came to the ground in mindless battle.

Korian shrieked as her clothing and flesh were ripped and torn from her. Her powers failed her, leaving her helpless—completely and utterly helpless against the overpowering weight and force of Anara's agent of revenge. Time stood still. Nothing existed—only the sharp spears of teeth. Korian heard her own skull crack and all was darkness . . . . . . .

"NO!" Ryan awoke suddenly from her night-terror. She was sweating and shaking. Panic constricted her breathing. The bridge between nightmare and reality had not yet been crossed. She fought and fought to free herself of death, but her muscles wouldn't move nor would her voice cooperate. Frozen.

Slowly, the morning light filtered through the hallucination to free her of her imagined trap.

Leslie sat up cautiously. She knew it was unwise to disturb a night-terror victim. For the third time in their short period of living together Ryan had again suffered a frightening dream episode. For the third time she did not invite consolation or soothing. Leslie hushed her concern and waited.

She knew she was brave enough to ask her lover about the contents of the dream but she held back. As she watched Ryan's chest stop heaving and her shaking subside there was still something separate and apart about this woman. Secrets veiled in mystery.

Ryan wouldn't allow herself to be comforted. She denied that she needed it. The bedcovers snapped away from her, she rose quickly and disappeared into her bath.

2

Still so early in their relationship, Leslie had only the conventional means of consolation available to give to Ryan: tender arms to hold tight and soothe, a full feminine bosom, soft verbal caresses and security. If offered, they would be refused coldly. If asked for, they would be given gladly and wholly. Ryan had approached her a meager few times in search of the renewal and strength Leslie had to offer. Otherwise, relief was sought in a violent dissipation of energy.

Leslie hugged her knees and the covers to her and listened to Ryan taking a shower, then drying her hair. As with the first and second time Ryan had had this terrifying dream, Leslie refrained from giving voice to her theory about what or who was responsible for it. This wasn't the result of some ill-considered late dinner or suggestive reading material; Ryan didn't suffer in that way. The cause was as unseen as it was dangerous.

A moment had not gone by, while Leslie had known her, when Ryan had been free of the baneful presence of her enemy from beyond death.

Anara was more than vindictive, she was cruel. She was merciless in her attempts to make Ryan pay for betraying her three millenium ago. Korian, Ryan's former self, had arranged to have Anara murdered and even on this very morning, Leslie believed that Ryan was still paying for that deed.

She looked on silently as her tall, slender lover dressed with angry intensity. It was the same dream as before. This Leslie was assured of when she saw Ryan strap her holster and revolver about her upper torso then slip on her motorcycle jacket.

The subject of Anara was, at times, too volatile to approach. Leslie maneuvered around it.

"You're going then?" she asked sadly. There would be no bittersweet kiss of parting—only the troubled, violent look of torment that she would catch briefly before Ryan took swift leave of their peaceful home.

Leslie didn't know how much longer she could go on pretending that it didn't bother her. She was beginning to wonder if Ryan would ever voluntarily reveal the substance of her dreams and share the burden of their accompanying terror with her. There was much to learn and understand about her recondite mate.

—◦❖❖◦—

On a lingering, hot day, midway through the month of September, Leslie was taking a much-needed break from the ambitious project of establishing a new household. She had given up her law practice to give her new home her full attention. The sky was the severe, crisp blue that can only be seen in Colorado and only in the late summer. She didn't notice—her eyes were closed behind her sunglasses. This was one of her last chances to reinforce her bronze suntan, so the sky could wait for her attention.

In the lazy calm about her, she was drifting into erotic remembrances, calling to mind her lover and the excitement of their mutual desire. In thirty-three years of her life she had only dreamed of having such a lover. Now, as the roses filled her nostrils with their romantic scent and the suntan oil mixed with her light sheen, she shivered inwardly with pleasure.

The jade eyes that devoured her from moment to moment etched an image in her thoughts: the eyes of her lover. A slight smile and tiny moan accompanied her memory of the time she had tried to seriously resist the advances of her passionate mate. Her resistance had been squelched immediately by the sudden removal of the Paris original she had been wearing. An ache insinuated itself between her legs as the thought of how her dress had been forcibly ripped from her body, exposing her to the loving, heated attack of need they both were party to daily. She drifted deeper into her tremors of lust.

The air stirred unexpectedly and the water in the swimming pool lapped against its concrete restraints. Confident, purposeful footsteps were closing in on her repose. The sound of boot heels making steady progress over the brick patio took her breath away.

The footsteps came to a halt beside her chaise lounge. She did not open her eyes, but stayed in her somnolent state of arousal. Her lover went down on one knee and deliberately moved inside her small peach bikini bottom with a knowing hand.

Leslie's hips began to rock and she hissed quietly. She did not speak or in any way acknowledge her lover's presence. Her body took what it wanted from the slender fingers invading her moist need.

Passion would always peak quickly for Leslie the first time her lover touched her in a day. Perhaps the second or third encounter would find her sustaining her arousal, but always the first had a mind of its own. Her hips moved steadily faster and her breath deepened. Distant moans echoed in her mind and it was over. Her sex seized the instrument of its pleasure with pulsing contractions.

The footsteps disappeared, leaving her to recover in peace.

—◦◆❧❦◆◦—

Ryan was sitting at her oversized desk paying bills, which she disliked doing. Much of the furniture that filled her study had been her father's before his passing. She had learned to find a warm reassurance from the nearness of his possessions instead of the searing pain of his absence.

Patrick O'Donnell's portrait hung proudly above the mantel in the study and mirrored Ryan's thoroughbred handsomeness. Ryan became more like him each day. Stray white hairs were finding their way into her fierce black mane, amplifying the effect. Her pale Irish skin defied all attempts of the sun to darken it, and remained in stark contrast to the black clothing she always wore.

She had avoided the chore of maintaining her estate for all her thirty-two years, until now. Leslie had insisted that she take an active interest in her personal and business affairs and, because she could not refuse her lover anything she asked, Ryan was paying bills.

She was more than glad for the interruption of her scantily clad lover who was standing in the doorway with a satisfied smile on her face.

Leslie closed the large double door to the study behind her and walked over to join her lover. "Mmmm. That was nice."

Ryan laid her pen down and stretched her upper body against the high-backed leather chair. "What was?"

Leslie rested her buttocks on the edge of the desk and crossed her legs at the ankles. The heels of her shoes dug into the thick oriental carpeting anchoring her weight. She inspected her manicure as she answered, "You touching me out by the pool."

Ryan had never acquired the habit of keeping cigarettes in boxes about the house as Leslie had learned to do. She preferred instead to keep them in their pack in her shirt pocket. She took one out and lit it mischievously. "How do you know that was me?" She watched Leslie's perfect form shiver slightly as her golden fringed eyelids lowered sexily.

"No one knows me that way. Only you can make me come like that." Leslie prepared herself to look into Ryan's thrilling green eyes. It very often took courage to seek them out directly, so strong were their effect upon her. This was one of those times. She found a playfulness in them and she relaxed.

Ryan saw the sparkle in the grey eyes that never failed to move her and continued. "Did you see me touch you? How can you be sure, counselor?" she teased.

Leslie drew automatically upon her experience as an attorney and answered, "If it please the court, I should like to submit evidence to substantiate my claim."

"Mmmm." Ryan looked her lover up and down, scanning the exquisite tan from the strapless heels to the sun-lightened blonde curls. "The court is very pleased."

"May I present exhibit A?" Leslie reached over for Ryan's hand, brought it to her and savored her arousal clinging to the long, bony finger, then held it to Ryan for her inspection. "Is this, or is it not, my sweet scent?"

Ryan inhaled deeply of the lust fragrance and sighed. Then, nonchalantly, "I believe it is, counselor."

"I rest my case." Leslie smiled sweetly and feigned superiority.

Ryan reached her arm around her lover and urged her to sit on her leg. Leslie took her place on Ryan's lap and waited for the verdict.

Ryan pretended to deliberate for a moment before answering. "The court finds in your favor." She followed her proclamation with a gentle, approving kiss.

Leslie noticed a telegram on Ryan's desk. Her unquenchable curiosity diverted her attention. "What's that?"

Ryan reluctantly drew her interest from her lover to the wire in question. "Do you remember what Susan said about my tax shelters?"

Leslie recalled what her ex-law partner had warned against when they last met to work on Ryan's corporate structure. "She said that you needed more and that you had better hope none of your oil wells come in."

Ryan handed the telegram up to her lover. "Two of them did last week." Her voice was devoid of feeling. It was by design that her wealth had taken a sharp increase. She decided, prior to buying McKinley, the vast mansion and estate they now occupied, that more money was needed to live as she intended. Just as no person said no to Ryan, neither did the Universe. Her request was granted immediately. She felt no concern whatsoever about the exorbitant taxes she would most likely be saddled with because of it. She, a naturalized citizen, felt a special pride about her adopted country. She would pay the taxes. But her lover wasn't pleased.

Leslie shifted on Ryan's leg. "Oh, Ryan. This late in the year? We're going to have to do some creative hustling to get around this. It's a good thing oil prices are down." She looked at Ryan sternly and reminded her yet another time, "If you had been keeping track of your investments all along, this wouldn't be a problem."

Ryan never took offense from Leslie's reprimands. It tickled her to see her mate's face transform into serious attorney, ever the business woman, shrewd and quick. Ryan was shrewd herself, but hated business. For many years she had allowed others to run her affairs. The only interest she took in any of her enterprises was to enjoy the bars, restaurant and flight service that she owned all or part of. Otherwise she had spent her days in the sky. Her nights had most often been spent in bed with a beautiful woman.

She ran her hand up Leslie's shapely back, paused to untie the string of the bikini top, traveled upward to the remarkable neck and loosened the bow at its base. Leslie ignored the slight tugs on her spine. She was waiting for Ryan's reply. The dexterous hand found and eliminated the bows on the hips. "Sweet dove, I did it for you. Everything I do is for you." Ryan locked her entrancing eyes on the peaceful windows of Leslie's soul and hypnotized her.

Leslie forgot her displeasure, and her chest started to heave with the power of her reawakening. The bottom of her suit disappeared through her legs and the top slid down her front into Ryan's willing hand. She heard the garment fall atop the papers on the desk. A spasm shook her when Ryan's thin lips circled the pink nipple on her conical-shaped breast. Her spine tightened with yearning as the point of Ryan's talented tongue flicked her rigid femininity.

Ryan gathered Leslie up in her arms and carried her over to the leather couch that stretched out in front of the fireplace. She sat down carefully and laid back into the firm armrest and crackling cushions.

Together they left the world behind and journeyed to their secret pleasure palace of lust and intimacy.

"Enter." Ryan's voice held a residue of desire in its resonant command.

The door to her study opened timidly and Corelle entered as she was bid. She remained near the door and blushed deeply at the sight of Leslie's nakedness and Ryan's disarranged shirt.

Her position as Leslie's personal servant brought her in contact with her Lady's lovely body on a regular basis. While performing her tasks as servant, Corelle felt only admiration and awe of Leslie's beautiful form. When she was reminded directly of its carnal purpose she was embarrassed by her own need, and it showed. She remembered her errand and curtsied quickly before speaking. "Miss O'Donnell, there is a call for you. Miss Barbara McFarland."

Leslie brought herself to her feet and smiled at her young servant. Ryan sat up and lit a cigarette, ignoring her shirt. She tore her gaze from her bride and looked at Corelle. It was as if for the first time she noticed that Corelle was part of her household. Immediately, she saw the desire in Corelle's gold-flecked green eyes. She traced the line from them to her delighted spouse and smiled to herself. "Fine." She rose and smoothed her short coarse wave back into place with both hands.

Corelle's eyes looked her way for a brief second then swept down to the floor quickly when she saw the niveous patch of flesh between Ryan's small breasts. Ryan had never before been so blatantly immodest in her presence and it shocked her. She turned to leave but Ryan stopped her.

"Corelle."

Corelle's legs tingled every time she heard the command in that Irish voice. Her own heritage tugged at her and made her long for more. She heeded the address demurely. "Yes, Miss."

Ryan's attention once again was focused on the object of her intense love. "Bring your Lady a gown, please."

"Aye, Miss." Corelle left quickly.

When the door closed behind the petite servant Ryan laughed quietly. "I love embarrassing her. How old did you say she was?"

Ryan's laugh always made Leslie smile with pleasure. She was grateful Ryan could laugh at all so soon after the death of her close friend, Rags. She joined in with a giggle of her own. "She's nineteen."

"She's well-bred in front, isn't she?"

"Ryan!" Leslie scolded. Ryan could still shock Leslie with her off-hand comments. Indeed, Corelle was quite busty for a woman of such slight features. Unconsciously, that had been why Leslie had hired the delicate immigrant. She was well-pleased with Corelle's gifted ability to serve and respond to her needs. It was a rare relationship.

Ryan was still shaking her head in amazement. She was surprised at herself for not having seen it before. Corelle was in love with Leslie. Corelle looked younger than nineteen. Perhaps it was her round face or her ability to look alarmed, yet shy, at the same time. Surely it was the mass of chestnut hair that framed her head in careful swirls that hid its true length.

"She's here on a green card, isn't she?"

Leslie glanced at the flashing light on the phone and back to Ryan. "Yes, she's the niece of a friend of Bonnie's," Leslie reminded her spouse edgily, referring to Ryan's long-time housekeeper.

"You're certain she's that old?"

"My dear, with the trouble you've gotten into with young girls, believe me, I verified it." A touch more impatience showed in her voice. It annoyed her that Ryan left people hanging on the telephone. She, in her genteel way, thought of it as rude.

Ryan took her cue and walked toward the phone.

Barbara McFarland, Ryan's attorney, had learned to occupy herself while she was on hold for Ryan. After seeing how vast McKinley was, she could easily understand why several minutes would pass between the time a member of the staff answered her call and when she would finally get Ryan. She had been Ryan's attorney for many years and had gotten her out of several jams. Yet another one had cropped up today. This one they expected.

Ryan pushed the flashing button and picked up the receiver. "Hi, Barb. What's up?"

"Good afternoon, Ryan. Sorry to bother you, but I heard from David Martin's attorney today. He's contesting Rags' will."

Ryan pinched the bridge of her nose while she fought off the fleeting incursion of grief at the mention of Rags and her tragic death.

In spite of all that had passed between Ryan and Rags they had been close and loyal friends. David Martin, Rags' erstwhile parole officer, had never tired of trying to exploit that friendship by attempting to expose to the public any and all of Ryan's (and Rags') unusual psychic talents as well as the merciless interfering presence of the spirit from beyond the physical world, Anara.

Leslie watched Ryan's face darken as the conversation developed. She waited expectantly, on the verge of jumping out of her skin from curiosity. Ryan hung the phone up thoughtfully, oblivious to Leslie's anxiety. Leslie cleared her throat cautiously. She wasn't always sure when to interrupt Ryan's concentration. They had only been living together for a little more than three months and she was still adjusting to her complex mate's habits.

Ryan looked up suddenly and apologized. "I'm sorry. I was off again, wasn't I? David is contesting Rags' will. He claims she never would have attached a codicil preventing him from publishing his findings on her case. Damn! Why doesn't he just give it up?"

Corelle entered quietly with Leslie's gown and helped her on with it. She saw the agitation in Ryan's eyes and the concern in Leslie's and left gracefully, as though she hadn't been there.

"He was at the reading. I can't imagine why he would question it." Leslie reconsidered the extent of Ryan's tension and knew more had gone on than she knew. Her infallible logic brought her to the source quickly. "It was an authentic codicil, wasn't it?"

8

Ryan lit a cigarette and passed her fingers through her hair. Leslie shifted her weight to one foot in response to Ryan's unconscious action. It was a habit that openly announced Ryan's discomfort with a situation. Ryan exhaled agitatedly and shook her head. "No, it was forged."

Leslie sighed and rubbed her temples. She knew that if David were to succeed in lifting the court's ban on publishing the results of the many years of work he'd done with Rags, he would also succeed in ruining the peace and harmony of her life with Ryan. She was beginning to be grateful that Barbara's ethics weren't as rigid as her own. "What does Barbara suggest doing?"

Ryan stood and began to pace the room. "She wants to let him. I agree. If we do anything to try to stop him, it will just fuel his suspicions. She can stall him with various tactics that won't seem too obvious. He would have to call in an expert to detect the forgery, which he'll no doubt do. Actually, it's just as well that he is contesting at this time. It will keep him off the scent of what has really gone on."

Leslie sat on the couch and composed her nerves. She knew that if she could relax, Ryan would too. She took a deep breath and plunged in. "What do you mean? What has really gone on?"

Ryan stopped in her tracks and realized what she had just said. She regarded Leslie closely before continuing. "Lady, I don't like involving you in my criminal activities. You're better off not knowing what I've done."

Leslie tried to remain calm. "I'll be the judge of that, Ryan. We're in this thing together. I want to know."

Ryan never ceased to marvel at Leslie's determination and loyalty. "If I tell you, you'll be an accomplice to a larceny," Ryan advised giving Leslie a chance to change her mind.

"Ryan," Leslie insisted.

"Very well." Ryan walked over to a wall cabinet and unlocked it. Inside were numerous reels of tape recordings. She took one out to show Leslie, then joined her on the couch. "I arranged for all David's notes, manuscripts and tapes to be replaced with bogus material. These should be the originals."

Leslie held the tape in her hand and inspected it. She knew what Ryan had in mind and was somewhat relieved. "Should be? You're not sure?" Ryan was normally very thorough; it surprised her that Ryan didn't know.

"I haven't listened to them yet." Ryan sounded sad and anxious.

Leslie remembered her conversation with David several months earlier. She knew that if the recordings were genuine they would reveal intimate conversations and hypnosis sessions between Rags and her parole officer, David Martin. If Ryan were to listen to them, she would have to hear Rags' voice and face up to all or part of her grief over her loss. Leslie felt a pain in her heart when she considered it.

Ryan didn't deal with grief. She swallowed it and locked it away. This worried Leslie greatly. Rags and Ryan had been close friends for several years, despite the inhumane nature of their relationship. Their kinship had transcended their struggle. Although it wasn't safe to bottle up the pain and anger, Ryan couldn't be persuaded to do otherwise. She insisted that every moment spent with Leslie was precious and shouldn't be marred by anguish.

Leslie had only herself to give to Ryan, and she could see by the strain on her lover's face that she was needed. She rose to the occasion and offered her help. "Do you want me to listen to them for you?"

It was clear by the surprise on Ryan's face that she hadn't considered the possibility before. She took a deep breath and began to relax. She couldn't answer verbally—words failed her. She nodded her head gravely. Leslie placed her hand on Ryan's knee reassuringly, and stood to put the tape back into the cabinet with the promise that she would attend to the chore in the near future.

## 2

. . . . . . Sanji's hands were entrapped in cuffs behind
her back. Her feet were braced apart to absorb the shock of
the three-tailed whip that was burning her firm breasts. She
was bound by her extreme need: the need to be conquered
by the passion and Irish tyranny of her master, Ryan.

This was not pain, but pure rapture bursting from every
nerve and every pathway of her brain. The leather thongs
seemed to slice her tender nipple, when indeed they would
not even leave a mark, so skilled was Ryan's administration
of frenzy.

Ryan was losing her control, falling into the abyss of
ecstasy. Sanji's rabid screams were closing in on her sensibility, building her sexual tension to a feverish summit. . .
She fell into bed with the black sex goddess and humped
her wildly. Together they abandoned their grip on reality
and rushed to the darkness of their insanity, moaning and
screaming deliriously in unison. Ryan was suddenly and
violently embraced by her . . . . . .

orgasm and she woke from the force of it. She gathered the bed linens in
her hands and tried to catch her breath. Her body treated her to waves of
seizures that pushed her to the border of unconsciousness and created a
loud ringing in her ears. Finally, her labored breathing gave way to the
bliss of sleep.

Watching all this, with no small amount of concern, was Leslie. The
intensity of Ryan's release had awakened her as well. This was the one
thing she had hoped would never happen in their relationship. She was

familiar with waking in the middle of the night from a desire-filled dream. Dreams of Ryan filled her nights during the months when they were not able to share their lust. She was aware that such dreams were for something needed, wanted, and desired, but unavailable.

How was it that Ryan could have such an experience when the woman she loved was lying next to her in the dark night? Leslie had never denied Ryan anything she had asked for sexually. She pondered this, looking back to the days when they first touched and how the sparks of love and passion had set them afire.

Ryan was more violent and intense then, more willing to instruct her in new ways of joining together in lust. Leslie was learning quickly the art of being a submissive sex partner conquered by Ryan's imperious needs.

Ryan's behavior toward her had altered gradually and become more loving and gentle. Although Ryan made many demands upon her, she could see now that Ryan was holding something back.

Was this a dream of what Ryan wished to share with her but was prevented from doing by love, or was it of another? It was dawn before Leslie fell back to sleep, unresolved and unsatisfied.

Brigid was in the semi-trancelike state that accompanied her creativity. The real world was a place that existed on the periphery of her mind when she was deeply involved in her ceramics. She used the sensations that filtered through her concentration to enhance the intoxication of being one with her art. On this day she was most aware of the heat of her kiln. Her shop was designed like a greenhouse, open and light, with fans and vents strategically placed to control the temperature. She kept it overly hot on purpose. She was sweating profusely, as she would in a sauna. This technique kept her weight under control if her work didn't.

She took advantage of the times when Star was away on speaking tours to shed some of the pounds that had accumulated from the rich and plentiful cooking her lover was known for.

An added benefit was the low-key sexual arousal coursing through her veins and escaping through her pores. In Star's absence, Brigid would wear very little in the way of clothes. A white muscle shirt and scanty jean cutoffs accented her broad shoulders and long leg.

Brigid had never been able to bring herself to wear shorts around other people. It drew their attention to her missing leg and made them feel uncomfortable. Even Star would sense a certain embarrassment if too much attention were focused on Brigid's handicap.

Brigid had the large heart of an artist and was painfully, but not bitterly, aware of this so she only indulged in free dress when she was alone. She enjoyed the way her sweat soaked through the fabric of her shirt and exposed her high-set, firm breasts. It quickened her breath from time to time when she became aware that her sex was barely covered. After a profitable afternoon of work she planned to retire to her bedroom to take care of her arousal.

She had seen a pale yellow flower growing near the barn and was working to match it for a glaze. Many of her colors were taken from the bounty of the mountains around her farm. Nature felt good to her so she tried to return the favor and give something special to life with her ceramic creations. The door to her shop squeaked open and jarred her. She whirled around on her bench and exclaimed, "Jesus! You startled me."

Dana closed the door behind her and stalked slowly into the shop toward her redheaded prey. "Darling, just anyone could walk in on you like that. Doesn't it worry you?"

"No," Brigid answered candidly. "You look nice, but you're going to wilt like lettuce in here." She was glad she knew how to control her emotions around Dana. It was a struggle at the very least, but for ten years she had managed not to reveal her feelings for the auburn presence coming toward her. Still it was impossible to stop looking at Dana without undisguised fascination.

"I'll take my chances." Dana was intrigued by Brigid's appearance. Like most people, she had never seen Ryan's cousin with so little clothes on. For the first time she saw what had kept Star so close to home for so many years. She stood next to Brigid and glanced at the glaze in progress, then turned to work her magic on the artist.

"What brings you up here, Dana?" Brigid tried to keep the excitement out of her voice. For a decade she had longed for Dana's unbelievable indigo eyes to look at her as they were just now.

"We *are* neighbors. This is just a neighborly visit, Brig." Dana's voice was sweet and alluring.

Brigid laughed to herself. The ten miles between her farm and Dana's mountain home didn't qualify them as neighbors. She wasn't fooled by the sleeveless, taupe dress clinging to Dana's heavenly body either. She knew what the seductress was up to, but she wasn't going to stop her.

Dana's voice grew more silky with each sentence. "I hear you're finally going to do a show. How was our famous art dealer, Marguarita, able to do what I've been trying to do for years?" She smiled at Brigid's self-conscious response. She was finally able to say something that would make Brigid look away, removing her disturbing gaze and allowing her time to stare with her own fascination.

"I was ready to be talked into it, and she saw it."

"Well, I'm glad someone was able to." Dana was impressed by Brigid's physique. Her groin pulled at her with excitement when she realized just how broad and muscular Brigid's shoulders were. Indeed, the Irish artist was quite muscular all over. Her upper body had a dark tan filtering through the freckles on her glistening skin.

She had come prepared to be repulsed by what had been left of Brigid's leg after her tragic auto accident eleven years before. She wasn't. Instead, she was thrilled by the sight of wispy red hairs peeking out of Brigid's shorts. She hadn't expected to enjoy seducing her friend.

Brigid wasn't worried about the outcome of Dana's scrutiny. If Dana were put off by her handicap it would spare her the infidelity she was longing to commit. No other woman could hope to persuade Brigid to break faith except Dana. This would be Dana's only opportunity to capitalize on Brigid's weakness for her. If she didn't act now, Brigid would forever and always be on guard against it.

Dana was no fool. She would have gone through with the seduction even if she weren't enjoying it. She'd done it with other women, many times. But she was more than enjoying it; she was beginning to want it.

Brigid's hard nipples were showing clearly through her sweat-soaked shirt. The fabric was plastered to her and underscored her shapely, athletic breasts. Her chest was heaving with desire, making it impossible for either of them to ignore it. She finally glanced sideways at Dana. "What are you staring at?"

"Your shoulders. I didn't realize they were so broad."

"I am six foot, you know."

Brigid's work was refined and unweighty, not like the heavy pottery that was popular in the West. Dana couldn't imagine how her fancy kept in such exquisite shape. She motioned to the work. "Did you get all those muscles from doing this?"

"No. I got them from working on the farm."

Dana was still perplexed.

Brigid laughed bitterly. "Who do you think takes care of this place? I'm not a cripple, Dana. Star is a lot of help, but I can manage nicely on my own."

"I didn't think you were, Brig," Dana reassured her quickly. She knew as well as anyone how defensive Brigid was about her independence and ability to take care of herself. "I just don't think about you doing anything besides your art."

Brigid mentallly smoothed her hackles. She wasn't going to waste this opportunity by letting her pride rule her actions. She reached for her crutches, slipped her arms into the metal clamps and rose to her full height. She looked down at Dana and narrowed her eyes slightly. Her voice was husky and menacing. "You like muscles, don't you?"

Dana was caught off guard by Brigid's veracity. No one had ever been a step ahead of her before. She recovered quickly and formed her simple sensuous answer, then let it pass erotically over her shapely peach-colored lips. "Yes."

Brigid locked her steady grey eyes onto Dana's blue pitfalls and felt a spasm of pleasure overtake her. She decided she had had enough of the game. "Let's go inside. You're starting to fade."

Brigid felt her excitement building as she followed Dana into the back door.

Dana stopped to block Brigid's progress into the house. She turned softly and looked deeply into Brigid's eyes.

"I need a shower, lady," Brigid insisted half-heartedly.

Dana reached down with her mischievous fingers and gently touched some of the hairs escaping the confines of Brigid's shorts. "I think not."

"Sssss." Brigid sucked in her breath and let it out with a sharp moan. "Oh god, Dana." Her eyes came ablaze and caused Dana to reconsider her errand.

"Brigid, I. . ." Dana took a tentative step backward.

Brigid wasn't deterred by Dana's faint heart. She corralled the beauty with her metal crutches and began herding her into the guest room. "You'll not be teasing *me*, Miss Shaeffer."

With the guest room door closed behind Brigid, Dana lost touch with where she was. She no longer cared.

She didn't know how they became naked in bed. She didn't know how her inner thighs were able to stand the strain of Brigid's wide pelvis. She didn't know how she bore up under Brigid's solid weight. She didn't know how Brigid's splendid hands explored and caressed every part of her body. She didn't know how many ways she heard her name called—reverently, urgently, animalistically, ecstatically. She didn't know how loud and maniacal her own screams were. She didn't know how Brigid's veteran mouth opened and delighted each of her orifices. She didn't know how her excitement exploded and peaked time and time again, then swelled to demand more. She didn't know how their passion merged into one final, mind-searing, exhausting orgasm that thrust them jointly into drugged sleep. All she knew was that only one other woman had ever made love to her so completely: to mind, body and soul.

Brigid settled into the pillows behind her back and watched Dana dress with a knowing eye. "So, when did you start adding married women to you list of victims?"

Dana feigned shock at the suggestion.

"Don't look at me like that. I don't have any illusions about you, Dana. I know you aren't going to leave Del—that you want your kicks and that's all I'll ever be to you."

Dana let her breath out, then sat back in her chair. She realized that Brigid had her number, but was disarmed by the absence of bitterness in the redhead's voice. "Why do you put up with me then?"

Brigid sighed deeply as if it hurt to admit it. "Because I'm in love with you."

For a brief moment, Dana was genuinely surprised and sincere. "You? I thought Star was your one and only."

Brigid ignored the mention of her lover. "You know, I still regret the day I introduced you to Ryan."

"Don't be silly. That was ten years ago." Dana was trying to hide her wonder at Brigid's admission.

"That doesn't make me any less a fool. If I had seen your power hunger then, I would have stolen you off to some faraway land and never let you come in contact with Ryan and her kind."

The conversation was becoming dangerously revealing. Dana tread lightly. "What are you talking about?"

"My dear, I fell in love with you the moment we met but, like an ass, I let you meet Ryan. With her you got your first taste of what it was like to control a woman of power.

"The trouble with Ryan was that she wouldn't give up her airplanes for you and let you have the complete control you wanted. Then you discovered that she doesn't have any ambition. Enter Delores Rhinehart, who has plenty of ambition and will let you have all the control you want. Everybody knows Del is headed for the State House and that suits you, too.

"I don't have a chance with a woman like you except that you like to control strong women, too. You'll get tired of me and that will be it. No, baby, I'm going to enjoy you for as long as it lasts," Brigid declared.

Cautious still. "What makes you think I'll be back?"

Brigid laughed derisively at her friend. "You will. You want something and you'll stick around until you get it. My treat."

Dana saw no more reason to be defensive. There was nothing left to defend. "And you will still love me?"

Brigid's voice was turning acidic. "Always. But you will never love me."

"You're bitter."

"Wouldn't you be?"

Dana put her shoes on and stood. "Yes." She didn't feel any sympathy for the artist, but she understood the painfully honest feelings.

"But not sorry," Brigid prompted.

"No," Dana agreed in a rare moment of candor.

"Then we understand one another." Brigid shifted her weight and the tone of the conversation. "Actually, I'm glad you waited to get around to me. I appreciate you much more now than I would have before. You are better than my fantasies and I'm glad."

Dana smiled in response to one of the rare, *sincere* compliments she had ever received from a victim and walked out of the room, closing the door softly behind her.

## 3

"Sanji!" The brunette's exclamation was echoed happily by the other dancers in the locker room. Sanji's surprise arrival after several months' absence was welcomed by all of them. Three of her fellow dancers crowded around her to express their delight and reassure themselves that the young Jamaican woman was well enough to return to the rigors of their modern dance troupe.

A blonde, who had turned twenty-six shortly after Sanji had, quizzed her. "Are you sure you want to come back? It's only been three months since the funeral."

Sanji nodded her head solemnly. "Yes. I need something to do to take my mind off Rags. This is the best thing for me." She walked toward her locker and took her sweatshirt off.

Her three friends gasped in unison. Before them, exposed by Sanji's backless leotard, was a ravaged, ruined back. "My god! What happened to your back?" the brunette asked. Sanji's black friend sized up the damage immediately and walked toward her sadly.

Sanji turned around suddenly, utterly surprised. "What are you talking about?"

"Girl, there is only one way I know of to get scars like that—a whip. What was that bitch Ryan thinking of when she did this?" the black woman accused.

"Ryan?! What has she got to do with this? I've had these scars for years." Sanji couldn't understand what was being said to her.

"Years? Honey, seven months ago your back was as pure as a baby's butt," the dark dancer informed her.

Sanji shook her head confoundedly. "Rags told me that they had been there for a long time." She looked up to the brunette, pleading for help.

Everyone felt protective toward the troubled Jamaican, as though she were unable to care for herself.

"Yeah, I'll bet. Covering for Ryan probably," the black woman persisted. The brunette signaled to her out of Sanji's line of vision to let up. She was trying to telegraph Sanji's distress.

"Ryan couldn't have hurt me. She's done nothing but show me kindness. She took care of the funeral, she's paying all my bills and she's always been around to talk whenever I've needed to," Sanji extolled.

Another dancer entered, unaware of the direction the conversation was taking. "I swear, I am going to find myself a multi-millionaire to take care of me the way you have, and blow this place."

Sanji felt weak. "How do you know she's rich?"

"Get serious, Sanji. You joined this troupe three years ago and all we have ever heard from you is how wonderful the great Ryan O'Donnell is. I'm sick of it."

Sanji sat down on a bench firmly, filled with disbelief.

"I've only known her for a few months."

The other dancers looked at each other suspiciously. They were mystified. The blonde ventured forth with some compassion. "Sanji, dear. Perhaps what happened to your back did something to your memory. Don't you recall living with Ryan for two years before you moved in with Rags?"

It was as if Sanji had pulled the curtain that blocked her recollections back slightly and looked inside. Soft stirrings and sensations eased into her heart and she began to remember. Tears filled her eyes and she covered her mouth with her hand.

Sanji never let anyone get close to her, so the others could only guess what was going on in her mind. The one person she wanted to get close to was Ryan. She, who was always so unapproachable, was always on guard around her.

The gap of love was beginning to be bridged and Sanji was seeing that the woman she had recently fallen in love with was the woman she had always loved. Her voice quivered. "I didn't know."

The black woman joined in smugly, "See, that proves it was Ryan who messed up her back and probably ruined her career."

"No! No way. It couldn't have been her. You're wrong!" Sanji neared the borders of panic.

The brunette soothed her quickly. "You're right, baby. It couldn't have been. Maybe it was Rags." Again she raised a hand to still the black woman's objections.

The black dancer stopped her rancor short and benignly handed Sanji's sweatshirt to her. "Here, put this back on. If Vernon sees this, the only job you'll get dancing will be teaching knock-kneed brats to square dance. We're going to have to do some fancy footwork to keep this quiet. Don't worry, sugar, you can count on us." She helped her frightened friend up and led her into the rehearsal hall to work out. She knew that with some healthy sweat and a few good groans all would be forgotten.

Socially, Susan Benson was always easy-going and congenial. Professionally, as a corporate tax lawyer, she was all business. Because of her genius in the field she was quite often employed by the very wealthy. She was comfortably at ease working odd hours in other people's homes, but spending Saturday morning with her ex-law partner was a special treat.

Her brow was tight with concentration, but she was far more relaxed than Leslie was about making sense out of Ryan's neglected corporate structure. Scattered about, on the desk and floor, were the tax papers for the last six quarters. She calmly sipped her coffee and ignored the disorder and mess she had made of Leslie's office.

Beneath the chaos, the natural elegance of marble and lush carpeting rivaled for attention in Leslie's eye when she joined her friend. She had claimed the room nearest the attached greenhouse for herself. McKinley had many rooms that would have served nicely but none would smell of moist earth and gardenias year round the way this one did. Exotic plants spilled out of the greenhouse into every corner of her office and at times made it hard for her to work. Their loveliness tempted her to while away the hours just staring at them, ignoring her self-appointed chore.

In the seven years that Susan had been in practice with Leslie, she had convinced herself that she had grown accustomed to Leslie's striking beauty. But when she glanced up from her work and saw Leslie in a low-cut, ivory lounging outfit sitting casually on a pale peach Victorian couch, she knew she was fooling herself. No one could get used to seeing that, she thought. She admired Ryan for trying.

She looked back to her work and turned the page. Her interest was aroused anew by what she was reading. She shook her head from time to time with amazement. Ryan was more clever than she had thought.

"Les." Susan sat back in her chair and tapped her fingers on the arm. Leslie looked up, "Hmmm?"

"I thought Ryan sold Cary's to Brigid." She scanned the form again to make sure she was reading it right.

Leslie walked over to her desk to see what Susan was concerned about. "She did. In April, if I remember right."

"Look at this. At the beginning of the second quarter the bar is listed dba Cary's and it's a partnership with Rags. Fine. Then it's listed dba A New Leaf."

"That doesn't make sense." Leslie was confused.

"Well, sometimes people hang on to a property until the end of the quarter to simplify their taxes. That's what I thought Ryan was doing until I read on." Susan turned each successive page to illustrate her point for Leslie. "Near the end of the quarter, just after Rags died, the partnership

19

was dissolved. Sole ownership reverted to Ryan, then the business was absorbed into Emerald Incorporated and becomes indistinguishable from any of the other bars Ryan owns. The taxes were paid at the end of the quarter and here are the forecasts for this quarter's taxes. She never sold that bar, Les." Susan's eyes met Leslie's widened saucers.

"You're sure?" Leslie was beginning to feel her skin flush.

"I'm afraid so."

"Does Brigid know this?"

"She has to."

"And Barbara?"

"Barbara's questionable ethics are authored throughout Ryan's business affairs. You can bet she had something to do with this."

"Rags had to have known. Ryan never did anything unless she knew about it." Leslie was growing more resentful by the minute. It bristled her that Ryan hadn't told her. She took the papers from the desk and left the room briskly in search of her deceitful lover.

Her robe billowed and snapped sharply in her wake. Her heels rang out angrily on the rose marble floors as she carried her delicate frame purposefully across the mansion to Ryan's study. She walked in and dropped the papers indignantly on Ryan's desk.

Ryan had heard her lover's resolute approach and felt her furious vibration before she arrived. She steeled herself for a confrontation by willing her body to relax. She glanced calmly at the papers, then up to Leslie's disgusted expression. Her ebony eyebrow raised slightly and she turned to read the tax forms.

She needed only to scan them to know how much Leslie had found out. Her fingers found their way into her hair and she sighed. "Leslie, there was a reason for this." She looked up at her fuming wife. She was serious and determined to make Leslie understand.

"There had better be. For starters you can explain why you didn't tell me."

"You were too close to it. I could see that you would tell Star and that would have defeated the whole purpose."

"Of course I'd tell Star. Ryan, she deserves to know that Brigid doesn't really own that damn bar. How could you do this?"

Ryan didn't make an effort to calm her lover. Leslie had every right to be angry about the deception. "I was trying to help Brigid. She couldn't handle having Star gone, even if she was the one who kicked her out. This was a way to get her to come back and it worked.

"We had to take away the stigma of Rags and me owning the bar to get Star to end her boycott. Once she ended it, then there was no reason for Brigid to make her unwelcome," Ryan recalled.

What had been a stopgap effort to save Brigid's relationship with her lover, Star, had taken on a life of its own. While the furor over a popular women's bar being owned by two women with scandalous reputations would have eventually died down, Brigid's deterioration over the loss of her lover would have only worsened. Ryan still felt that the deception had merit.

"So you cooked up this scheme and Star is the brunt of a cruel, heartless joke!" Leslie seldom raised her voice but Ryan could make her angrier than anyone.

Ryan was struggling to keep her tone in check. She proceeded a little less calmly, "It was Brigid's damn idea. All I did was find a way for it to happen. There was no way in the world that Rags was going to sell that bar to Brigid or anyone else. It was too important to her. She needed that income for her victim restitutions. Barbara talked her into going along with a sale on paper and she agreed to lay low.

"Brigid was desperate and in a lot of pain. You would have seen that yourself if you hadn't been so unhappy at the time." Ryan lit a cigarette and tried to deal with the adrenalin coursing through her veins. She needed Leslie to understand.

Leslie was still too hurt to fully grasp the purpose of the charade. "Poor Star. She thinks that bar is Brigid's. You let her rename and redecorate it. She even makes some of the decisions about the direction the bar is going. Can't you imagine for a minute how deeply hurt and humiliated she'll be when she learns of this?"

Ryan lost her battle with her temper. She stood up sharply and her voice carried well beyond the confines of the study. "Go ahead, Leslie. Tell her, damn it. Satisfy your need to be honest and just." Ryan picked up the receiver of her phone, using it to illustrate her point. "Call her right now! Hurt and humiliated? You want to see hurt? Watch what happens when you tell her. Did it occur to you that the first thing she'd do would be to leave Brigid? Hurt? You can count on it. Hurt like nothing you've ever felt."

"Ryan, don't. Please." It frightened Leslie when Ryan lost her temper. Ryan had been known to turn violent and more than one person bore the marks of her wrath.

She knew that Ryan was right. She was being unreasonable in wanting Star to know the truth. If Star did find out, she would leave Brigid and that would be the end of one of the most beautiful relationships she knew of. As always, Ryan's anger made hers look foolish by comparison and she relaxed. "I'm sorry. I wasn't thinking. You're right. Considering the circumstances it was the only thing you could do. I won't say anything to her about it and I'll explain it to Susan. She'll stay quiet, too. Please forgive me, Ryan. Please." Leslie unconsciously drew upon her courtroom experience to lend authority to her plea. She could see that she was beginning to have some success.

The flare in Ryan's eyes began to dim and the muscles in her face started relaxing. The receiver was replaced slowly. She didn't speak until she was sure she could do so civilly. She closed her eyes and took a deep breath to calm herself. She gathered Leslie up in her long, powerful arms and held her silently for a moment, smoothing Leslie's soft blonde curls.

Then she gazed lovingly into her restful, dovelike eyes.

"Lover, you know what questioning my judgment does to me. I hate getting angry with you, even if you are exquisite when you're sore at me." Ryan's smile accented her fine bone structure and purebred jaw line.

Leslie did know better than to question Ryan's reason for anything. More than one person had warned her and she had seen first-hand how explosive her mate could be at times like this. Still, it was the fire they generated with their passion that attracted them to one another and kept their relationship lively.

"I wish you didn't frighten me so when your temper flares. You really are marvelous to watch." Leslie was smiling now, too.

"I couldn't hurt you, angel. You are my heart. I would never forgive myself if I ever hit you. I'd sooner tear this mansion apart, stone by stone, than raise a hand to you in anger." Ryan's tone was sincere. She loved Leslie more than life itself and the thought of hurting the magnificent woman she was holding, in any way, frightened her. Her temper was far from being totally under her command, which worried her greatly. This episode served to show her just how much work she had to do.

She didn't transmit her worry to Leslie; instead she sealed their reconciliation with a firm, consoling kiss.

4

Where did you find this place? It's so private." Dana was amazed that it felt good to be honest with someone. Brigid's clarity had disarmed her completely, but in a relaxing way. With Brigid she could be herself, not the vixen queen she portrayed from sunup to sunset every day of her adult life.

"My father owns it, though I doubt he realizes it. No one ever comes up here except me when I want to be alone." Brigid turned her attention to her painting. Her brush moved about the canvas with alacrity and ease. She doubted that hers was the first portrait done of Dana, but her practiced eye told her that this was the first time Dana had posed nude.

They had chosen a sunny opening in the aspen grove to picnic on French wine, herbal tea, cheese and bread. About them, prepared for autumn to turn them gold and crimson, ferns and scrub oaks gathered about to witness Dana's radiance.

The winds held their breath in awe and the birds of inspiration guided Brigid's hand. Nature was not jealous of the art that rivaled her own as it created itself on canvas.

Dana sipped her wine sensuously. "What changed your mind about coming out of your reclusive lifestyle to do a show? You've always been so shy about your work."

"This may sound odd," Brigid continued on, undisturbed by the conversation, "but it was Rags' funeral."

"You're right, it sounds odd." Dana didn't like to think about the horror of either Rags' life, such as she knew of it, or her unpleasant end. She was sincerely curious about Brigid's sudden interest in the outside world so she held her tongue. "Why did you attend the funeral? You had nothing but distaste for Rags. That was never any secret."

"I went to console Ryan. Although I should have known that she wouldn't let anyone see how upset she was." She looked up from her work for a moment to seek Dana's understanding. She hadn't spoken of her reaction to the stark funeral to anyone. Not even to Star. "It was pathetic, Dana. Besides Ryan and me, the only people to attend the funeral were Leslie, Sanji and that jerk, David Martin. Of course, he had to be there because he believed he cared about Rags. Sanji believed she loved her, and Leslie was there for the same reason I was, for Ryan. But Ryan was the only one who ever really liked or cared about Rags. That isn't what bothered me. I was shocked by the coldness of it." Brigid shivered and looked back to her work.

"Funerals aren't noted for being warm events, Brig."

"That's true." Brigid nodded her head slightly. "I've just never been to one that didn't at least have a religious service or a priest to preside over it." Brigid wasn't devout at all. Still, she clung tenaciously to her beliefs for herself and never imposed them on others. "There was nothing at all for her. It was spooky."

"That doesn't sound like something Ryan would do. She's a bear about details, and ceremony is very important to her." Dana was baffled by what seemed like inconsistent behavior on the part of her ex-lover.

Brigid paused for a moment. It unnerved her how well Dana knew and remembered Ryan. "That was my feeling as well. Ryan insisted that Rags' spirit fled the instant of her death and that there was no reason to commend her soul to the other side. She said that all she was doing was dispensing with the body."

"That's scary, Brig. Do you believe her?" Dana was losing her interest in posing and was starting to squirm.

"You know better, Dana. Ryan isn't like other people—she has always known about things like that. Of course I believed her."

Brigid had come close to finishing what she needed to do with the painting. There were things about Ryan that Dana didn't know and she had to be careful about what she said to her. Her concentration was unconsciously diverted from her work. "I don't really know why she even bothered to go to the cemetery, unless is was for Sanji's sake. She told us to leave her at the grave and she stood there alone, saying something. Then she joined us and it started to rain."

Brigid had known since early childhood that her cousin was what The Church called a heretic, a pagan heathen. She had her suspicions that Ryan had spoken the Old Tongue over Rags' grave and that it was Ryan who had made it rain. Raining the tears she could not shed. Brigid kept her suspicions to herself, as she had always done. She shook her head of the memory and tried to answer Dana's original question. "Anyway, I was real upset by the whole thing. It had never occurred to me that anyone could leave this world so quietly."

"I wouldn't like it to be that way for me." Dana had stopped posing altogether and was getting comfortable. Brigid hadn't scolded her for moving as other artists had, and she was grateful. She didn't want their afternoon spoiled, although the conversation was on the edge of disaster.

"Me either. That's why I decided that I wanted to make a name for myself in this life. I realize it's narcissistic, but I want people to take notice when I die. So I'm doing a show this winter and I'll probably do many more as time goes on. It isn't worth it to be so shy about my work. It's damn good. I'm warming up to the idea of receiving some appreciation for it while I'm young enough to enjoy it."

Dana raised her wine glass in assent. "Hear, hear."

Brigid smiled and lifted her cup of sun tea in reply.

"Can I look yet?" Dana's curiosity prickled on her skin.

"Sure." Brigid held out her hand to caress Dana's slender waist. "It isn't done yet, but I can finish the rest from memory."

Dana gasped when she looked at it. It had been many years since anyone had seen a painting done by Brigid. It wasn't Impressionistic nor was it the work of a Realist. It was somewhere in between. As she stared at the foliage about her body she was taken by the vitality and crispness of it. Brigid had captured the intense feeling of the autumn air that sharpened their senses and made the day so beautiful it hurt.

When she looked at the image of her body and face it shook her. Here again, Brigid had portrayed what she saw to perfection. The absence of boundaries, the seductive sensuality, the youth frozen in time. "Oh, Brig. I had no idea you could paint so wonderfully."

Brigid forced herself to look at Dana instead of away as she usually did when she received a compliment. She suppressed the modest reply and said what she felt. "I had the best possible subject. I'm glad you like it."

"I love it. Do I really look that young?"

"Exactly." Dana, at twenty-nine, still looked nineteen. "In three years, when you're my age, will you still look like a teenager?" Brigid wasn't flattering Dana in the least. She was as accurate in her portraiture as she was in her assessment of people and their motives.

Dana nudged Brigid's ribcage with her naked hip. "I hope so. I'm getting chilly. Come warm me up, you luscious hunk."

Brigid moaned from the force of the sudden passion tugging at her belly. Her nipples hardened under the fabric of her sportshirt and rubbed against it as her chest began to fill and empty with desire. Dana had reawakened the animal in her, the animal she had caged and locked away in its prime when she lost her leg.

Her stump had never been an issue with Star, but Star was that way. Finding that a woman like Dana, who was anything but compassionate, could see past her handicap, had an actively positive effect on her self-image. Brigid was learning to accept herself as a desirable, adept lover.

Even though Dana's motives were questionable, her responses were not. Brigid joined the siren on the blanket and loosed the wild animal upon her. The crumpled ferns made a soft mattress for them, making it easier for Dana to absorb Brigid's heated lechery.

Their Sapphistry was celebrated in the quaking aspen leaves about them. The dotted shadows began to pass over their inverted, entwined bodies as they fervently kissed one another's sex. Neither of them thought of anything but the consummation of their pleasure.

Instinct brought them together and played out their lust and chemistry with the same flawless purpose as the wind that shimmered the leaves. For its own enjoyment.

The shadows had grown dangerously long into the time when they would be missed before they could bring themselves to gather the props of their tryst and return to their homes.

Dressed in a dark brown, woven suede pant-skirt and vest which covered a blouse the color of fresh cream, Leslie was supervising the planting of bulbs in the raised diamond-shaped garden before her.

She found it restful to watch the proceedings, mentally imagining the following growing season and its Snowdrops, Crocus, Hyacinth, Iris, Columbine, Flax and Gypsophila blooming in their predestined order dazzling the senses with a calculated display of blue and white.

She cut short her meditation when she noticed Ryan out of the corner of her eye. She turned to look in the direction of Little Dry Creek, the stream that eased a path through the south end of McKinley's undulating acreage, where her lover was seated on a fallen poplar. Perched on Ryan's shoulder was a large, black bird that she couldn't identify from a distance.

She excused herself from her chore and walked down the new stone pathway she had designed that would one day be lined with intoxicating lilacs, but today led, unadorned, to the small grassy area behind where Ryan was sitting. As she neared her lover, Leslie felt herself hesitate. It was a feeling she could not purge from her system and came every time she felt she was invading Ryan's privacy.

Ryan had told her it was silly to feel that way because they were one— the same person. Ryan saw no boundaries between them, no separateness. Still, there was a part of Leslie that was in awe of her lover and made her heart flutter when she approached her.

She could see now that the bird resting on Ryan's shoulder was a crow, and she didn't want it to fly away when she came near. Her curiosity prevailed and she joined her lover. To her amazement and delight, the bird remained.

It was cool and relaxing in the shade of an ancient willow. The shrunken trickle of water in the stream slid silently through and over the exposed roots of the grand tree. The crow broke the quiet with a throaty comment, and Ryan nodded her assent with a warm smile. The bird hopped down to her knee to get a better view of the new arrival.

Leslie had an open mind and was highly intuitive. She knew the bird had spoken to her mate and had been understood. In the few short months they had been living together she watched with pride and fascination as Ryan grew more relaxed and centered. It was becoming commonplace for Ryan to exhibit unusual abilities and Leslie no longer found herself astounded, and never skeptical. "What did it say?"

Ryan ran her finger over the majestic bird's chest feathers. "He recognizes your energy as being equal to the dove in his world." Ryan's eyes were distant, yet receptive and warm, as she looked toward Leslie.

Leslie felt deeply complimented by the crow's observation. It drew her closer to Ryan to be sharing this special moment. "I didn't know you could speak with animals, Ryan. It's wonderful."

"I've only bothered to learn to speak with birds. They interest me and we understand one another." Since infancy, Ryan had been aware of her kinship with the feathered creatures of the Earth and at age seven had begun to learn to fly airplanes so she could join them in the sky. It was a love affair that influenced her every action.

This consanguinity with birds filled Leslie's blood too, although she was just beginning to become aware of it. It drew Ryan to her and kept her there—in harmony.

Leslie moved closer and touched Ryan's pale hand with her sensitive fingertips. "How long have you been able to do this?"

"I can't remember when I didn't know how. Except for the years I was under Rags' influence, I've always done it. It used to drive Brigid crazy. She wanted to tell my father and her parents, but I wouldn't let her." Ryan smiled at the memory of her childhood antics.

"I wish I'd known you then. Can you call them to you?" Leslie was enjoying this new facet of her involuted spouse.

Ryan laughed. "Yes. I remember the time Brig and I were rock climbing on the western slope. She kept daring me to call hawks and falcons every time we would come across one. She loved watching them swoop down on me then land ever so carefully on my arm."

"Didn't they get annoyed by being called for no other reason than to entertain Brig?"

The crow echoed Ryan's laughter with a noisy caw. "No. Birds like to play as much as animals do. They thought it was great fun. I got the last laugh that day. She dared me to find an eagle, but she never thought for a minute that I could do it. I wish you could have seen the look on her face when I did. I got an adult female bald eagle to come to me. She only stayed long enough for us to get a good look at her then she took off. I thought Brig was never going to close her mouth again."

Leslie giggled with delight at the image she formed in her mind of the unflappable redhead being taken so off guard by her cousin's mischief.

"Why did you call him?" Leslie reached out and smoothed the feathers on the crow's head. They were soft.

"I didn't. He came to me to be healed. He had a sinus problem."

The bird ruffled its wings and spoke confidently.

27

"Yes, she does. I'm lucky," Ryan agreed with the bird.

To Leslie: "He's glad you believe in me. So am I." Ryan put her arm around Leslie and hugged her gratefully.

The bird flew gracefully away, sensing their need for privacy.

"He was beautiful, Ryan. I never realized how attractive they are."

"They're a much maligned bird, undeservedly so. Crows are highly evolved and extremely intelligent. I've learned a great deal from them about having too much pride."

"I've always wondered if you had the power to heal. Your touch is so relaxing. Is that something else Rags kept you from doing?"

"I couldn't even think around her, much less heal. I was just beginning to understand diagnosing and healing when Father died. Needless to say, I lost interest in it, which suited Rags just fine. She couldn't afford to have me develop any of my strengths."

Leslie studied Ryan's face carefully, watchful for signs of pain. It was an expressive face that had changed for the good and bad since their marriage. The mysterious eyes were clearer and less remote. The mouth was graver but quicker to turn to a smile or laughter. A new furrow was engraved above the brow, but the weariness of spirit had vanished, unmourned.

Grief had taken its toll on Ryan's noble features, but the nourishment of Leslie's love was busily countering its effects. It was, however, still a stalemate.

"Does it bother you to talk about her?" Leslie had avoided the subject, much against her natural curiosity. This was the first time since Rags' funeral that Ryan had actually spoken directly about Rags. Leslie had only started listening to the tapes of Rags' parole sessions (destroying them as she went along) and hadn't learned enough to satisfy her. She had seen first hand how frightened Ryan had been of Rags; how frightened everyone was of Rags, including herself. But Ryan was a strong woman and it mystified Leslie that Rags had gained such total control over Ryan's life. As Anara's agent of revenge, Rags had been very effective.

Ryan stood and sighed distressfully. "You know I've thought about this quite a bit and one of the things I've realized is that I'm not going to stop feeling this way about her." She turned to face her peaceful, compassionate mate. "Leslie, you need to know what lengths Anara has gone to in the past so you won't be shocked by what she does in the future. I can't protect you from this any longer. She isn't just after me any more." Ryan lit a cigarette and shored up her courage. "She's after you, too, because you have taken my part, and you need all the information you can get to arm yourself against her."

Leslie settled herself on the fallen tree and schooled herself to stay relaxed. She had learned early on that if she let it show a thing upset her, Ryan would clam up and it would be doubly hard to reopen a sensitive subject. Many times she had to become completely dispassionate to keep the flow of Ryan's revelations uninterrupted.

Ryan watched Leslie's beauty settle into firm resolve and she continued. "If you are going to hold your own against an enemy, it's essential that you understand how they think. I've known for a long time that you want to learn how Rags gained and kept control over me and my life. I've weighed the suffering you'll know from hearing about how she did it against the peril it would put you in to remain ignorant of it, and I've decided that I have to risk hurting you now in order to make you stronger later."

Leslie was not of faint heart. "How did she go about it?"

This was the test. If Leslie held fast now, Ryan would know that she hadn't rushed her. "Torture," Ryan revealed neutrally, trying to soften the impact.

Leslie's face remained impassive and expectant. "That calls to mind prison camps and Germans."

"It wasn't that severe. Anara's strictest mandate was that I remain alive. That was no mean feat for Rags because when she found me nearly dead outside Cary's, I had absolutely no will to live."

"That doesn't surprise me knowing how much you loved your father and Dana. And losing them both within three months, I'm not sure I would have done any better. When she found you that night, what did she do with you?"

Ryan crouched beside the stream and tossed stones into it absently. "After she started my breathing again, she took me home with her and began the very long process of using me against myself."

"For instance?"

"You know how I feel about nudity. Unless I'm sleeping or bathing I have no desire for it at all. When I came to the next morning, I was naked as a newborn on the cement floor of her basement."

"She went into your mind and found out what you hated most and did it to you. Why didn't you leave?"

Ryan threw a stone angrily across the creek. "That's a little hard to do when you're in shackles."

Leslie's eyes widened and her hand came involuntarily to her high-boned cheek in horror. "Ryan, I had no idea. That's awful! How long did that go on?"

Ryan hung her head low. She couldn't help experiencing the residue of defeat and despair. "Two weeks." She winced when she heard Leslie moan. She forced herself to continue. "She called Phil and told him that she was drying me out. He was grateful that somebody was, but he never knew what was going on. He still doesn't." She snorted derisively. "Dry me out. She did that all right. I had been drinking myself to death for three months and she made me go cold turkey from alcohol."

Ryan couldn't bear to look at her lover while she spoke. It was far easier to seek the anonymity of the mountainous horizon. "I learned many things in those two weeks, but most importantly, I learned what pain was and how to beg. I begged her to let me die. I cried and pleaded with her.

29

The harder I sought mercy, the harder she made me suffer. You can't know what real fear is until you've confronted your own worst ones face to face.

"It always amazed me how selective she was about what to use against me. It was as if she knew exactly what she wanted me to feel." She finally looked at Leslie and saw the calm restored. "She was very careful to keep me from approaching psychosis. I think that's why she never used cats." Ryan sounded very much like she was just then discovering her persecutor's methods.

"But why should she when she had me convinced that she could, at any moment, realize my biggest fear by making it impossible for me to fly again?"

Leslie interrupted. She could see that Ryan was drifting with the memory and wasn't getting to the point. "Ryan, you were so terribly afraid of her. It was more than that."

"Rape," Ryan answered unexpectedly. "Every day, in one way or another, for six years she raped me. It was more than the whippings and beatings." Ryan drifted into the past again. "It was the constant, unmerciful destruction of my dignity. She forced me to violate myself because she knew it disgusted me. She humiliated me in public. Oh, god. She was always in my mind and I couldn't get her out. I had no privacy. No control. Nothing." Ryan relived the emptiness, fighting back a moan.

Leslie restrained her tears and the rebellion in her heart. Her voice shook in response to Ryan's pain. "Ryan, my love. Did she rape you . . . sexually?"

Ryan stood and hugged her ribs. "Yes. Oh, how I hated it."

Leslie despised having to remain apart from Ryan. She knew better than to approach her; Ryan was inconsolable until she was finished with her emotions.

"No one was happier to see Rags die than my doctor. I never told him what was going on, but he knew."

"How?" Leslie breathed.

"Because Bonnie found me unconscious in my bed one morning with a temperature of 104° and called him.

"I do not willingly submit to pelvic examinations, but I certainly wasn't in any condition to resist him. So, he not only found the welts on my back and thighs, but he found I was suffering from an acute infection caused by festered lacerations inside my pelvis. He's no fool. When he added all that evidence to the bruises on my wrists and ankles, he didn't have far to go to draw the correct conclusions.

"He, and three other surgeons, spent far too many hours putting my insides back together the time Rags turned on me. He knew," Ryan recalled confidently.

Leslie rubbed her temples. "Ryan, why didn't you have her arrested?"

"Believe me, I thought about it. That is when I found out Rags could read people's minds. She beat the tar out of me for just thinking it."

30

"Or leave?" Leslie felt as though she were belatedly pleading for her lover's life.

Ryan shook her head. "Where was I going to go, Leslie? Don't you think Anara would know where I was and send Rags for me? It went against everything I knew at the time to kill Rags or have her killed. She had me and she knew it."

"I can see how she got you in chains the first time. How did she keep doing it?"

"Rags could do more than read people's minds. She could manipulate them, too. She just forced me into unconsciousness and I'd wake up in hell," Ryan explained, wrestling with the memory.

"You never fought back?"

The sun was beginning to set and the air was turning cold. They both ignored it.

"That's where her true genius was. This may sound incredible to you, but it took me a year of spending my weekends in hell before I regained my will to live and my Celtic fight started flowing in my veins again. Thinking back on it, it was absurd to believe I was fighting back. I didn't have anything left to fight with. She had infiltrated and seized every aspect of my life.

"Really all I did was lash out with rage. Rather than let me get a taste of directing it at her, Rags started introducing other women into our sexual activities and I took it out on them."

"She was clever."

"Extremely. She shifted the focus of everything after that. The whippings stopped, along with the bondage. Instead, she taught me how to do it to others. She toned down the humiliation and quit making me violate myself. The damage was done, all that remained was to maintain the undermining of my will."

"But she didn't stop forcing you sexually," Leslie observed.

"Never. She took me the night she died," Ryan revealed quickly as though haste would lessen the effect of the truth.

Leslie gasped and her hand came to her heart. She felt faint. Catching herself, she restored her breathing to a more normal rhythm.

Many times during the beginning of her relationship with Ryan, Rags had invaded the sanctity of it. Never in her wildest dreams had Leslie thought of Rags as being that callous. She found her voice, though just barely. "When? How?"

Ryan found it harder than she imagined to go on. She was strained and struggling with the rage. "Out back of the bar. Normally she used the kitchen."

"What kitchen?"

"It's not there anymore. It was where the pool table is now." Ryan swallowed and clenched her fists to dissipate the energy. "Rags got her kicks out of watching me play pool or pick up women. It turned her on. So, right when I would be winning a game or succeeding with a woman, she would walk up to me and tap me on the shoulder.

"My heart would sink every time, but I always excused myself from whatever I was doing and followed her to the kitchen. On the way in there she made sure that I saw her putting that damn leather glove on."

"Why?"

"Because she knew I had eroticized it and the moment I saw her putting it on I would start getting hot."

"Ryan, you don't like butch women and Rags was about as butch as anyone I've ever seen. How on earth could you get hot for her? Or her gloves, which I've only seen you be frightened of?"

Ryan held up two fingers. "Both gloves, yes." Then she emphasized her point with one finger. "One glove meant she was after sex, not violence.

"I didn't get hot for her. My body did. That excited the hell out of her. She loved watching my body betray me. She knew, and so did I, that the minute she closed the door behind us, I would be ready for her.

"If she closed in on me and undid my belt and pants, then I knew she was going to make me come. She'd slip that damn leather gloved hand inside my pants and I'd come like a banshee all over that hot black finger of hers. I hated it, but my body would have its way. With or without my consent.

"If she undid her belt and pants I had to go down on my knees and submit to her pressing her sex into my face. There was no faking it either. I learned from the first that I was expected to be genuinely passionate and give my all to eating her. She made it harder because she was fond of saying vile and vicious things to me while I did it.

"My body never failed her. It always gave her what she wanted. That was what made it good for her—watching me crave what I hated."

They both fell silent, entrapped in their own emotions. Ryan struggled with her rekindled resentment. She knew she wasn't really in hell any longer. Now she was in heaven. She walked over to Leslie and drew her to her feet.

Leslie couldn't hold back her tears in the close comfort of Ryan's powerful body. Her own response was overwhelming and she let go her sobs of grief.

Few could be more soothing or gentle than Ryan when she chose to. Leslie felt the solace deep in her heart and settled down. She looked up and Ryan took her face between her hands and wiped the tears away with her thumbs.

"My angel, there is no way in the world I would have done this if there had been any way to avoid it." It made Ryan ache down to her toes to look into her lover's moist eyes. In her heart, she cursed Anara.

"I never could have imagined the horror of it or how you endured. Rags was barbaric and heartless," Leslie spat. "How could you possibly be friends with her?"

Ryan was definite, but warm. "Who Rags was and what she did were separate for me. No one else could see her as anything but a cruel, frightening persecutor. No one else understood her. I knew what she was doing and why. I could accept that she had to keep trying to break my will. That was her mission in life. She was still a human being and she had feelings.

"Through it all, Rags was intensely loyal to me as a person. In the end, she was sorry for what she'd done, and Anara is no doubt making her pay for not only failing in her mission, but caring about me."

Leslie's eyes widened slightly. "Do you really think so?" It hadn't occurred to her that Rags would be punished.

"I'm certain of it." Ryan held Leslie away and searched her eyes for understanding. "This has been a lot for you to handle at once and I want to help you with it. I'll be able to talk about it in the future without getting caught up in the leftover emotions. I'm okay now. Are you?"

Leslie accepted Ryan's handkerchief and dried her face. She swallowed the lump in her throat before answering. "It won't be easy to keep this in perspective if I dwell on it. I want to understand it, and I will in time. For now, I'm all right."

Ryan looked at her watch and chuckled. "Bonnie's probably set the whole household on its ear by now. She never could deal with my being late for dinner. Hungry?"

"Starved. And cold. I didn't even notice it had turned dark." Crying left Leslie feeling empty and drained. A warm meal would work wonders. She slid her arm around Ryan's firm waist and they walked up the path to the dinner that waited impatiently to restore them.

# 5

Phil Peterson leaned back in his shopworn chair and watched Ryan park her motorcycle in the lot outside Peterson's Flight Service.

He thought back to when Ryan turned fifteen and was finally legally old enough to drive it and how upset Patrick O'Donnell had been over the whole affair. By that time Ryan had been soloing in single engine airplanes for years and wouldn't be denied the hulking Harley. She got her way. She always did.

It amazed Phil that a woman of Ryan's wealth would still be riding the same machine seventeen years later. But Ryan loved that old bike and she took loving pains to keep it in good running order, preferring it to any number of cars she had had over the years.

This was Ryan's first lengthy absence that wasn't cause for worry for him. No funeral, or mysterious illness, or excessive drinking had kept her away from her vocation these past few weeks. For once, her leave had been by choice. He was still glad to see her back. He missed Ryan—they were close friends and shared a passion. He had taught her everything he knew about flying and then some. Yes, he missed her terribly.

He smiled at her when she entered. Always in black, from her leather jacket to her boots. Even as a young person she had insisted on wearing that color which was thought to be morbid by her peers, mysterious by adults. But everyone liked Ryan immediately so they looked the other way, calling her eccentric.

"Hey, stranger. Good to have you back." Phil's clear voice rang out through the room. He had developed its authority over years of shouting above the noise of turbines and props.

Ryan clapped him on the shoulder and drank in the pale blue sparkle in his eyes and the rich warmth of his leathery skin. She straddled a chair next to his desk and lit a cigarette. Phil was one of her constants in life. Something she could count on. "It's good to be back. It always is." She nodded to the pilots in the lounge area who took notice of her return. They thought of her as more than just their boss. She was a fellow pilot and they shared a deep sense of comraderie. This was Ryan's family, but she had a new family now and she was torn in her allegiance.

"I don't have a flight for you today, buddy. Things are pretty slow for a Tuesday," Phil told her.

Ryan locked her friend with her serious eyes. The smile left his face. "Phil, I need to talk to you about that." Ryan took a deep inhale of her cigarette to settle herself.

Phil put his pen down and returned her look. "What's wrong, Ryan?"

"Nothing. It's what's right. I'm not going to fly commercial flights anymore." Ryan tried to hand it to him as easily as she could, but the effect was still the same. The shock wave pulsed through the entire room and caused a stir everywhere it went. The other pilots never really eavesdropped on conversations—little could be said in the converted hangar that stayed private. They stopped what they were doing and some of them walked over to hear Ryan's explanation and support Phil, whom they knew wouldn't take it well.

Phil was speechless and shaken. Ryan ignored her audience; they had as much right to know as Phil did. She leaned closer to her mentor and spoke softly. "Phil, I can only afford to have one obsession in my life and even that isn't safe to do. I never thought I would see the day when I would care about something more than I do flying, but I do."

"Leslie?" Phil's voice was distant and pained.

"Yes. I can't explain to you how much she means to me."

"You just did." In a quarter century, Ryan had not let another human being come between her and her religious devotion to aviation. Phil had assumed it would always be that way and he would have Ryan to himself for the rest of his days. He couldn't have prepared himself for this if he'd tried. There was no way to conquer a rival who had already tasted victory and was consuming the spoils.

He had to admit it to himself. The honeymoon wasn't going to be over—the bloom wasn't going to fall off the lily. Ryan had, at last, found her one true love. It was time for him to step aside and let Ryan have the happiness she deserved. He was glad he liked Leslie or he might be tempted to hate her for this.

He wouldn't have wanted anyone to deny him his Sarah. She was the love of his life and had been for thirty-five years. It was Ryan's turn to get back some of the love she had given in her life.

He cleared his throat and picked up his pen again. He tried to tap away the sound of reality ringing in his ears. "She's one hell of a woman, Ryan. You'd be a fool to hang around here when you could be with her. Does this mean you're not going to take over the business when I retire?"

Ryan dropped her cigarette to the floor and stubbed it out. She couldn't look at him while she broke his heart. "You know it does." Everyone was silent for a moment, as though they were mourning the passing of a tradition. Finally, Ryan spoke again. "Phil, you're fifty-five years old. You've put your sons through college, you have Sarah and the home she always wanted. You're a success in every sense of the word. I don't have to tell you what most men your age are facing now."

Some of her co-workers shifted their weight nervously. She was saying what many of them wanted to say, but couldn't. Phil had always worked too hard and they were starting to worry about him. Phil knew as well as anyone that his peers were dropping like flies around him from heart attacks. He had been in far too many hospital rooms and to enough funerals to know what he could expect if he kept up his pace much longer. He nodded gravely.

"It's time you started enjoying all the work you've done in this life." Ryan turned slightly to address one of the pilots, a short man with large eyes. "Davis."

"Yo," he answered.

Ryan pointed to the morass of paperwork on Phil's ancient desk. "How much of this do you know how to do?" She knew the answer, but she had to be forceful with Phil to get her way.

"Most of it, Ryan. Phil hardly ever lets me do it though," Davis replied with a small measure of resentment in his voice. It was true that Ryan had been picked over a decade ago to succeed Phil. No one doubted her ability to do it, but very few believed she wanted to be saddled with the responsibility. Davis wanted it and had been trying to find an opening in Phil's heart for years with sparse results.

Ryan stared purposefully at Phil while she spoke to Davis. "Call the office supply place and order yourself a desk and whatever you need to perform your duties as vice-president of Peterson's Flight Service. You've just entered a new tax-bracket, starting today."

Davis' eyes widened and his ambitious face broke out in a broad grin. Those around him began to congratulate him on his good fortune.

Then Phil spoke. "Just a damn minute, O'Donnell. I get a say in this, too."

Ryan cut him off before he could gather steam. "Fine. Let's vote on it. I own one third of this business and I assent. You own two thirds of the firm so you get two votes. The part of you that wants to enjoy life votes in Davis' favor and the part of you that thinks you're indispensible and can't delegate authority says nay. Two to one, Phil. You're outvoted." She followed her coup by rising to her feet and grasping Phil's arm to help him up too.

"I don't know about you, but my employees earn their money. Davis, sit down and get to work. Phil is going with me to take a spin in his Stearman."

Two of the pilots closest to them laughed at Ryan's pun and joined in

37

with her to push Phil out the door.

"Ryan, she needs spark plugs and I have to check the altimeter."

"We can do that, too. Let's go."

As always, Ryan got her way.

Leslie was awake, although her eyes were still closed. She took inventory of her surroundings to see what had awakened her. The first sense to come aware was her sense of smell and it was delighted by the soft, clean scent Corelle had sprinkled on her pillow when she turned down the bed.

Then she listened carefully for any sound that would have disturbed her and she heard it. Ryan's halted breathing next to her. Then a soft moan, and her heart sank. Another dream.

She turned quietly and forced her eyes open. The room was dark and peaceful. She knew Corelle was asleep two rooms away and the housekeeper, Bonnie, would be resting soundly in her apartment on the first floor. There was no bird chatter outside their window, so she knew it was the depth of the night.

A second moan bypassed her worry and went directly to the seat of her desire. Her own breath quickened to match her lover's.

Ryan's eyes were quivering under their lids, and her sensuous lips were responding to her nocturnal visions. A small hiss passed over them and Leslie found herself drawn under the bedcovers in search of her part of the passion.

Ryan's womanhood beckoned to her as the sky calls to birds. She visited the raven silkiness and partook of its goodness regularly, though never often enough to satisfy her. She edged her way down Ryan's sinewy length and lodged herself between her powerful legs.

She kissed Ryan's sex lightly and it came alive for her. At once, Ryan's pelvis began to rock slowly, demanding satisfaction. Ryan's body had developed a greediness for Leslie's creative tongue—a hunger that could short-circuit the dream tempering of the body.

Leslie held her mouth above her quarry and waited for it to rise insistently, hungrily, to be touched again. Her breath stuttered when she felt Ryan's nether lips press against her mouth and she sped to the insanity of her own need. She knew all the secrets to fulfill her lover, but this one, she knew best.

The first taste of Ryan resembled an aged, unblended scotch, but quickly turned, with help, to the sweetness of an artichoke heart. It was palatable and addicting. Leslie couldn't get enough, although she gorged herself wantonly each time. She quickly was lost to the intoxication and floated away.

. . . . . . . "Master, please. I beg of you. Please, it's been so long."

Tiny, thrilling seizures darted through Ryan's muscles as she listened to Sanji's pretty Jamaican accent address her fervent petition.

Ryan inhaled casually from her cigarette and let the smoke trail slowly out of her nostrils. To Sanji she appeared calm, almost bored. Inside she was bordering on dementia.

Her heart pounded in her ears from the excitement of looking into Sanji's agonized face. It was a virtual mask of entreaty with its strained muscles and shimmer of sweat. She didn't know how much longer she could bear to look into the soot-black eyes deeply submerged in tears and looking very much like stars trapped in bubbles. How perfect she was in the ageless posture of supplication: her long fingers interlocked prayerfully above her satin throat.

Ryan felt herself drawn to Sanji's naked vulnerability like a lemming to a cliff. Her eyes devoured the supple curves and tight planes of the well-trained dancer. As a child returns to its mother, Ryan's gaze fell upon the heaving chest and it impossibly beautiful breasts, twin planets whose axis Ryan could no longer resist touching.

With her cigarette lodged, forgotten in the crook of her fingers, she bent to reach the tempting nipples and rolled them cruelly between her thumbs and forefingers.

Sanji's eyes enlarged and her fingers tightened so that her knuckles nearly showed through her dark skin. She was determined to corral her desire and pass this test of concentration. Her speech almost faltered but the words came. "Please! I'll serve you better than I've ever done. Master, I'll do anything. Take anything from me, I beg you." She could not have pleaded more ardently if it were for her life. "Let me kiss your wonderful sex. You have made me wait an eternity. I implore you, show kindness to me." The chance to perform cunnilingus on her Master was always the carrot dangling before her, the greatest reward for her faithful service.

Ryan's face hovered directly over the tormented sex-goddess and remained indifferent, but the time was fast approaching when she would no longer be able to maintain the facade. She was galvanized by the excitement Sanji's sincerity and desperation brought to her.

She plucked her fingers from the aggravated black nipples and straightened herself. Her head fell back on her shoulders and an overpowering gasp escaped the depths of her being. Her cigarette fell, unnoticed, to the tile floor. It was happening, she couldn't stop it now.

The electric rushes ripped through her bloodstream and bottlenecked in between her legs. The throbbing backed up into her chest like rush hour traffic, hot and volatile. Her skin began to ignite like signal fires. Then the quaking started and she knew that if she didn't do something soon, she would break out in a cold sweat and unmanageable shaking.

She could no longer tell how long she had forced her slave to kneel, begging for the ultimate favor. She only knew the spell was cast and the magic held true. As each time before, Sanji's adjuration blazed through her like a brushfire and consumed her reason. The uncut narcotic of madness and desire ravaged her.

Her hands trembled, nearly out of control, as she struggled to unfasten her belt buckle. "Jeeesus," she whispered. She knew her limits. "You finish it, bitch. I can't."

Sanji continued to beseech her Master as she undid each button of the black jeans and slid them sensuously over the tortured flesh of Ryan's long legs. Her anxious mouth awaited permission with difficulty, but nothing prevented her from consuming the prize before her with her eyes. She memorized each shining hair and inhaled deeply the tangy aroma.

Ryan swayed closer to the hungry face, drawn by the magnetic chemistry, guided by the palpable force field between them. She caught herself just as the hair of her sex made contact with Sanji's moist lips. "You'd like that wouldn't you, slave?"

"Master, yes! Please." Sanji's voice was beginning to shake and break up. Her craving was coiling around her throat like a snake. With a concentration that belied her need, Ryan managed to sit on the bed. She leaned back on her elbows and smiled fiendishly. Her knees were spread. All was ready, lying in wait.

Suddenly, Sanji was seized by the fear that for all her prayer and appeal, she would be denied. She clutched her breasts and wailed mournfully, "No, Master! Please, don't deny me. I beg of you. I cannot bear it." She was on the verge of weeping openly when she heard Ryan chuckle cruelly.

"Do it, baby," Ryan demanded.

Sanji felt as though she would swoon from the pinpoint agony of finally being allowed to taste her Master's lust. It forced her into a heightened sense of awareness that made everything clear and vivid.

Her full mouth drew near and her sultry breath blew the sable hairs like a breeze through tall grass.

Ryan hissed loudly. In her intense state, the gentleness of it almost hurt. "Ohh god, Sanji."

Sanji smiled inwardly. For a few fragile moments she was in control of the action and she would be allowed to prove her worth. She knew that her Master would never be more ready than now to survive her ophidian kiss. Her lips grazed the burning sex which brought about a fierce moan from Ryan, followed by another and another—each getting deeper and more insistent as she drew closer to her ultimate goal.

Ryan was entranced by the seal-brown skin rubbing against her alabaster thighs. She watched Sanji's face transform itself from utter despair to shrewish contentment. The sight of their opposite colors joining as one in breathless need thrilled her so that sweat beaded on her brow.

Suddenly, the serpent tongue made its way into its den and began dancing with mindless frenzy.

Ryan's elbows failed her and she fell back upon the bed with a deafening scream. The poignancy cut through her like a lance piercing her brain, then rewarded her endurance with ecstasy. She grabbed fists of wiry hair and yanked Sanji's head into the perilous depths of her urgency. It was from here that Ryan took back control of the action as she locked her thighs about Sanji's face and made her aroused mouth but a brutalized receptacle for passion.

"Oh god! Ohhhn." Ryan tossed her head furiously from side to side as her fever heightened. "God, baby. You're driving me wild!" She bucked and writhed mercilessly and without regard for the mouth she was violating.

Sanji lost touch with reality. Now her true talent took the foreground . . . her ability to withstand pain and savagery. For her, all that existed was rapture. Nothing fulfilled her more or gave her purpose in her life than to sacrifice herself for her Master's pleasure. This wronging was all that was right for her.

"Take it, bitch. Ooaan. Take it," Ryan commanded. For Sanji there was no choice. She had to endure any and all things her Master forced upon her. Willingly.

Only incoherent raving reached their nerve centers as Ryan stepped up the pace of her defilement. Their minds blanked of conscious thought and all became a frantic focus of ecstasy.

Pure fire penetrated Ryan's brain and her body acted on its own to evict the mouth of the sex-goddess. The vacated space was instantly filled with a firm, womanly globe. Her mighty thighs seized and crushed the breast as she was overcome by a disabling orgasm.

Sanji was used to this treatment . . . . . . .

41

but Leslie wasn't. She fought against crying out as her delicate breast was locked in a vicegrip between Ryan's legs.

Ryan had been ungentle with her in the past, but never anything as severe as she was experiencing now. Leslie was frightened by the intensity of it. A few more unbearable moments passed as Ryan finished having her way, then began to loosen her grip on her unsuspecting wife.

Ryan's breathing was still labored as she entered into awareness of what she had done. Her eyes came open suddenly and she pulled the covers aside. When she saw Leslie in the position that, heretofore, only Sanji had taken, she shuddered inwardly. She relaxed her leg muscles and released her unwilling captive, then gathered her up in a silent caress.

She smoothed the blonde head lovingly and searched the darkness for forgiveness. She could not bring herself to speak of her dream-life transgression. Instead, her body pulled her into its contentment and relaxation and finally deep, satisfied sleep.

Leslie was no longer uncertain about the meaning of Ryan's dream. While there was never any doubt in her mind that she was able to satisfy her lover sexually, as she watched her slender mate rest so peacefully, she knew something was missing.

Their lovemaking always brought them together as one spiritually, answered all their emotional needs, and aroused them mentally. Until now, Leslie believed that physical gratification was guaranteed as well.

Leslie rolled slightly away from Ryan and let her sleep on, undisturbed. For the first time she was able to see beyond the physical scars Rags had left on Ryan's besieged body to the intangible ones. Scars no less rugged or lasting.

This was the body that Rags had exploited and trained to have an appetite and needs independent of its occupant. Needs that surpassed Leslie's ability to satisfy.

She felt tears well up in her eyes when she realized who did know everything about satisfying these foreign-born exigencies. She had never liked Sanji from the first moment that she had regarded her as a rival for Ryan's attentions.

Sanji's frequent visits to McKinley were always colored with borderline strife and unmasked suspicion. It was beneath Leslie to openly exhibit her feelings for the Jamaican, even in private to her lover. Ryan felt obligated to look after Sanji and Leslie respected the arrangement, but she was not happy about it. She succeeded in her efforts to conceal her animosity from Ryan, who sometimes missed even the most painfully obvious feminine signals of discord. Not so with her all-female staff. Ryan was never alone with the intruder.

In her heart, she knew it wasn't possible for her to deny Ryan anything that she needed, which spawned a new sense of helplessness in her.

She lay motionless, considering the selfish alternative, until sleep reclaimed its hold on her and freed her of her irresolution.

# 6

For years, Fridays had been a welcome ending to David Martin's work week. This one seemed more like a collapse, a miscarriage of purpose. He stared through the foliage covering the window that had been his for the last thirty-six years. If he focused properly, he could see the outline of the Capitol building against the gloomy overcast sky.

He tugged at his well-worn pipe and shook his head, defeated. With a large sigh, he looked at the blank page before him for the hundredth time that afternoon. Thumbing through page after empty page in the notebook that had once contained copious notes and speculations, he stared in disbelief.

He wondered to himself how he, a man who was as tough as any of the parolees he counseled, could have been such a fool. The tape reel continued to labor on silently behind him, saying nothing. Blank. Everything was blank.

Nearly a decade of interviews and hypnosis sessions with his only female parolee, Rags, were gone, but not far gone if his suspicions held true. Only one person was both clever enough and had motive enough to liberate the physical evidence of his life's work.

He closed the notebook and began to pace absently in his small, booklined office. No doubt remained that Ryan was at the bottom of this effacing larceny. She had won yet another round in their ongoing bout: the hopeless court battles, the defamation of character, the corrupting of potential publishers. All this and more he had endured and survived and never thought to protect his notes from vandalism. Fool indeed, he thought to himself.

He promised himself that Ryan would not succeed this time. He was more certain than ever that Rags' will had been tampered with. If only he could prove it, he would have a chance of convincing the authorities to take him seriously and pursue an investigation against his nemesis.

Her wealth, her damnable wealth, and willingness to use its influence had undone him and his efforts for years. This time, she would not win, he would make sure of it.

Christine knew that she had never pedalled her ten-speed so hard in her life. In two months she would be old enough to have the car her parents promised her for her sixteenth birthday. Until today, having that car was the biggest concern in her young heart.

Vehicle exhaust filled her overtaxed lungs and burned them in places she hadn't known existed. She pushed herself up the hill on the boulevard toward Seven Lakes and understanding. It was hard to see in the dusk, but she didn't care. Her eyes were filled with tears and she sobbed openly in between her outraged curses against her parents.

In the months since she had been forcibly separated from Ryan, the ring Ryan had given her as a token of love was her only consolation. In the evenings, while she studied her schoolwork, she allowed herself to wear the delicate diamond and gold band. The comfort of its closeness eased the longing and anguish in her heart.

Her love for the older woman was as complete and beautiful as adolescence would permit. And no less intense. She knew it was a forbidden love and that Ryan had been arrested for it. Illegal though it was, she knew it to be sweet and genuine. It took no special insight to tell her that what her parents forced her to do was equally unlawful, but empty of love.

As headlights and streetlamps began making sporadic appearances along her tortured path, she suffered anew from the thought of her only link to true love being robbed from her. Her mother had caught her with the ring and, her desperate pleas to the contrary, the inscription inside it had revealed its origins and it had been taken from her.

The overactive emotions of youth sped her to the top of the hill without the strength of dinner. Hope of Ryan's sure, steady solace sallied her blindly to the gate of the exclusive older residential subdivision.

When the guard didn't immediately open the massive iron gate upon her approach, she bore down on her brakes and stopped sharply. He came out to greet her. "Whoa there, missy. Where do you thing you're going?"

She straddled the bike, trying to catch her breath and comprehend why the guard was questioning her. "I want to see Ryan," she managed to reply through her pain-constricted throat.

The guard shook his head sadly. He liked the young blonde and scoffed at the torrid rumors he'd heard about her and Ryan. "Sorry, missy. I can't help you. Miss O'Donnell moved away about three months ago."

Christine stared at the aging man with disbelief. Her mind began to reel senselessly with despair. The words "moved away" pounded and crackled inside her brain until she could not think. All that stood between her and utter hopelessness was gone. A sharp emotional stab of pain in her heart weakened her knees, but did not prevent her from remounting her bicycle and heading mechanically for the street.

She heard his voice cry out, "No, missy, look out!" then everything went dark.

The guard felt sick as he heard the hollow thump when the car struck the distraught girl. The bicycle collapsed and became entangled under the wheels of the vehicle and Christine's body landed thirty feet away in the middle of the road. A second car came to a squealing halt, barely a foot from her. Traffic came to a panicked, grinding halt behind both cars.

The guard, a veteran of two wars, kept his head and stepped into his station house to call the rescue squad. That duty performed, he rushed to Christine's aid, calling out to curiosity seekers to leave her alone.

She was badly injured, and he could tell instantly that most of the danger was in what looked like a serious head trauma. Already, the sound of sirens put him at ease as he administered what first-aid he could.

The driver that hit her was crying and someone was comforting her. Another was directing traffic around the scene. Finally, the ambulance reached them and the rescue squad took over the guard's attempt to assist, which left him free to respond to the horror of the situation.

"Oh god, missy. Please live. Please." He began to weep uncontrollably for the bloodied virgin face and mangled body. He didn't even know her name. He wanted to do something to relieve her suffering and couldn't.

The ambulance personnel gathered her up and sped away while the police stayed behind with their unpleasant investigation.

--·◆⟨⟩◆·--

Ryan was restless and nervous. She had been flying earlier in the week, but the steadily building tension migrating through her system hadn't ebbed. When the sun began to disappear behind an amethyst wall of mountains, her condition took an unexplained turn for the worse. She left a half-eaten dinner and mildly worried spouse behind to indulge in a cleansing drive on her motorcycle, a drive that led her to a small theater near Larimer Square.

She wasn't sure what brought her there. Normally the dramatic arts held no appeal for her, preferring life to the portrayal of it. She took a seat near the front of the darkened theater in between dances and read the program. The upcoming dance was listed as an original piece choreographed by a member of the troupe entitled "Temptations Lost". When she read the title of the dance she felt the irony. Surely, there was no better way to describe the star of the dance. The heavy velvet curtains parted her thoughts as they parted to reveal the fragmentary set.

Bathed in an orange-red light three women and four men held reaching positions as a triangle tolled its tiny bell in a discordant beat. When a sad clarinet took over, one of the male dancers recoiled into a backbend over the lichen-covered boulders that served as the focus of the set.

The other five dancers, dressed as he was in fawn-colored leotards and tights, responding to his action, gravitated toward him. They left Sanji alone on the opposite end of the stage, aloof and staring into the beam of light that illuminated her.

As always, Sanji could bind Ryan in a spell with her sultry seduction. Ryan took little comfort from the knowledge that she was not alone in the dizzying mesh Sanji wove around her audiences. Her perviousness to Sanji's wiles had taken root in the core of her being long ago. She was glad that Sanji was unaware of her presence.

All eyes rested on Sanji's dramatic pose. Her long fingers were frozen gracefully below her line of vision in a characteristically feminine attitude. The lines of her supple body were accented by her dull, brick-red outfit. The only movement perceptible to the eye was the easy rise and fall of her bosom.

The fawn brindling down her front and leg, held slightly behind her, called to mind the echoes of flames. Her hair was gathered in a gold spiral headpiece atop her head, and her dark eyes were highlighted with gold-flecked eyeshadow. It took the breath away.

A cymbal vibrated to a crescendo as she slowly lowered her long arms and began to turn her body toward the others. The focus of her eyes remained fixed on the light source until the sudden entry of a violin. A pirouette overtook her body, then she catapulted herself across the distance between her and the others. Her approach was climaxed by a grand jeté, landing in a fixed pose of distant concern for the recoiled male.

A French horn joined the violin in a quiet serenade as Sanji held her hand out to him and bewitched him with a gentle, inward curl of her finger. He slithered off the rocks to join her and Ryan squirmed in her seat.

The other dancers took random positions of forest trees while Sanji induced her partner to weave in and out of them with halting backward strides. Piano, cello and harp joined in to create a deceptively pastoral theme.

Sanji allowed herself to melt into the arms of the male who bristled with detailed muscles. Her firm breasts mashed against his unforgiving chest and she looked into his eyes longingly. Ryan's jaws clenched with vague resentment.

Although none of his activity had yet been vigorous, his face was glistening with sweat. Maintaining his professional detachment from his partner took more out of him than the most strenuous workout. The audience was responding to his real life temptation. There was a communal faltering of breath as he returned her desire-filled look.

Try as he might, he could not ignore the certainty that Sanji's eyes could not look at him, or any man, with earnest. Try as she might, Ryan could not ignore the knowledge that the look was meant for her. Nor could she dislodge the tick of jealousy sucking her reason through her epidermis of control.

The dance picked up pace with a flurry of rejoicing that involved all the dancers. Pink was added to the lighting, and Sanji's skin picked it up coquettishly.

The audience nearly gasped audibly when they realized that the music and tone of the dance had transformed into a searing struggle between the temptress and her prey without a visible transition to warn them.

Fanned by the dark wings of Hypnos, the prey raised his fiery fancy above him in a one-arm lift. Sanji tilted his chin up to her with a snakelike finger and bared her teeth with a wicked smile. Slowly, his eyes grew large and he lowered her to the ground into an arabesque.

The music turned sinister, which precipitated the other dancers into undulating attitudes of appeal on the part of the prey. A depraved smile crept over Ryan's face when she let the power of Sanji's command of the plot, the dancers and the audience course through her. She savored the deliciousness of knowing how completely she mastered Sanji, who was in turn manipulating her. She narrowed her eyes and the simmering in her groin burst into an autumn brush fire that could consume prairies and everything in its path. She saw now why she encouraged Sanji to wear blues and silver—to cool the perpetual furnace.

Sanji was, by now, too hot to touch and the male dancer recoiled into a series of spins that propelled him toward the rocks like a tempest-tossed ship. The moment before he was due to hurl himself into them, he recovered, and stood stock still with his feet braced apart and his hands splayed out near his hips.

As if caught in the crossfire, the other dancers faded into the floor, seemingly out of sight. A tear formed and slid down his cheek. It's twin found its way down Sanji's shining face. The crowd was rapt with anticipation. The lights went out and the curtain closed. After a stunned pause, the patrons burst into spontaneous appreciation. Three curtain calls ensued, but Ryan didn't know it. She left the moment the curtain broke the spell.

—··◆❧❀❧◆·—

"Sanji, you were perfect!" exclaimed the choreographer as he burst into the dressing room. He was well heard over the excitement of the crowd gathered in the narrow room. "You had them in the palm of your hand from first to last." He turned his bright expression to the director, Vernon. "I told you, this dance was made for her. Like a tailored glove, it fit!"

Sanji smiled broadly and replied, "Mosley, I wasn't the only dancer out there, you know."

"Yes, yes. You were all wonderful. Thank you," he responded generally and enthusiastically to everyone about.

The theater owner entered with an enormous bunch of white and blue Siberian Irises in his arms. "Sanji, these came for you, hot stuff."

"Oooh, girl, they're beautiful," Sanji's friend cried out happily.

Sanji's eyes were as large as her smile as she received the flowers gratefully. She read the card and her knees gave out, making her sit involuntarily on the dressing table behind her.

"You were excellent. I was thoroughly bewitched. RO."

Only once before had Ryan taken the time to watch her dance and never before had she sent flowers. This much Sanji had no trouble remembering about her past.

She was thrilled and confused at once. Her heart wanted the sentiment to be a declaration of love and not merely an act of appreciation. Bewitched. That was how it had always been between them. Her mind began to flood with memories, all pleasant and exciting. She stared lovingly at her flowers.

She was shaken from her reverie by a petite voice. "Sanji, we're dying of curiosity. Who are they from?"

"Hmmm? Oh." Sanji smiled and replied wistfully, "Ryan."

The two dancers who disapproved of Ryan grumbled, but the others chimed in with teasing and congratulations. "She's after you, hot stuff," the owner encouraged. "I thought I saw her out there. I'll bet that was her Hawg parked in front."

The caterer arrived and shouted, "Who's got the munchies?"

Sanji realized that she was ravenous and was one of the first to reach the cart after handing her flowers to the set decorator for safe keeping. A new hope filled her heart as she satisfied her appetite, rewarding herself for a job well done.

## 7

"Is Susan coming over today?" Ryan asked absently. Her attention was engaged by the sales promotion brochure she was reading.

Leslie nursed her coffee and turned the page of her newspaper. Her eyes scanned the headlines. "She had to stop by the office first. She'll be around shortly."

Ryan didn't acknowledge her answer, so Leslie looked up from her reading to see why. Ryan seldom indulged in the sedentary custom of coming to the breakfast table in a robe. It was a practice of which Leslie was the primary offender. She marvelled at her mate who, even on a Saturday, was up with the sun and neatly dressed before she had her coffee.

Not so Leslie. After years of college and law school, followed by several more of law practice, she wanted a much-deserved break from daily routine. She was grateful that she and Ryan had in common a dislike for lovemaking early in the morning. It made taking the first meal more relaxed for them and predictable for the cook.

It was for this reason that Leslie had concentrated heavily on the decor of the sun porch where they dined in the morning. She made plentiful use of glass and the color theme centered around fern green and a flat white to extend the airy feeling of the windowed room.

The masonry wall on the north side of the room was covered with bougainvillaea that flourished in the diminished southern exposure. Ryan commented once that their delicate pink flowers reminded her of Leslie's lips. The eastern windows were what gave Leslie the greatest enjoyment. Sunrises continued to be, as for all previous residents, McKinley's crowning glory. The unobstructed view of the unbroken skyline presented the viewer with daily opportunities to relish Nature at her best. Leslie planned her mornings around them and had no difficulty persuading her lover to join her. "What are you reading?"

It was some time before Ryan noticed Leslie's question. She had continued to feel out of balance, and a disagreeable sensation that refused to go away had wedged itself into her awareness. She sensed pain so she called her cousin to make sure all was well with her. It was. Before, when she felt achy for no discernable reason, it had been due to suffering on her cousin's part—suffering she could not avoid herself.

Not being able to identify the source of the distress made her nervous. Every form of escape she tried, including absorption in reading, failed.

Leslie cleared her throat tentatively and Ryan's head came up. "That must be fairly interesting. You haven't touched your meal."

Ryan blinked at her tepid eggs and felt nauseous. Her nervousness was building. She hesitated to reveal it to Leslie until she could identify its cause. She handed a glossy photograph to her instead. "Phil is thinking of buying a Citation III, the new jet Cessna has out."

Leslie looked at the sleek jet and appreciated Ryan's interest in it. "It's very appealing and beautiful. Do you want to add it to your fleet?" She stared at the elegant plane a moment longer before handing the photo back to Ryan.

"If she is as good as Cessna says she is, it would be well worth the time to get the factory training on her." Ryan pushed her plate away to be taken by the servant who appeared to refill their coffee cups. "Do you think my Lear would be jealous?"

Leslie smiled at the question, but answered quite seriously, "Anyone or anything that had to settle for less space in your heart would be jealous of a newcomer."

While pulling a cigarette out of a pack with her teeth, Ryan sighed. She eyed the picture of the well-laid out control panel. "I think I would rather," she paused to light the cigarette, "make my heart larger so everyone got enough of what they needed." Ryan was once again preoccupied. Her extremities were beginning to go numb and a sense of urgency was forcing its way into her concentration.

Leslie couldn't decipher Ryan's mood, which appeared to be worsening steadily. As she debated about disturbing her again, she thumbed through the newspaper, canvassing the headlines. One caught her eyes and she began to read the article below it.

TEENAGE GIRL STRUCK, IN CRITICAL CONDITION. Midway through the first paragraph she shuddered and turned the page quickly. She tried to mask her shock to keep from arousing Ryan's interest.

Ryan's empathic abilities had increased many-fold in recent months to a level far superior to where they had been before tragedy had closed off all but the basic ones. She knew of her lover's apprehension immediately. She placed the hand that held her cigarette over the newspaper to prevent further pages being turned.

Their eyes locked and Leslie surrendered the section of the paper. Ryan took it and opened it back to the page that had caused her lover's distress. Her eyes fell directly on the article. She read it quickly, twice. Her nervousness came to a rolling boil, but at least she could pinpoint its source. Finally, an agonized groan erupted from her deepest heart. "Oh, Chris." Her voice was filled with pain.

"Ryan, don't get involved in this. You'll be asking for trouble," Leslie pleaded.

Ryan returned her plea with an expression of shocked disbelief. "You can't be serious?"

"I can, and I am. You would be walking right into a possible restraining order or suit for harassment."

"Did you read this?" Ryan pointed to the article impatiently.

"Only the first two lines. I stopped when I realized who it was."

"This accident happened in front of the guard station at Seven Lakes and the guard is quoted as saying Chris was looking for a former resident. If she hadn't been looking for me this wouldn't have happened, Leslie." She emphasized Leslie's name as she always did when she was annoyed with her lover's contrariness. She tossed her napkin on the table and stubbed her cigarette out angrily, then stood to leave.

"Where are you going?" Leslie asked, somewhat vexed.

"Christian Memorial," Ryan replied in kind.

"If she's in intensive care they won't let you see her." Leslie continued to try to dissuade Ryan from being rash.

"We'll see about that," Ryan called on her way out of the sunroom.

—·◦→◌⋛⎰⎱◌←◦·—

Ryan walked up to the nurse's station and leaned on the counter. An attractive brunette nurse was updating charts and didn't notice her.

Ryan spoke softly to avoid startling the woman. "Jennifer."

Jennifer recognized the voice and a small spasm of pleasure rushed through her, much against her will. She raised her head slowly, gathering her professional fortitude. "Ryan." Then she sat back in her chair abruptly and shook her head. "You. I might have known."

Ryan's eyes bored into her, expecting her to elaborate.

"Last night our young patient regained consciousness for about thirty minutes and the entire time she screamed "Ryan" at the top of her lungs. She just about undid us all, especially her parents. Then she lapsed into a coma. It was you she wanted, wasn't it?"

"Yes," Ryan answered without feeling. She had to remain detached and under control to get what she wanted to help Christine. "Is she still in a coma?"

"Unfortunately. She isn't responding well to treatment." Jennifer pulled her sweater closer. "I'm worried about her, Ryan."

"How bad is she?"

"Two broken legs, a broken pelvis, fractured hip and some minor kidney damage. They stopped the internal bleeding and she has a serious concussion." Jennifer suspended her ethics temporarily to reveal Christine's condition. Her intuition told her that Ryan could help.

"Is there pressure on the brain?"

Jennifer looked sadly in the direction of her young charge. "They haven't found any, and there isn't any real reason why she won't come around."

Ryan trusted Jennifer's intuition. "What do you think it is?"

Jennifer lowered her voice and leaned closer to Ryan. "I've seen this a couple of times before. I think she's lost her will to live. She isn't injured that badly."

Ryan couldn't keep the pain from filtering through her expression. It was too great for her to contain. Her love for Christine had always been a gentle, sweet thing that served as a life preserver in her hour of greatest need. She owed Christine her life. "You have to get me in there to see her, Jennifer."

Jennifer had tended Ryan's tortured body years before in this same ward and had grown closer than was wise to the stubborn Irishwoman. She didn't need to mention that Ryan's own lack of desire to remain on Earth was what she based her diagnosis of Christine on. That was gratefully behind them now.

"You know the rules—only the immediate family," Jennifer protested, furtively glancing about to see if anyone was paying attention.

"If I can get their permission, can you get me in there?"

She knew Ryan wasn't going to give up and would go over her head as far as need be to get her way. There was no point in making a fuss. She looked at her watch and sighed. "Yes. If you hurry. The doctors will be making their rounds soon and, frankly, I don't think she has much time left."

"Where are the Lathams?"

Jennifer motioned over her shoulder to the waiting room. "In there and not in very congenial moods. I can bet they don't care much for you."

"The feeling is more than mutual. I'll do what I can." With warm appreciation she added, "Thank you, Jennifer."

When Ryan walked into the waiting room Mrs. Latham groaned and sat heavily in a chair. Mr. Latham stopped pacing and his face became animated with anger and resentment. "What are you doing here? I told you to stay away from my daughter."

"I want to help," Ryan replied evenly.

"Help! It's your damn fault she's here in the first place. If I could have you kicked out of this hospital I would. You are not going to touch that girl. Ever!"

Mrs. Latham pulled at her husband's coattail. "Brody, keep your voice down. This is Intensive Care. Please."

"I realize that I am, in part, responsible. What I don't understand, Mr.

Latham, is why she was coming to see me. You told me that she understood she was never to see me again."

Mrs. Latham groaned again and began to cry.

"Zina, stop it. You did the right thing." His tone was not comforting. Both he and his wife had not slept since coming to the emergency room the night before. His temper was shorter than usual. He turned on Ryan again. "Where do you get off giving her a ring? That is disgusting!" he spat.

Ryan felt her jaw muscles tighten. She spoke clearly but with enough menace to make Christine's burly father reconsider his attitude. "Where *is* it?"

Mrs. Latham opened her purse and took the delicate band out. She began to cry again. "I was going to give it back to her. I was so upset when she ran out of the house. If I had known she was that upset . . . now she doesn't even know we're here."

Ryan took the ring that belonged to her mother prior to her giving it to the angel that lingered near death in the next room. It reminded her of the tenderness and purity of Christine's love. She relaxed and tried a different approach. "Can we think about Christine for a minute instead of our personal differences? Your daughter is dying, Mr. Latham. I believe that I can intervene."

Ryan's brutal words took the wind out of Brody Latham and he slid into the chair next to his sobbing wife. He had known Christine was slipping away, but couldn't admit it. To have it spoken made it real for him, something he could deal with rationally. The doctors had been of little help and he was growing desperate. Any offer of assistance, however distasteful, was better than helplessly watching his only child die. "What can you do?" he asked gravely.

Ryan pulled a chair near and sat with them. Her tone was deeply serious. "I need your cooperation for it to work. She needs hope, a reason to fight and live. You can give her that."

"How?" Mrs. Latham hung on Ryan's every word.

"I'm going to give her back the ring. It won't do any good if she believes that you'll take it away again. It's clear she's capable of some fairly desperate acts. That is partly because she is young and partly because she is a very passionate individual.

"I will stand by my word and stay away from her after today. You need to allow her the space to live out her passions until she finds someone else whom you approve of. Believe me, there are worse things she could do than wear my mother's wedding ring. Can I trust you in this?" Ryan looked them both squarely in the eye with so much intensity that they were bound to the pact before they realized it.

"Yes," they replied in unison.

Ryan hastened to capitalize on their receptivity. "Fine. Now you must also promise that what I plan to tell you and do for her will remain in complete confidence."

They nodded their heads anxiously.

"I can bring her out of her coma and relieve the stress on her system to the extent that she can recover on her own without the staff getting suspicious."

They accepted her statement without questions. Ryan had a way of communicating that bypassed skepticism. Mr. Latham asked, "How are you going to get past the staff? You aren't related to her."

"I've already taken care of that. Just tell nurse Jennifer that you consent to let me see Chris, and she'll take care of the rest."

He did and Ryan was quickly ushered into Christine's room by Jennifer. "Hurry, Ryan," she urged and left her alone with the injured girl.

Christine's frail body seemed lost in the tangle of monitoring equipment and tubes. Her hair was matted and her skin looked yellowish and clammy.

It hurt. "Oh, baby. I'm not worth this." Ryan swallowed the lump in her throat and went to work. Her conscious mind let go and allowed her inner self to contact Christine's spirit. "Chris. Come back. I need you."

Her answer was swift and joyful. "Ryan!" Then suddenly, a deep sadness flooded the room. "I can't go on. They won't let me see you or love you in any way. Please, just let me go." Christine's soul sounded unusually fatigued for one so young.

On the edge of her spiritual peripheral vision, Ryan could sense a presence: a white-eyed intruder, waiting patiently in the shadows. Ryan could sense the energy of her enemy, Anara, nearby but dared not break her concentration on Christine to make certain. Ryan addressed Christine. "Special soul. Perfect love. You have a purpose in this life and I need you to fulfill it."

"I need *you*. I can't continue on without knowing that I can't love you." Christine's spirit was weak and distant sounding.

"There is another . . . Chris! CHRIS!"

The monitors beside her bed fluctuated dangerously for too many seconds. Ryan tried not to panic. If Jennifer or any other member of the hospital staff interrupted her, she would lose Christine's battle before she began. The door opened. "Christine, come back. I beg of you! Your caretakers have agreed to let you express your love, silently and for as long as you wish." Ryan's higher self spoke swiftly and forcefully, and the monitors settled down. Jennifer looked on fearfully. She trusted Ryan and prayed she would succeed in saving the youth. Holding fast against an emergency, she stood quietly in the doorway and watched.

"There is another. Someone who will need you more than I ever have. Someone whose darkest hour you must brighten with your pure and generous heart."

Christine's heart was pure and generous, and responded immediately to Ryan's distress. With great courage, she replied, "For you, my love, I will return."

"Blessed Be," Ryan prayed in gratitude.

Anara's menacing presence disappeared and the crisis dissipated. Ryan cut short the correspondence between souls and laid her hand upon the blonde head. She concentrated keenly and eased the trauma in Christine's brain. Christine herself opened the door of her coma and returned to semi-consciousness.

The machines busily recorded her new brain activity and Ryan sighed with relief. She took the delicate hand between hers and restored the ring to its rightful owner. "Rest easy, my sweet."

On the way out of the door Ryan touched Jennifer's arm; they shared a mutual look of deep gratitude, then Ryan disappeared.

—◦⟶✦⫾ ⫾✦⟵◦—

Brigid looked up from the magazine article she was reading to see if Christine was awake. Ryan had asked her to be there and reassure the young girl when she became coherent.

Christine had been pronounced out of danger and moved to a medical surgical ward for care. Her private room was cheerful and filled with flowers from family, friends and teachers. Christine was immensely popular and well-liked. Brigid was glad for some time alone during the day when most people had come and gone already. She, better than most, knew what Christine was going through and had to look forward to for the duration of her stay. She turned the crackly page and tried to concentrate on what she was reading.

"Brig?" Christine's voice was faint and shaky.

Brigid closed the magazine slowly and smiled. Her chair was as close to the bed as was possible, and she had a clear look into Christine's blue eyes. They were bloodshot, blackened and had a feverish sheen to them. "You gave us quite a scare, little lady. Welcome back."

Christine tried to moisten her lips unsuccessfully. Her tongue was as dry as her lips. Brigid reached for her crutches and stood. She took a lemon swab and moistened the parched lips for the third time since she had arrived. Christine looked decidedly grateful.

"Where's Ryan?" Her heart's desire meant more to her than the longing for water.

"She was here yesterday. She had to promise your parents that she wouldn't see you. . . don't cry. Look." Brigid held up the tiny hand to Christine for inspection. "Your folks thought better of taking the ring from you. They promised Ryan that you could wear it whenever and as long as you like."

Christine pulled her hand from Brigid's and clutched it safely to her bosom. She took strength from the nearness of the ring and the solid, confident voice of her visitor. "I'm thirsty."

Brigid held up the swab. "This is it, kid, until they take you off that bottle."

Christine moaned and tried to sit up. She was dismayed when she couldn't. She tried to take inventory of her surroundings and the condition of her body, but her mind wandered too much. "My head hurts."

"That's a good sign. They'll probably let you have more pain killers now that they don't have to worry about masking any symptoms. Are you understanding me at all?" Brigid probed.

"I think so. If I can't see Ryan, how come I can see you?" Christine could hear her own voice pounding in her head. She didn't want to ask for a nurse. She wanted to be alone with Brigid.

"Because your parents think that I have a younger sister that goes to school with you. I told your mother that I knew what you were going through and I wanted to help. She took one look at me and stopped asking questions."

Christine found that nodding her head was a mistake but she was pleased that Brigid went to the trouble to manufacture a sister to be with her. "Oh. Where are they?"

"At home asleep, I imagine." Brigid found the control for the bed and raised the head of it slightly. "Better?"

Christine replied softly that it was.

"Your poor mother doesn't have a clue about how to take care of you. I've shown her two or three things just this morning. I've never seen anyone look so relieved. She has all but turned you over to me. I'm no nurse, but I know my way around a hospital bed," Brigid reassured her patient.

"Are they mad at me?" Christine struggled with her words but she knew instinctively that her emotional situation was the key to her recovery.

"They aren't mad at you. They're frightened of you. I don't think they had any idea of how passionate you can be. You can count on them to tread pretty lightly around you for a long time."

With the painful honesty of youth, Christine forged ahead. "Do you think they'll stop making me have sex with them?"

Brigid had the double-edged privilege of being Ryan's confidant and had learned, over the years, some horrifying things about Ryan's life. Among the worst was hearing of Christine's unhappy arrangement with her parents. She was not at all sure about the extent of the Latham's callousness, and this was the first she'd heard that the threat of blackmail hadn't discouraged their activities. She marshalled her horror and responded with hope. "I believe they will now. They are starting to come to a sense of how special and precious you are and that you *are* destructible."

"I hope so," Christine added resentfully. She was starting to hurt badly all over.

Brigid saw courageous tears forming in the sensitive blue eyes. "I think the doctor probably left instructions to increase your medication if you asked for it. I'll get a nurse. It won't take much to convince her that you're ready." Before she left, Brigid saw a tear fall off the ghostlike cheek that once housed a perky rose coloring that made the entire face seem more alive than life itself. She fought down the gourd in her throat and cursed the ravages of living in a complicated world.

In the weeks that followed, Brigid would be a regular visitor and advocate. She encouraged Christine to be positive and active. She visited Christine in physical therapy, where she had spent agonizing hours herself once. All in all, she was the difference between an unbearable recovery and a bearable one for Christine. It felt good to Brigid to be able to do something to help someone directly instead of sitting back, helplessly, watching circumstance destroy someone. Brigid began to feel a new life flowing through her veins and was grateful to Christine for the chance to help.

# 8

"David." Bennet Waterton's patience was wearing thin. "There isn't a judge in this town that will issue a search warrant for McKinley. It would be pointless. *If* the evidence were there, as you claim . . ."

"It is and you know it," David Martin insisted.

The young city attorney clenched his teeth in exasperation for a moment before going on. "It would be destroyed by some member of Ryan's staff before an officer could get in the front door."

David was beginning to sense that something more than red tape was holding up his attempt to prove Ryan was behind the theft of his materials. He was determined to get to the bottom of the matter. "Come off it, Bennet. It isn't as though she has never done anything illegal."

Bennet took an antacid tablet from his desk and sucked on it pensively. "Okay. So we pick her up every couple years on morals charges. They're always dropped and everyone looks the other way. That doesn't make her a thief."

"What about her history of suppressing information? Did you see one word in the papers or one picture on the news about Rags' murder? Two separate judges have presided over the censorship hearings resulting from her attempts to keep me from publishing Rags' story. There's intent," David pressed.

"Ryan O'Donnell makes a religion out of keeping her name out of print. Wealth, good lawyers, and connections make that fairly simple, but not illegal."

David lit his pipe purposefully and snapped at the ambitious attorney. "Okay, okay. I'm getting too old for these games. What is the real reason that you won't help me?'

A disgusted sigh freed itself from Bennet's squat frame and he looked skyward. "You're as bad as she is about getting to the truth."

"She. Who?" David demanded.

"Leslie."

Disbelief shook David's head with a palsied tremor. His brief encounter with Leslie had shown him her courage and determination, but not any dishonesty. "She couldn't have been to see you," he maintained anxiously.

Bennet placed his elbows firmly on his desk and intertwined his fingers under his chin. He fixed David with his eyes and added cryptically, "She didn't have to."

A look of subterfuge beamed on Bennet's face. David had seen it many times on lawyers, doctors and politicians. It was starting to make sense to him. "I don't suppose she did. DU Law School, wasn't it?"

"Yes," Bennet admitted. "I'm not ashamed of having gone to school with her, David. She's a damn good attorney and is very highly regarded around here."

"Hmmph." David stood and emptied his pipe into the ashtray in front of him. Their eyes met on a plane of challenge as David absently filled his pipe again. "I know you better than that. You're too cutthroat to play good 'ole boy games unless you've got something to gain. What's she got on you, Bennet?"

"I owe her, old man. She's half the reason I got this job."

"Spill it," David urged with sheer disgust. All hope of legal recourse against Ryan had just slipped through his fingers.

Bennet's eyes hardened along with his voice. *"She* didn't want it."

David rubbed his left arm, which was feeling numb and tingly, as he digested, defeatedly, Bennet's answer.

—◦→⛬⛬◦—

October began with a fast-moving cold front that forced temperatures near freezing and eliminated all doubts about the capricious nature of Denver's weather.

Ryan had kept her promise and shortly after Leslie agreed to marry, she found herself installed in a newly-vacated position on an influential Board of Directors. Leslie came to breakfast dressed in a tailored tweed suit, ready for her twice-monthly meeting.

Ryan preferred her in less business-like attire, but she admitted that Leslie looked as elegant as ever, so she didn't mind.

Ryan liked to read at the breakfast table. She was enjoying the Christie's art catalogue as much as she was her steak. Her appetite had returned full force as soon as Christine was reported to be on the mend.

"Hmmm!" Leslie exclaimed through the melon in her mouth.

Ryan's concentration popped like a bubble. "What?"

Leslie swallowed and smiled broadly. She read a birth announcement aloud from the paper. Ryan was still puzzled. "Don't you see? I just became an aunt again. My youngest sister this time!" Leslie was bubbling with pride.

Ryan stared, amazed. This was the first time that she had ever had to deal with the reality of Leslie's exile. It was beyond her to reconcile her mate's joy over a child she would never see with the brutal actuality of her status within her family. She and Leslie were vastly divergent about their attitudes on the subject of familial love and loyalty.

The middle child of nine, Leslie had never been allowed to feel special or unique and she envied Ryan's only-child status. Ryan had never seen her as anything but special and unique, and treated her as such. Leslie's childhood wounds were healing rapidly under the constant care of Ryan's kindness and devoted attention. She, in turn, was puzzled by the expression of wonder on Ryan's face.

"How many of these nieces and nephews have you ever seen?" Ryan quizzed.

No one had ever questioned Leslie's creative approach to her banishment from her family. As before, Ryan was showing her something about herself that she had not seen or had refused to. The process was seldom comfortable; however it invariably occurred in an atmosphere of love and trust. She answered, subdued, "I saw two of them born before . . ."

"Before the great ancestor issued the edict that the *entire* Serle brood was to wash their hands of their inverted progeny! I'm sorry, angel, but it makes me angry that you're reduced to reading obituaries and birth announcements to keep track of your family. You deserve better." Ryan steered clear of her own anger—she wasn't sore at Leslie.

"I'm not the only one that has paid a high price for her affectional preference. At least I didn't get cut off from a personal fortune," Leslie consoled herself defensively.

"At least Brigid has the good sense to be bitter about it. She doesn't torture herself every morning over her coffee. Brigid only has to deal with avoiding her parents. All the rest of our relatives are blissfully tucked away in County Donegal, Ireland, so she has never met them. That doesn't compare with the dozens of relatives you've got living right here in Denver. I suppose you were going to send this new arrival a gift?" It sounded like something Leslie would do. She was generous with the people she cared about.

"I've always sent money," Leslie explained evenly.

"Do they cash the checks or return them?"

"They cash them."

"It's fine to accept your money, but not your love," Ryan marvelled. She reflected for a minute before going on. "You know it isn't the money I care about. Every penny I have is yours, but, just this once, I'd like to see the maiden aunt keep silent. Let them worry about you this time."

Leslie took a cigarette from her case. Ryan reached over with her gold lighter, opened and ready to assist. Ryan never made such actions seem like habits. Each time was noteworthy and one of the secret ingredients of her magic with women.

"I couldn't," Leslie insisted.

"You could, but will you? All I ask is that you think about it before signing on the dotted line." Ryan appealed to Leslie's natural reason. She was assured her suggestion might take hold by the thoughtful expression on her lover's face.

Leslie dropped the subject through her watch. "I have to go."

Ryan rose and gathered her up in her arms for a memorable kiss.

Tuesdays were the one day of the week they spent apart, Ryan going her way to fly with Phil, and Leslie hers to Board meetings and shopping. They both felt the need to make token contacts with the outside world, but it made parting no easier.

"Have fun," Ryan closed.

"You, too." Leslie purposely avoided looking into the inviting jade eyes, lest she lose her resolve. She turned and left quickly.

Ryan smiled and sat down to finish the balance of her fruit and coffee. Barely a half an hour passed while she contemplated a Pissarro that might be happy in the O'Donnell art collection when Sanji walked in to join her.

Sanji was wearing the sultry lynx coat Ryan had given her two years earlier and had undone the native braids she had been wearing. Instead, her hair was fixed loosely behind a silver-blue headband that pulled the front of her coiffure snugly against her head. The effect resembled a peacock-in-mating show.

Ryan made no bones about expressing her preference on the subject of female appearance. It didn't go unnoticed by her that Sanji was wearing her hair in the fashion that she liked best. She looked Sanji over with a practiced eye and nodded approvingly. "You look nice."

Sanji was pleased. "Thank you."

"Have you had breakfast? You may join me if you like." Ryan motioned for her to sit.

"I've eaten, thank you."

"If you're going to stay, take your coat off at least."

Sanji lowered her chin and eyelids seductively. She stood with her weight on one foot and with one knee bent coyly under the coat in Ryan's direction. Ryan's eyes were focused on hers as she slowly undid the leather belt and let the coat fall softly to the floor. Sanji's heart began to pound harder in her chest as Ryan's eyes grew large and her breathing stalled.

Ryan was not easily taken off-guard or shocked. Sanji had managed to do both. Ryan's breathing resumed, at a more difficult pace, as she stared openly at Sanji's exceptionally desirable body—in the flesh.

The onslaught of electric impulses traveling the well-scored pathways from heart to groin and back threatened Ryan's faithfulness. An alarm went off in her mind and she stood swiftly, threw her napkin on the table emphatically, and took off for the inner house.

With the fleetness lent to her by her profession, Sanji pursued, followed closely by Corelle who had been observing from a discreet distance.

Sanji caught up to Ryan in the main hall, grabbed her by the arm and spun her around to face her. Ryan was already seething, and being handled disrespectfully by Sanji put the Jamaican in more peril than she knew.

Ryan's voice was sharp and dangerous. *"Put* your fucking clothes on, Sanji. You're a guest in my home."

"It would seem that I've always been a *guest* in your home," Sanji retorted acidly, with pinpoint accuracy.

She scored a hit. Ryan's tone and attitude reversed suddenly in response to the term that described the status of any woman who had lived with her between Dana's tenancy and Leslie's.

Ryan's eyes narrowed warily. "What are you talking about?"

"I've begun to remember things," Sanji informed her unflinchingly. Ryan turned her head slightly toward Corelle, but her eyes were measuring Sanji and the extent of her recollection. Her eyes darted to Corelle who was standing nearby. As with every other time Sanji visited McKinley, a member of the staff was never out of the field of vision. Using the full extent of her authority, she spoke to the slight servant. "Leave us."

Corelle hid her dismay and backed out of the large hall toward Leslie's office, leaving Ryan completely alone with Sanji.

Ryan returned her penetrating gaze to the object of her inquisition. She had to know where she stood with the islander now that she claimed her memory was restored. *"What* have you remembered?"

Sanji relaxed. One of the first things she sniffed out when she breeched the gap in her memory was why she was never alone with Ryan. This was her chance and she attacked swiftly. "That this torch I've been carrying for you isn't a new thing. That we were mad for each other."

"What else?" Ryan asked, more at ease. She could see the angle Sanji was shooting from and she began to feel safer. She made the mistake of loosening her defenses.

"We lived together and it was wonderful, Ryan." Sanji's body was beginning to glow like methane gas. Her breasts drew near to Ryan then withdrew rhythmically as her breathing revealed her growing need.

Ryan's physical need forged ahead in the race for control over the situation and her gaze descended with short stutters until it rested longingly on the Jamaican womanhood. Her own chest rose and fell in urgent reply. "I'm married now, Sanji. I don't need this."

Sanji understood Ryan's emotional attachment to Leslie and she accepted it to the best of her ability. She had grown accustomed to her unrequited love for the handsome tyrant she was bedeviling. She knew that Ryan's value system and emotional makeup allowed for only one woman in her heart and that space was more than adequately filled. She also knew that Ryan's sexual makeup demanded more than she was getting or she wouldn't have gotten as far as she had.

"I know you don't. But, you want it."

Ryan made her second mistake by looking back into Sanji's eyes. From the first, Sanji's hazy eyes were corruption incarnate. Ryan had mainlined Sanji's raw opiate for far too long. It was impossible to stem the tide. The sorcery ignited her nerves. "You bitch," she cursed.

"You *want* it," Sanji stressed.

Ryan's response was not spoken, but hissed. "Yes."

Carefully, without pause, Sanji took Ryan's hand and placed it on her hungering breast. Her own arousal pressed in on her sobriety, then turned her blood into a volatile substance. She managed one last reasonable statement. "Then, take it."

The sparks began jumping between them and brightened the air like heat lightning. Ryan gripped the breast and dug her fingertips into the flesh ravenously. "Ohhh," she moaned. The nipple hardened like a prod in her palm, and she hissed through her teeth.

Cradled safely in Sanji's other hand was her insurance policy. She opened the small brown bottle and let the scent reach Ryan's nostrils.

If Ryan hadn't noticed before, she did now. Sanji felt her excitement struggle free of its reins. She knew that if Ryan took the poppers from her and indulged, then she was assured of being taken sexually.

While Ryan's hand became melted white frosting on Sanji's smoldering breast, her other hand took the inhalant. She didn't need to watch what she was doing—it was as automatic to her as blinking. After giving Sanji a healthy dose, she absorbed the fumes deeply, too. The result was to push them both beyond the point of no return.

The Board members were relaxing quietly in their seats while a slide presentation was being prepared. A secretary approached Leslie. "Miss Serle, there is a call for you on 3602."

"Thank you," Leslie replied. She picked up the receiver on the multi-button set before her and pushed the appropriate button to take the call. "This is Miss Serle."

"Oh, milady. The saints be praised," Corelle began, then proceeded to frantically describe her situation in excited Gaelic.

Leslie kept a calm exterior that masked her annoyance and interrupted her personal servant sternly, to the mild amusement of her fellow Board members. "Corelle. Speak English."

"Oh. Oh. Beggin' your pardon, milady. Ye know I would not disobey you for any reason." Her English began to improve as she went along. "You've instructed us, one and all, never to leave Miss O'Donnell alone with the Jamaican. She's here now, and Miss O'Donnell bid me to leave. I had to do as she said. Please don't be angry with me," Corelle pleaded.

Leslie felt her cheeks redden and her nostrils flare. "You did the right thing. I'll be there presently. Thank you for calling." She hung up the phone and addressed the others calmly. "Gentlemen, a problem has arisen that requires my immediate attention. I must excuse myself." She stood and closed her briefcase. "I would be most grateful if someone could send the minutes over afterwards. Good day." She walked airily out of the room as though nothing were wrong at all.

Corelle was young and full of youthful yearnings. What she had seen of the shameless seduction opened the door wide to her own need. Her suppressed desires wrestled free of their years of careful confinement. Without regard for her own modesty or station, she ventured out of Leslie's office. An indescribable force drew her toward the great hall. Her steps kept pace with the steady carnal cadences that grew louder as she drew nearer.

Her absence of experience in areas of the flesh kept her from coming any closer than the outer circle of the energy field created by the errant coupling before her. She did not notice Bonnie standing in the doorway of the dining room frantically trying to get her attention. It was too late for Bonnie to save her from the awakening of passion in her innocent heart.

There, lying on a nineteenth-century Persian carpet, was the dawning of recognition for Corelle. For as long as she could remember she had fueled her self-pleasuring with abandoned fantasies. Faceless lovers taking her with wanton and tireless need. Faceless until now. For now, and always, that lover's face would be the fierce, Irish visage of her employer, Ryan O'Donnell.

Helplessly, she endured the volcanic stirrings that gripped her as she watched another take what she wanted.

Sanji's body was taut and shimmering. Ryan was lying partially on top of her, kissing her mouth savagely. One hand had clenched a fistful of springy hair and yanked Sanji's head backwards, arching her neck vulnerably. The fingers of the other hand plunged mercilessly into her sodden furrow. Ryan's hips rocked in syncopation with the well-tuned sex instrument, performing a duet of mastery and yielding. Sanji's inflamed moans were drowned in the rising wash of Ryan's.

Suddenly, Ryan pulled free of Sanji's wonderful mouth to raise the level of passion to one more urgent and violent.

"God," she exclaimed breathlessly. "Damn, I've wanted you." She let Sanji's hair loose and reached for the small bottle next to her head. Her breathing was as hard and unforgiving as her eyes.

Sanji let her neck muscles relax. With her great talent for courting danger, she gazed into Ryan's sovereign jade eyes with a sideways look of challenge.

The desired response was swift in coming. Ryan narrowed her eyes and slowed the pace of her invasion to a dangerous circular movement designed to prepare Sanji's womb for a more brutal attack. "You cunt. You run wild through my dreams like you had the right to, taking me places only you know how to find. You sneak through the back door to my thoughts and I can't get free of you."

The prickly nap of the carpet irritated the skin of Sanji's buttocks and shoulderblades as she began writhing uncontrollably in response to the threat in Ryan's voice. She raised her head slightly to partake of the drugged fumes that would relax her muscles and remove any conscious resistance to the assault on her person.

Ryan eased down Sanji's nimble body to gain leverage, then drugged herself fully. In the darkness of their combined need, Ryan's hand became a fist and forced its way into its badly missed home. "Jesus, you're hot," Ryan wailed.

Sanji's eyes had grown large, then rolled up into her head briefly from the pain. She made a choking sound in her throat that reminded her attacker it had been some time since she had last been used so cruelly. It was of no consequence to Ryan, who simply reinforced the sex goddess' altered state and went about the business of taking what was hers.

Together they slid into oblivion—lost in a tangle of screams and entreaties, dangling on the precipice of eternity.

Ryan pummeled the walls of womanhood viciously. "You're burning me, baby!" she cried as she was overcome by the searing fire that scorched her flesh.

Sanji inhaled in deep, hoarse gasps and exhaled with ear-rending shrieks that penetrated the most distant corners of McKinley. She clawed the carpet desperately, rocking back and forth maniacally.

It had been overlong for their return to the land of madness, and their bodies snapped under the strain. Sanji's back arched with a sudden paroxysm and a blinding orgasm seized her being. Her climax was so urgent and insistent that she pulled Ryan over the edge with her.

Ryan recovered quickly and ripped her hand from Sanji's raw and abused cavern. Sanji sucked in her breath and grimaced but didn't cry out. Ryan's passions were unstable immediately following an orgasm. If Sanji let it be known that she wanted more, she could count on Ryan to stall out. If she remained quiet and open Ryan might float into a puffy cloud of compassion or, as easily, be coaxed to ascend to a higher altitude. She was encouraged when Ryan climbed on top of her and started to grind her denim-covered pubic bone into the debauched womanhood beneath her.

"God, I love hurting you," Ryan admitted passionately. She reached into her back pocket for a handkerchief and dried the sweat from Sanji's eyes. They were glazed but attentive, and Ryan penetrated their depths with determination. She raised up by arching her back and bracing her hands on Sanji's shoulders. Her pelvis continued to undulate slowly as she spoke.

"While you're busy remembering things, do you recall who your Master is?"

Sanji's heart skipped a beat, then settled into a frantic pounding in her chest. She knew what came next and she had not dared hope to be so fortunate. She replied in a clear voice, "You are, Master."

Ryan's voice was powerful and dark. Her words were music to Sanji's ears. "For how long?"

Sanji answered sincerely, from her innermost being, "As long as I live."

Their eyes were locked tightly—nothing else existed apart from them. "That's right. And I can take you . . ." Ryan pulled away, then thrust her bone into Sanji's to reinforce each of Sanji's answers.

The replies came through heartfelt moans. "Time."

"Any . . ."

"Place."

"Any . . ."

"Way."

"You will obey me at . . ."

"All times."

"In . . ."

"All things."

Sharp jabs of arousal ravaged both bodies as the oath continued.

"Because you are my . . ."

"Oonn, slave."

"I am your . . ."

"Master."

"Open up to me," Ryan demanded throatily.

Sanji pulled her knees toward Ryan's shoulders to open herself and render her body totally vulnerable. Ryan collapsed her arms and wrapped them under her slave's shoulders, then gave in to the power of conquering.

The position was Sanji's favorite because it was the one that allowed her to hold Ryan. She wrapped her arms tightly around the slender ribcage and locked her ankles in the air above them. Her supple, responsive muscles answered the wild humping with perfectly timed bucking. Again, they met in harmony on the demense of dementia.

Ryan's sonorous moans escalated and echoed in Sanji's ear. The feeling of her Master's hot breath in her hair undid her and she began to beg. "Master. Oh, Master," she cried urgently.

Her permission was swiftly given. "Come on, slave. Give it to me," Ryan induced.

Sanji continued to answer Ryan's need through the near paralyzing contractions of her release and beyond. Her eyes opened and she smiled blissfully at Leslie who was standing next to the Louis XVI hall table, watching them.

Ryan reached her summit moments later. Her contractions were accompanied by a gutteral rendering of relief, followed by great heaves of satisfied exhales. Finally, she collapsed and Sanji went limp. When she could move again, Ryan lifted her head and began to kiss Sanji softly.

"That's enough, O'Donnell," Leslie scolded caustically. She had arrived at the beginning of Ryan's oath extraction and had been intensely aroused by what she had seen and heard. She could not bring herself to interrupt her lover or deprive her of something she so clearly needed. She was angry with herself for letting it happen, but moreso, for enjoying it when it did.

Ryan slid calmly off to one side of her slave and faced her angry lover. She reached inside her shirt pocket for her cigarettes, pulled one from the pack with her teeth and set the pack on Sanji's moist chest. Silently, she eased her lighter out of her pants pocket and lit her cigarette nonchalantly. She was deeply satisfied and relaxed.

For the first time, Leslie noticed Corelle. She had no way of knowing that her personal servant had just experienced a cataclysmic reaction that shook her young soul to the core. She spoke sharply to her employee and unknowingly frightened her. "Bring Miss Charles her clothes."

While waiting for Corelle to return, Leslie stared into Ryan's half-lidded eyes.

Corelle approached cautiously with the coat and Leslie noticed her. Her gaze darted from the coat to Sanji to the coat again. "Is *that* all she wore?"

"Aye, milady," Corelle answered timidly.

Leslie smelled the rat immediately. "Very well. Help her on with it and show her out. I'll be in my office if you need me." Leslie left the dirty work and Ryan behind to sort themselves out.

---

Brigid ran her sensitive fingers through Dana's rich auburn hair and sighed. She had never known such profound fulfillment with a woman until she allowed herself to take Dana. Her eyes searched the native pine panelling on the walls of Dana's guest bedroom with wonder. It was amazing to her how easily her values relaxed and how quickly they stepped aside in favor of her long dormant needs. There was no hesitation to break faith with her lover or unwillingness to do so in her good friend's home.

The sheets and quilt rustled softly as Dana began to stir from her sex-drugged sleep. She nestled her head on Brigid's broad shoulder and smiled happily. The elegant mountain home she shared with Delores was comfortable and warm. She enjoyed bringing her afternoon lovers into her own environment. It was more relaxed and she kept better control over the action. More than one woman had likened the bedroom to a spiderweb, deftly spun to seize victims while the queen sucked dry their juices.

Brigid had no thought of the price she would pay for the privilege, only that it felt good. In the back of her mind she knew the spider kept her dwelling free of debris—that the finished hulls fell to the ground, forgotten. She traced the line of Dana's divine, peach lips with her finger and the end seemed remote.

The genuine affection in Brigid's steady grey eyes made Dana uneasy. She was going to miss the strength and excitement the artist brought to lovemaking. Brigid had a face that required study, and she found herself studying it a great deal. It had a bold bone structure with a keen, square jaw and prominent cheekbones. Wideset eyes graced the stern, narrow nose—a lucky feature that descended down both sides of the proud lines. The refinement it brought to Brigid's unique face mirrored the character it brought to Ryan's. Dana decided that it was the bleached eyebrows and lashes that made the difference. They chased away the Irish gloom and took the edge off Brigid's imperturbable nature.

"Del's lucky," Brigid whispered gently.

Dana shifted and stared at the ceiling. "Some don't think so."

"They're fools. I'd put up with your infidelity. I always wondered why Del did, but now I know."

"We have an understanding. She only asks that I be discreet and stay healthy," Dana provided dispassionately.

"She doesn't feel cuckolded?"

"Everything has its price. She loves me and wants me to stay, so she puts up with it. As well as I'm able to love anyone, I love Del. She has what I need and is free about giving it to me. I learned a long time ago, that isn't easy to find, so I stay." Disappointment in life was a bitter pill Dana dutifully swallowed each morning. Some people drank away their disillusionment, Dana offered hers up on sacrificial fornication.

"Do you sleep with her?" Brigid wondered aloud.

Dana wasn't appalled by the question. She had been asked before. "Of course I do."

"Is she good?"

"I wouldn't stay if she weren't. She's tender and loving, not exciting like you or Ryan." She cast the bait deftly on the surface of Brigid's ego and watched it float downstream. She knew Brigid had no idea how like her cousin she was, and she felt a strange thrill from being the one to point it out to her. She rolled her tongue along the inside of her teeth and waited for the tug on the line. It wasn't long in coming.

Brigid took Dana's chin in her hand and turned her face up to her penetrating gaze. "No one has ever compared me to her before. You're dreaming."

"Who's had the chance to, hermit? You're every bit as intense as she is. At least Ryan has the grace to spread the wealth around. You ought to be ashamed of yourself, hoarding it all these years. Star doesn't know what she has up there. Or does she?" Dana cocked her head coyly for emphasis.

"You're mad, Dana. Ryan is charisma itself. Charm incarnate," Brigid insisted.

Dana sat up and braced her weight on her hand. Brigid wasn't going to get away from her without reshaping her image of herself as a lover. It was essential. "So are you, when you want to be. Ryan doesn't have a corner on the market. I don't know what it is about you two. Maybe it's that thick Irish blood or maybe you just picked it up from being around her all your life. Brig, you are just as appealing as she is."

The indigo in Dana's eyes seemed to bleed out of the confines of their pupils and fill the whites from lid to lid. They were mesmerizing. Brigid was losing ground in her attempt to discount Dana's words. "My dear . . ."

"Don't "my dear" me, MacSweeney. The only difference between you and Ryan is Ryan's reputation. She can't walk into the main terminal at Stapleton without gathering flight attendants like lint. When was the last time she walked through the Polo Club without some sticky debutante crossing her up? Why doesn't she *ever* accept party invitations?" Her last question demanded an answer.

"Because even straight women make fools of themselves trying to get her into the spare bedroom," Brigid replied sardonically.

Dana looked down quickly to keep Brigid from seeing the wicked smile form on her face. She had done it. She had called up the spirit of Brigid's Irish competitiveness.

"That's right," Dana encouraged sweetly while she smoothed her sharp fingernails over Brigid's bare chest. "But believe me, lover—you could bed any one of her admirers with equal ease."

Their eyes locked, then Dana lowered her eyelids slightly. "Even that pretty little black girl I hear she's so fond of." Dana was reeling in the catch.

Brigid shook her head and whistled. "Whew, she's hot."

"What am I? Ice cream?" Dana blew her a phantom kiss.

After a long, serious look that could burn away any falsehood, Brigid put her hand behind Dana's head and pulled the seductress to her. "No, baby. You're molten lava." She didn't say anything more. Their kiss dissolved into tremors and quakes of urgent need that would not be denied.

Dana saw her seed germinate. She hoped the weed would grow tall and strong, never seeing a scythe or plow.

# 9

Fast moving eyelids. Rapid breath. Awareness. Leslie held herself tightly against the furtive passion. She had fallen asleep on the couch in her office. Now she lay in the darkness, disturbed and confused. Her nether lips tingled and throbbed in response to the familiar touch of her own hand.

What manner of power did this Jamaican queen have that she had unrestricted ingress into the dreams of others? What exemptions had the border patrols granted her? Leslie refused to accept blame for her night-time visit from Eros. She would not let herself claim desire for the sublime submissive who had so perfectly acted out her natural part in the great hall earlier that day.

Undisclosed appetites surfaced and were denied recognition. Leslie had so recently learned of, and accepted, her need to be dominated; such needs were still so precious there wasn't yet room to comprehend these unfamiliar stirrings. She returned to slumber before discovering that submission showed two faces to the initiated.

$$—\circ\!\!\rightarrow\!\!\text{ᚷᚻᚻᚷ}\!\!\leftarrow\!\circ—$$

Bonnie wasn't normally awake at two in the morning, but the unsettling mood of the household kept her awake. The light was on in the master suite and she knew Ryan wasn't sleeping either. She stood in the doorway while she caught her breath from climbing the stairs to the second floor.

Ryan's tastes had prevailed when the time came to decorate the master bedroom. The theme of ecru and chili pepper that had graced her last bedroom repeated itself here with a bold richness. Gone were the antique

71

brocades. Instead, vertical stripes riveted the drapes and upholstery. A grand, ornately carved, teakwood bed took center stage, flanked by matching nightstands and Waterford lamps.

It was a large room, adjoined by separate baths and vast walk-in closets. Near the window seat a round table and two chairs stood ready for the occasional meal taken in private. In the window seat, staring out into the darkness, sat Ryan, fully dressed.

The ice in Bonnie's drink settled and attracted Ryan's attention. She turned reluctantly from her reverie to welcome her friend. In a home full of strangers, Bonnie's plump face was a glad sight. She smiled at the stout woman approaching her and tried to remember when Bonnie's thick braid had started becoming more white than black. The first eyes she saw in life were Bonnie's homey blues. They were sadder now and certainly too tired, but refreshment none the less. There was beauty there once, slipped away, untouched and unused.

Bonnie set her drink on the dresser and poured Ryan a brandy. "Join me in the national past-time?" she asked cordially with her pronounced accent.

"Sure," Ryan answered, relieved. Suddenly, a drink sounded good.

Bonnie handed her the snifter and pulled a chair close. She sat down wearily, but her smile was cheerful.

The hand that held Ryan's drink rested on her bent knee and she settled into the cushions behind her. She lit a cigarette and sighed. "Bonnie, how can you drink that stuff?"

"County Cork's finest whiskey to me. The devil's brew to you. It's all in the blood, lass," Bonnie teased. "You're not really Irish at all, you know. Can't get you near a horse or a dog."

"I don't like domestic animals," Ryan responded in kind.

"Won't wear wool."

"I'm allergic to it."

"Don't like mead or ale."

"Yuuk." Ryan curled her lip playfully.

"It's better than that horsewater you drink," Bonnie insisted.

"Domestic beer makes me a happy drunk," Ryan slurred her speech mockingly. It was a game she and Bonnie had played since Ryan had learned to talk. Bonnie liked to keep Ryan humble about the over-refinement of her purebred lineage.

With her whiskey tipped in toast, she added, "But a drunk through it all."

"I'll drink to that." Ryan saluted and laughed. "You're just trying to cheer me up because she isn't coming to bed, is she?" The question spiraled into earnestness.

"No. She's sleeping on the couch in her office."

Ryan looked away. "Damn."

"Hubris doesn't become you, Ryan," Bonnie scolded.

"I *tried* to talk to her, Bonnie. She just went into the greenhouse and started pinching spent blooms off the orchids and gardenias. How do you combat that? No one has ever given me the cold shoulder before and frankly," Ryan searched her surrogate mother's eyes, "I don't know how to deal with it."

Inside, Bonnie was chuckling. She was glad Leslie had given Ryan a much-deserved ice treatment. It made Ryan think. Her face kept her counsel and offered up understanding instead. "You've met your match with her."

"So . . . I've been told," Ryan agreed caustically. She was frustrated by her lover's behavior. She would have preferred an open fight that cleared the air and absolved her of her guilt. The silence baffled her. "Did she eat?"

"No more than you."

"Bonnie, what do I do? How can she ever forgive me? Infidelity. I never thought I would see the day," Ryan chastised herself. She had already punished herself more than anyone could have or would have.

"That isn't what she's upset about," Bonnie revealed.

Ryan stopped mid-inhale and stared cautiously into the sensible, blue eyes. She had a way of making people continue talking without asking them to.

Bonnie knew all Ryan's looks better than anyone. If she followed the subtle shifts and nuances closely, she could often determine what went on in her charge's complex mind. She could tell Ryan was on unfamiliar turf and she knew why. "For being a woman, you certainly don't understand them very well."

Ryan nodded her head gratefully. Although there were times it was inconvenient to be so well understood, more often than not, it was a blessing. "Even Rags had them figured better than I do, and she was less of a woman than I am."

"Leslie never expected you to avoid temptation. She's upset because her pride is hurt," Bonnie related compassionately.

"Her pride?" Ryan asked softly.

"Sanji outsmarted her."

Ryan stretched out on her side, facing Bonnie. Her face was expectant like someone waiting to be told a bedtime story. She motioned with her drink for the explanation to continue.

"Why do you think Leslie has never openly objected to Sanji coming here?" Bonnie quizzed.

"I never thought about it. Why?"

"She knows you have an obligation to take care of Sanji, so she could hardly keep you from seeing her. Leslie is no fool, darlin'. She didn't want you driving across town to see Sanji in her home—she wanted Sanji over here where she could keep an eye on her."

"I've already proven I can't be trusted," Ryan interrupted bitterly.

Bonnie clucked. "You aren't listenin', Ryan O'Donnell." The full name stretched out in the universal display of motherly disgust. "It wasn't you she mistrusted. It was Sanji. She opened our first staff meeting with explicit instructions that no one was ever to leave you two alone for even a minute. She explained to the others, and I echoed it, that you have a definite weakness for that . . . I won't tell you what she called her. We all knew that if Sanji managed to get you alone it would come to this. Sanji is clever and she beat Leslie at her own game." The expression on the pale face told her that the puzzle pieces weren't fitting together for Ryan.

"Are you certain that's all she's upset about?"

Bonnie took a sound swallow of her drink before going on. "There's more. Leslie is sensitive, and she would have preferred it if you had chosen some other part of the house to give in to your weakness. I think you would have been safe if I had done my job better." Bonnie had spent a lifetime covering up for Ryan's transgressions in the loyal fashion required of her station.

Ryan gave Bonnie another look.

"When I saw what was happening I herded the staff out to the servant's quarters. Then I discovered I had a lost lamb. When I came back to find her, I found Corelle not ten feet from you, in a daze. I tried to get her attention, but she didn't see me. It wasn't possible for me to just walk up to her and snatch her away, so I left her there. I'm sorry."

"Oh, brother." Ryan shook her head sympathetically. "Poor kid. I probably scared the crap out of her."

"You did something. She's as skittish as a sheep," Bonnie noted.

"Does Leslie know?"

"She called me to her and asked why Corelle was there. I had to tell her."

"Yes, yes. I've really done it this time, haven't I?" Ryan stood and refilled her drink. She paced the room for a moment then collapsed in the window seat with a defeated sigh. "Now what?"

Bonnie set her empty glass next to Ryan's ashtray and started to roll her ring around her finger. "Petition for forgiveness."

"You mean beg," Ryan clarified shortly.

"You could do well to learn," Bonnie urged.

Ryan closed her eyes for a long moment before replying. When she opened them, they were filled with pain. "I know how to beg. I know every trick, every approach, every manner of begging there is."

Bonnie's mouth was open and her eyes were ablaze with incredulity. She had never known Ryan to fabricate anything, but she couldn't believe her ears. Still, she saw the misery lodged in Ryan's enigmatic eyes.

In hushed tones, Ryan explained herself. "Bonnie, don't you think Rags taught me how to beg for mercy in the most unmerciful ways possible? She was an artist at it. I promised myself, when she died, that I wouldn't let someone put me in that position again. I can't beg Leslie. I just can't."

Neither of them could bear the subject any longer. Ryan quickly changed it to something without pain. "I'm grateful to you for helping me

74

understand what is going on." Her heart and eyes softened for the hearty woman who had served her since she drew her first breath. "I take you for granted, don't I?"

"A wee bit." Bonnie shrugged a shoulder. "I don't mind. You were an easy child to raise and you've never done an unkind thing or spoken meanly to me. You're generous to a fault. Who could ask for more?" A broad smile opened up her face and returned the color to it.

"You're so devoted. I'm awed by it. You could have married, had children of your own, instead of giving your youth to me. Why didn't you marry? You could have had any man you wanted." Ryan was amazed at herself for not having asked before. When her father was alive, she was too young to be curious. After he died, she was too upset. Being married herself made her wonder why her loyal caretaker had foregone the pleasure.

"No I couldn't, lass. The one man I wanted didn't even notice me." She tried to keep the sadness out of her voice.

"It's probably because you spent all your time with me. Who was he?" Ryan had failed to pick up on yet another obvious female distress signal.

Bonnie smoothed the nap on her robe then rubbed it against the grain repeatedly while she debated about telling Ryan the secret she had harbored lovingly for thirty-two years. She knew Ryan would never guess, but if Ryan related the piecemeal information to Leslie, the counselor would figure it out. It was better heard first hand. "Your father." A mild catharsis flowed through Bonnie's veins and lightened the load on her heart. She knew Ryan would understand.

"I never knew," Ryan whispered with head bowed.

A long silence ensued as each woman searched her heart, looking for the proper way to proceed. Bonnie ventured in. "He's with his sweet Devnet now, which is where he always wanted to be. I'm sure he'll forgive me from where he rests."

"Is loving someone a sin, Bonnie?" Ryan couldn't sanction the Christian idea of sinning, even less so if loving was counted among them.

"No, 'tisn't," Bonnie reproached herself firmly. Second only to raising Ryan as a boy was Patrick O'Donnel's insistence that the staff keep their catechism to themselves. Then she chuckled to herself. "I see so much of myself in your young Corelle. God love her. I hope she doesn't do as I did. It was all right for me, but she's so young."

"I fear you're too late, old woman," Ryan mused.

"You?"

"Leslie."

Bonnie laughed out loud at that. "That beats them all. Heavenly Mary, I must need glasses for sure. I thought that look in her eye was innocent devotion. Poor lamb. It comes full circle after all. It doesn't bother you?"

Ryan smiled genuinely. "No. Half a dozen people are in love with my darling wife. What can it hurt?"

Bonnie rose to go to bed. She had an uneasy feeling that Ryan would live to take back her words. She made no mention of it. "Get some sleep. You can't accomplish anything looking for the sun to come up."

"You know me better than that," Ryan assured her.

"I do, I do," Bonnie agreed, as she padded out of the bedroom. She herself would wear blisters in her fingers with rosary beads the balance of the night, praying to her God that Ryan would hold on to her moment of happiness for all time.

Leslie arose in the morning with no appetite and a great need to soak in a hot bath. She lounged thoughtfully in the herbal-scented water that filled her large marble sunken tub.

The only sounds in her boudoir were those of Corelle moving about as she prepared to assist Leslie out of her bath. Corelle was not her ebullient morning self. Instead, she was withdrawn and spoke only when spoken to. Her behavior drew Leslie out of her self-absorption to take notice.

She studied the younger woman for signposts. The tailored uniform of grey linen and starched white bib and cuffs accented Corelle's luxuriant figure in a way that made Leslie smile. The pins in her plentiful hair clung against all odds in their proper places. Tiny, fragile hands performed in a magical way each task asked of them. The eyes were averted—there was something wrong.

Leslie stepped out of the bath, revived. Her smarting pride was purified. Corelle wrapped her in a downy towel and stepped away meekly. After drying herself vigorously, Leslie slipped into the painted silk robe Corelle held out for her. "Mmm. I feel much better, thank you." She pulled the robe to her and sat at her vanity to have her hair combed out.

Midway through the grooming, Leslie stopped her servant and turned to address her. "Corelle, what is wrong, dear? You're as nervous as a bride," she asked with gentle concern.

Corelle shook her head demurely, saying nothing.

Leslie moved aside on her bench to make room. "Sit with me."

"Aye, milady," Corelle answered unhappily. She sat with her back to the vanity and worried the brush in her hand, still trying to avoid her employer's gaze.

"Please tell me what is bothering you so." Leslie placed her hand on Corelle's cheek and turned the young face toward her inquiring eyes. Leslie's insatiable curiosity and natural dignity created a comfortable forum that often proved irresistible "Is it what you saw yesterday?"

Corelle swallowed her fear and nodded. Finally, their eyes met. Corelle's were blanketed with resolve. "Milady, I beg you to release me from your service."

Leslie gasped and looked away. Her words chafed in her throat. "Is what you saw that repulsive to you?"

A long silence separated them. Leslie agonized over the thought of losing her personal servant. She began to realize how close she felt to the youth and how important she was to her. Similarly, she could not bear the idea of being thought of as loathsome or vile. Corelle was tormented and unsure about how to explain her reasons for abandoning her post.

"Very well, Corelle. I couldn't abide you seeing me or my love as repugnant." Leslie stared into the mirror and fought back her tears.

"Oh no! That is not how it is. I cannot find the words to tell you how I feel. This is terrible." Corelle stood and tried to run away, but Leslie caught her by the arm. She came to her feet and confronted her servant firmly.

"Corelle, wait. You must try. I have to understand this."

Corelle liked to be handled sternly and she responded to the treatment. "Milady, please forgive me. Your love for Miss O'Donnell is as pure and good as hers is everlastin'. I would not come between you ever. Oh, my heart, but I have sinned against your love," she cried plaintively.

"How?" Leslie's voice bordered on danger.

"I just stood there," Corelle began to recall, "like my feet had been nailed to the floor. New and strange feelings overcame me and swelled my heart until I thought it was going to burst. I was, I was," she started to weep, "jealous. Of that, that . . ."

"Wench," Leslie whispered.

Corelle pulled a hanky from her pocket to catch her tears, "I was swept away by the power of Miss O'Donnell and I found myself wanting to be taken like that by her. Oh, this is unbearable," she sobbed.

Leslie pulled her close and soothed her. "There, there. It isn't awful or horrible to feel that way." She was trying to console herself as much as her servant. "It certainly isn't cause to leave us. Stay, Corelle. You'll begin to feel better soon and everything will be fine."

Leslie remembered what Ryan had told her about the passions of youth when she felt the force of Corelle's plea. "No, I cannot. I cannot. Please, I must go."

"Shhh. I'll let you go, darling. I'm sad that staying is so painful for you. I'll miss you terribly." Leslie stroked the round face she was cradling to her bosom.

"Milady, I'll miss you, too. Please understand. This is for the best, I know." Corelle took deep comfort from Leslie's voice and the closeness of her body. She grew still and compliant at last.

Leslie held her away and searched her misty green eyes. "Will you give me the customary two weeks? I need you." Corelle's leaving couldn't have come at a worse time for Leslie.

Once she received Corelle's promise, she sent the distraught woman to bed. She, herself, had never been subject to extremes of emotions in her youth, but since meeting Ryan she had come to know how taxing they could be.

Leslie placed her brush on the vanity slowly when she saw her lover's reflection in the mirror.

Ryan approached calmly and stood behind Leslie. She was more relaxed from her walk of several miles about the neighborhood. Her relaxation was not so great that she felt at ease with removing her leather motorcycle jacket. It had been many months since she needed to wear it in her mate's presence. Armor.

"Where's Corelle?" Ryan placed her hands lovingly on Leslie's shoulders and rejoiced inwardly when she was not rebuffed.

Leslie rested her head on Ryan's chest and spoke to her reflection. "I sent her to her room to get some rest." After a frustrated sigh she continued, hushed, "Damn you, Ryan. She's asked to be let go because of you."

Ryan glanced at the door to Corelle's bedroom then back to the mirror. "Is she frightened?"

"No. Aroused. It seems she's discovered that your brand of lechery appeals to her and she doesn't want to be reminded of it every day," Leslie related with pure displeasure.

Ryan kept a straight face at great cost. "That surprises me."

"Why?"

"Because it's you she's in love with," Ryan revealed evenly.

Leslie turned sharply to confront Ryan directly. "Don't toy with me, Ryan. That's not funny."

"Just true," Ryan asserted firmly. "That's why it surprises me that she would leave so willingly. She hides it well. I only noticed it a couple weeks ago." She let go of Leslie's smooth shoulders and moved around to sit on the edge of the vanity.

"You don't normally notice that sort of thing," Leslie recounted.

Ryan lit a cigarette and sighed. "Maybe Rags left me a legacy after all. I don't think you need to worry about losing Corelle. Find her a position that she can get out of easily and fill hers with a temporary. She'll be back before long. When is she leaving?"

"Shortly after my birthday. Gratefully. I couldn't make it through this party you've planned without her." Leslie opened a jar of cream for her face and collected her nerves. It worried her that Ryan was wearing her jacket indoors. There had been no clue from Bonnie that anything was amiss—something she had counted on. She had, therefore, indulged herself in the full extent of her sulk, a bad habit grown worse during her many years of living alone.

"Does this mean you're finished being angry with me?" Ryan asked gravely. She searched for the doves of peace she hoped would settle into her lover's eyes.

Leslie stared openly. "I wasn't mad at you. I was mad at myself. I don't like being jealous. I like even less being outwitted by the object of my jealousy," she explained.

"She just said the right thing at the right time. It couldn't be helped." Relief began to filter into Ryan's speech and the muscles of her face loosened.

"Just what was the right thing?" Leslie inquired.

"She now has memory of having lived with me, although she didn't mention anything unhappy. She got my attention and capitalized on it."

"I should say. Are you going to tell her?"

Ryan put her cigarette out and shook her head. "Not unless she brings it up."

Leslie was glad it was a decision she didn't have to make. The air was clear between them and understanding brought them closer. A second look showed her the true condition of her spouse. "You don't look well. Haven't you slept?" she asked, vaguely amazed.

Suddenly, Ryan was extremely tired. She stood and walked toward their bedroom. "No. Or eaten, or bathed or changed clothes," she added to head off the inevitable third degree. The intense pain bled through her voice when she turned to address her lover. "Don't *ever* do this to me again, Leslie. You'll have to find some other way to soothe your pride. I cannot bear to be apart from you."

Leslie followed Ryan into the bedroom. "I'm sorry. I had no idea I was hurting you."

Her apology was unheard. Ryan hadn't removed her boots or pulled back the bedclothes. She had fallen into a deep sleep the moment her head reached her pillow.

"Les, you can be a real fool at times," Leslie scolded herself quietly as she watched Ryan's body unwind and begin to restore itself. "The only thing she has ever asked for was love and she gives everything she has in return. Your pride could never equal her pain. Isn't it about time you stopped letting it interfere?" Her answer came with a silent resolve to love Ryan *more* than life.

# 10

The eleventh day of the tenth month was a Friday. An Indian summer day to begin Leslie's thirty-fourth year.

Ryan stood at the end of the bed watching her mate sleep. Fresh from her shower, Ryan felt relaxed and somewhat playful. Since life had begun anew for her, she had learned how to have fun again and Leslie was as much her playmate as her soulmate. She was looking forward to making the day special for the woman who had made living special.

The warm aroma of coffee reached her and she reluctantly broke off her appreciation to see to its service. In the hallway, a young kitchen servant was arranging white spider mums in a vase on the tray she had prepared. Ryan addressed her pleasantly, "Is it here?"

"Yes, Miss O'Donnell," the servant answered in kind. "It just arrived." She handed a set of keys to her employer then waited to serve the morning refreshment.

"Thank you." Ryan put the keys in the pocket of her robe and waved the servant away. "You needn't bother. Corelle will serve it." The young woman nodded and left quietly.

Corelle was surprised when Ryan walked into her room. Her services were not required until later in the day, and then quite late, so Leslie had given her the morning off. Sleeping late was a luxury Corelle seldom had the chance for. Ryan's unexpected presence found her seated at her vanity fixing her hair and still wearing her sheer, sea-green nightgown.

Hip-length, chestnut curls cascaded down her back, forgotten. The chore of harnessing them into the full braids and swirls that normally graced her head couldn't be performed with shaking hands or a pounding heart. A hairpin fell from her hand to the floor as she turned her wide-eyed gaze to Ryan.

Ryan wore a full-length, black robe accented with a gold ascot about her neck. The gold piping and monogram on the pocket revealed Leslie's talent for design. All Corelle saw was the unbearable elegance and the hedonistic smile creeping across Ryan's masterful features. Her blush deepened when she became aware of her own near nakedness. Coquetry bled through her reserve. With a side glance, her greeting was sweet. "Miss O'Donnell, top o' the morning to you."

"It is especially nice," Ryan agreed. "And I know you have the morning off, but would you be so kind and perform a small favor for me?"

"Gladly." Corelle showed her bright teeth with an eager smile.

"I should like you to serve your Lady her coffee in bed. The tray is in the hallway."

Corelle stood and walked toward her wardrobe. "Give me but a moment to dress." She wondered how she was going to continue standing when she felt Ryan take her by the arm to halt her progress. She knew her trembling would reveal her need; she couldn't stop it.

The fulcrum in Ryan's arsenal of magic with women was a hauntingly persuasive look that the most frozen of hearts could not resist. Corelle was young, hot-blooded and Irish—no match for the sophisticated, experienced womanizer with a satin voice.

"Don't change a thing. You look very becoming just as you are."

Corelle sucked in her breath frantically, then exhaled hypnotically. "As you wish."

—◦◆⟨⟩◆◦—

Leslie's eyes and smile opened lazily. "Mmm. Good morning."

"Happy birthday, angel." Ryan leaned over and kissed Leslie's soft cheek. She helped settle pillows behind her lover, then walked to the door to allow Corelle in with her tray.

Leslie gasped slightly, then looked sharply at Ryan's mischievous expression. Her eyes betrayed her by refusing to linger there. Instead, they suited themselves and followed the path of appetite.

Corelle was never so graceful as when she dwelled in the domain of service. Her walk was free of sideways movement and her head held still as any fashion model. The tray in her hands was balanced neatly, but all was met with indifference.

Leslie had tunnelvision for the unbound breasts. Each step shook them with a gentle bounce that emphasized their generosity and brought their admirer fully awake.

The tray was set astride Leslie's lap, and Corelle's breasts hung provocatively before her hungry grey eyes. " 'Tis a grand day for a birthday, milady. May yours be happy and full of joy." Corelle fought to keep her professional demeanor and stepped slightly away from the bed.

Nature had paid an early call upon her juvenile body and turned it into a woman long before she was ready. Nearly half her life had been spent heavily covered with dowdy, shapeless garments chosen expressly to hide her womanhood. Now, in the company of women, she was free to dress as she pleased when she was off duty, which, by her own choice, was not often.

This, then, was the first time someone other than her own female relatives had seen her in such a revealing, compromising situation. It was not unpleasant for her.

Nor was it unpleasant for her employers. Ryan stretched out sideways across the bed with her head propped on her hand near Leslie's feet. She had the best view and she maximized it— enjoying both women enjoying each other.

"Thank you, Corelle. You look lovely this morning." Leslie eyed the full vision waiting to be dismissed over the rim of her coffee cup.

The neckline of the pretty negligee terminated at an empire waistband. Each breast was cradled in its own sheath of gossamer fabric, through which could be seen brown areolas larger than silver medallions fit with nipples that resembled small thimbles. They were hard and bulged out prominently.

Two pairs of intrigued eyes traced the line of the flat tummy to the junction of the legs. In defiance of the pliant nature of its owner, the coarse, dark sex-hair stubbornly proclaimed itself. The triangular patch forged out boldly then curled back on itself like drake tail feathers. The fabric rested on the shelf it created then tumbled over the edge, sharply outlining the extravagant, womanly profile.

Taken as a whole—the burdensome breasts, exaggerated nipples, plentiful hair and expectant hips—Corelle's body could easily be mistaken for a lifesize fertility charm. True to her race, she possessed a body created for childbirth and hearty, robust living—a body that did not fit the temperament of its inhabitant. Or the reverse, Ryan couldn't decide which. Knowing what it was to not fit, she sympathized with her.

Leslie's train of thought wouldn't progress beyond the quickening of her newly-discovered fetish. A fetish that was bound for growth into a full-blown obsession.

Ryan let the fixation take root for long minutes; then she dismissed Corelle gently. "You may leave us now. Thank you."

Leslie and Corelle's attention snapped and they whipped around to register what had been said.

"My pleasure," Corelle replied. She exited through the boudoir, traveling the shortcut to her own bed and secret deliverance.

The silence she left behind was broken by the chime that rang out when Leslie set her cup in its saucer. "You are aw-ful," she chided lovingly.

Ryan laughed so hard her sides ached. She recovered and wiped the moisture from her eyes. "Oh, angel. You had me praying you wouldn't nod your head even the tiniest bit. I thought surely your eyes were going to fall right out of their sockets."

"I wasn't *that* bad," Leslie insisted.

"Worse!" Ryan massaged her lover's feet through the bed covers as she spoke. "I've seen children in candy stores with more poise."

Leslie lit a cigarette and chuckled. "I suppose you're right. Have you ever seen anyone built like her? I haven't."

"Now we know where heaven is. The Irish countryside. It's probably crawling with giant tits and chestnut manes. Want to go?" Ryan raised her eyebrows quizzically.

"What? And leave all this behind?" Leslie waved her hand in a reserved sweeping motion. "Ask me again after I've had a couple drinks. I might change my mind."

"You're on. I must say, though, I'm not normally attracted to her type, but she wants it so badly, it wouldn't take much provocation to give it to her."

"Or to enjoy it. You planned this, didn't you?"

"No. I just saw a chance to sink the hook in a little deeper, so I took it. Tell me you minded," Ryan teased.

"I'd be married to the wrong person if that sort of devilry bothered me."

"I'm lucky, then."

Leslie moved her tray aside and stretched. "You're so calm this morning. I'd be a nervous wreck in your place."

"That's when you would discover how indispensable Bonnie really is. Believe me, she has everything in hand. My father didn't entertain on a large scale because our home was too informal. This one is designed for it, so the problems are minimized," Ryan reassured.

"You've always maintained that you're a poor host."

"If I have to do the work. As long as all I have to do is give instructions, I enjoy entertaining." Ryan paused to light a cigarette. "It would be difficult to own three taverns and a restaurant if I didn't. You aren't supposed to be worrying about any of this, lover. Your biggest concern today should be what time you want to eat dinner," Ryan instructed.

"Well, all right. I won't worry about a thing and just have lots of fun." Leslie was good at pampering herself. She was even better at letting someone else cater to her needs. Being the center of so much attention hadn't become real for her yet. She was quite relaxed.

"You're so obedient. I love it," Ryan bantered. "Not so for me though. I simply could not resist getting you a gift."

"Ryan," Leslie sighed. "I asked you not to."

"It's just a small one." Ryan feigned a plea. She took the keys from her pocket and handed them to her wife. "See, it fits in your hand."

Leslie gave a playful scowl, then looked in her hand. Her eyes widened with amazement. "These are keys to a Rolls," she observed breathlessly.

"A Corniche touring coupe. It's out front." Ryan smiled indulgently and shook her head. It tickled her to watch Leslie bound out of bed and into the window seat. She followed and looked over Leslie's shoulder at the sand-colored convertible parked on the brick horseshoe-shaped drive below their window.

"Oh, Ryan! It's beautiful! How on earth did you get it here so early?" She turned her sparkling eyes toward her lover.

"It isn't hard to do when the owner of the dealership is a neighbor and friend of the family."

Ryan, for all her generosity, could not be persuaded to go outdoors in her robe as Leslie had done. She stayed behind to dress while her excited mate dashed down the stairs and out the front door to inspect the lavish auto. After a hastily-eaten breakfast they went for a drive in it and reveled in its luxury.

"Your dress is here." Ryan walked into the boudoir and gave the garment over to Corelle.

Leslie was just finished with her bath and still relaxed. "Did Mrs. Crown come with it?"

"Of course. Your hairdresser arrived as well. They're waiting for you downstairs."

"Which means you want to see the dress now," Leslie guessed.

"You're good," Ryan congratulated Leslie playfully. She admired her spouse's powers of reasoning and observation. Life was much easier when she didn't have to explain herself quite so often. She leaned against the mirror casually and watched the expression on Leslie's face transform into one of surprise and vexation. Corelle zipped the back and stepped away to admire the gown.

"This is not the neckline I designed," Leslie informed Ryan sternly.

"Hmmm. I know." Ryan's voice was passionate and full of appreciation for the risque bodice. From where she stood the shimmering white fabric hid only the pink circles of Leslie's perfect breasts. "I told Mrs. Crown that I wanted to see more of you this evening. You look incredible." Ryan savored every detail of the gown authored by her wife.

The sleeveless dress fit snugly about the waist. The skirt hung from the hips in a straight, seamless piece of fabric that overlapped the pelvis and parted gracefully below the knees. The hemline originated at the right hip and came full circle in a sparkling scallop of sapphire blue sequins.

At Ryan's covert request, the square neckline had been lowered two inches and challenged Leslie's virtue. Leslie admitted to herself that it was an improvement and had a stunning effect; still she objected. "Ryan, I can't wear it this way."

Ryan's mind was set. She stepped up to her wife and pinched the nearly exposed nipples savagely. "You *will*," she demanded with narrowed eyes.

Leslie hissed through her teeth and agreed quickly to get the unexpected pain to stop. From the first time Ryan had forced her into submission, Leslie knew she was hopelessly addicted to the intense thrills it gave her to participate in her own undoing. Every day she was confronted with Ryan's indomitable will and had the serene pleasure of surrendering to it.

Ryan rewarded her with a lingering kiss, then vanished.

After dinner was finished for Ryan and the guest of honor, McKinley yawned and stretched for a short time before rousing for a night of festivities.

The classic house came alive to welcome guests, as few homes could, in the style and purpose of its design. Members of an all-woman orchestra warmed up in the ballroom, side by side with the female rock band that would alternate songs with them to provide a comfortable assortment of dance music for a cross-section of guests.

Servants bustled about under Bonnie's vigilant guidance. The distaff nature of the household made the existence of a butler impractical. Ryan preferred to greet her guests personally and set them at ease at the onset.

Leslie was resplendent. She stood to her lover's right, where she received arrivals with a poise and grace that was hers alone. Her style was the perfect complement to Ryan's charisma. An aura of harmonious cordiality settled over them and warmed everyone who came near.

Ryan's friends were as eager to meet the woman who brought her out of her mourning as Leslie's were to discover what manner of woman could thaw her virgin heart.

Women all, the guests hailed from every background and status. For this one evening they were brought together by their common interest in their hosts. Most had never attended a formal event, but none would pass up such a rare opportunity to dress in finery or see McKinley. Least of all, Brigid. Few were as glad as she to see Ryan quit the path of self-destruction that was dangerously near its end when Leslie had come into her tortured life.

This was a time of celebration for Brigid and she made the best of it. Herself in tails, she approached her cousin with a broad smile. Pain shortens the memory of times when life is good and carefree. Brigid had forgotten entirely how handsome Ryan could look when she chose to.

Ryan wore black tails, a white vest, shirt and bow tie. She stood tall, proud and confident as she extended her hand affectionately toward her closest friend.

Brigid took it firmly in hers and held on for a moment as she spoke. "This is one of the happiest days of my life." Her eyes sparkled with delight in answer to the thin-lipped smile animating Ryan's noble features. "To see you well and entertaining again is more than I ever dreamed possible!"

"It feels as good to me," Ryan agreed as she noticed Star standing next to Brigid. She studied her cousin's mate with her sophisticated eye for beauty. An eyebrow raised slightly and she nodded approvingly toward Brigid before greeting Star. Brigid's smile transformed into one of self-satisfaction and pride. It took some doing to raise one of *Ryan's* eyebrows.

"Welcome, Star." Ryan kissed Star's hand. "I'm so glad you could join us," Ryan opened silkily. The time when Ryan and Star hadn't gotten along was well behind them now.

"I wouldn't dream of missing a party given in Leslie's honor. Thank you for having us." Star began to relax and grow more comfortable in her once abandoned role of femme.

"You look heavenly tonight," Ryan observed genuinely.

Star had allowed herself to be persuaded into leaving her politics at home for one night. She hadn't owned a dress in several years, but Ryan chased away the discomfort she felt with wearing one.

Her gown was sky blue taffeta cut in the most flattering style for her healthy roundness. She wore a simple strand of pearls and the sharp lines of her face were softened by a neat, feminine hairstyle.

But, as water seeks its own level, the human eye seeks true beauty. It was never far from reach as long as Leslie was nearby. Ryan, Brigid and Star gravitated toward her in concert. Ryan closed her eyes briefly in serene appreciation of her wife. Brigid appraised the vision through the trained eyes of an artist. Star's eyes enlarged with amazement and awe. Each was breathless.

Lightbeams from the chandelier above them hailed down on the sapphires and diamonds of Leslie's necklace and bounced randomly about, impaling themselves on her slender neck and falling helplessly upon her seductive front. The pendulous lacework of diamonds held oval-cut stones which looked like iridescent blue flies snared in a web of dewdrops.

Leslie's original design of the dress served to showcase the jewels. Ryan's intervention made the jewels a showcase for the woman. For Ryan, the evening would yield frequent occasions to take delight from eyes inextricably locked on her spouse's magnificent breasts.

"You're staring. All of you," Leslie reprimanded jokingly.

"No more than anyone so far tonight, darling," Ryan reminded her.

"Brig, I am so pleased with the gift you made. It arrived this morning. I can scarcely describe how lovely it is. Day lilies are my favorite flower." Leslie distracted the trio by encouraging a hearty hug from the artist.

Ryan laughed. "Are you sure, angel? You only ordered three thousand of them."

"Leslie! You didn't?" Star gasped.

"I did." Leslie beamed. "I'm quite good at spending her money." She gave a quick, coy look at Ryan.

Ryan agreed with an utterly joyful laugh that ran clear and bright through the great hall where they stood. She could find nothing in her memory to compare with the happiness she felt at that very moment.

Leslie embraced Star warmly. Their friendship had grown over the years and had become something special and unassailable for Leslie.

"Thank you ever so much for the herbal bath bars. You know I've come to be quite dependent on them. I can't imagine what plain bath water is like any more."

"You better watch out, honey. She's wealthy enough to bribe you for your secret recipe," Brigid teased.

Star blushed. Brigid was the one person who knew her well enough to find ways to embarrass her.

Leslie took advantage of the blush to comment on Star's appearance. "Star, you look absolutely wonderful!"

"Thank you, Les. I'm certain that no one could be foolish enough to try to look as lovely as you. It can't be done." Star's telling remark proved to be true. Indeed both members of the happy couple were set apart by their elegance. Nothing less was expected by the friends of either.

—◦◆❖│◗◦◦—

"I don't feel so badly now about never getting anywhere with Leslie," remarked a party-goer standing on the edge of the dance floor.

"Why?" the woman next to her asked.

"Jeez. I was not only barking up the wrong tree, I wasn't even in the right forest," the consoled woman revealed.

"Yeah. We are a little out of her league."

"A lot! I don't think that even Del knew there was a diamond-studded rose at the core of that ice-castle."

"Where is Del? I'd have thought she would come," the second woman remarked.

"Shit. Are you kidding? Del hates Ryan like birds hate cats. I heard Dana tried to get Ryan in the sack and got a black eye in the process," the first woman related.

"Ooeee. A bitch like Dana won't let that go."

"That's for sure. I'll bet Dana's dying to find out what McKinley looks like. Too bad Del wouldn't let her come." Both women laughed sardonically, but quickly turned their attention to the orchestra once they stopped tuning their instruments.

All the guests had arrived, so the hosts were free to join them in the lavish ballroom. They glided onto the dance floor alone and turned to face one another. Leslie curtsied deeply and Ryan bowed from the hips in reply. Ryan gathered the love of her life in her firm grasp and the orchestra struck up Gounod's Waltz from Act II of "Faust."

Together the couple traveled effortlessly around the floor, jubilantly observing the first dance for the guest of honor. They gazed intently and lovingly into one another's eyes. The floor felt like puffy clouds beneath their feet.

The crowd was spellbound as they drank in Leslie's shimmering white dress and gloves, jewels, silver shoes and perfect coiffure. Ryan augmented the effect as she guided her partner confidently around the floor in harmony with the music. Many, including the principals, didn't want the dance to end. End it must, and those gathered there expressed their appreciation, then joined in to the strains of a slow, romantic song.

The night was underway. The music and champagne flowed freely in the collective bloodstream, heightening awareness and loosening morals.

The sculptured ceramic day lilies were lemon yellow. The flowers rested in an S-curve bed of dark green Scotch broom. The entire arrangement spilled over the edges of their crystal container like a frozen waterfall. Its final home would be the sitting room, but first it was on display on the mantelpiece in the ballroom.

As others had done throughout the course of the evening, Leslie admired the artwork with unabashed fascination.

Star approached her friend respectfully, as one nears a celebrant of the feast of the soul. Her voice was quiet and reverent. "She really outdid herself this time. I've never seen her spend so much time or work so hard on any piece before. If I didn't care as deeply about you as I do, I might have been jealous. She is so grateful to you for making Ryan happy. This was the best way she knew of to show her thanks."

"Oh, Star. It's magnificent! The detail on the broom is unbelievable. Each little ridge stands by itself, yet is a part of the whole." Leslie tore her gaze from the gift to look at Star. "I cried when I first saw it. Ryan was completely awed. You know that you're married to a master artist, don't you? I envy you being able to watch these creations come into being."

"I am fortunate," Star agreed. "I keep thinking that Brig can't possibly top her last work, but she always does." Star drew closer and lowered her voice gravely. "Les, she's been acting so odd lately. I'm worried." Star hoped Leslie would understand the strange behavior and explain it to her.

Star was like an adopted sister to Leslie. It was an arrangement that benefited both parties—the older woman sorely missed her family, the younger woman needed Leslie's levelheaded observations and guidance to keep life in perspective. Leslie took a sip of her champagne and schooled her face in the reflection of gentle concern. Her own quick worry simmered beneath the surface in a pool of foreboding. "How so?"

"Don't laugh, but she's started painting with oils. She gave up painting in high school and now, for no reason, she's taken it up again. And she's gone a lot," Star related anxiously.

"I don't understand. What do you mean by saying that she is gone a lot?" Leslie pried.

"She just leaves. With no explanation. Then when she comes back and I ask her where she's been, her answer is always testy and the same. 'Out,' she says. Moody," Star added suddenly. "One minute she's her normal peaceful self and the next it's like a maternity ward waiting room. I've found her pacing about, even in the middle of the night. She's nervous, irritable and unpredictable. There are times when I actually wish she would call Ryan and dig up one of those fights they used to start at Sergios."

"They may be overdue for a visit to Sergios. I can't tell. How long has this been going on?" Leslie toyed with her necklace.

"About a month."

"I need a cigarette and a refill." Leslie urged her friend toward the bar arm in arm to discourage dance offers. "She hasn't shown any sign of getting better?"

"Worse," Star emphasized. "When you invitation came she insisted that I wear this outfit. I wanted to wear a woman's tux, but she wouldn't hear of it. At least she didn't make me go with her to buy it." Star's discomfort threatened to begin anew and she didn't want it to. She was enjoying herself and had promised to leave her convictions at home. There would be time, later, to sort out and assimilate her impressions of the night's events. She hadn't expected to enjoy all the compliments and dance offers that came her way. Now she wanted to untangle her confusion about her lover's behavior, and Leslie was the best person to help her do so.

Leslie did see things clearly when she had the right information. "Star, I'm surprised at you. It isn't at all unusual for Brig to want you to dress so nicely for a formal party."

"You don't think so? Brig has never cared a whit about roles. I couldn't have lived with her for so many years if she had," Star maintained.

"It isn't a question of roles," Leslie instructed wisely. "For all her laissez faire, Brig is still, and always will be, a member of the upper class." Leslie nodded at the bartender in gratitude for filling her glass and lighting her cigarette. "And, for all her confidence and self-containment, there is still a part of Brigid that wants Ryan's approval. I thought she was going to burst with pride when Ryan showed that she appreciated how nice you look. I've discovered that a number of people have a deep respect for Ryan and her way of looking at women. To have Ryan admire you was probably one of the nicest things to have happen to Brigid's ego."

Star laughed heartily and dissipated her nervous energy. "It didn't do my ego any harm either. You're right. I'm overreacting to this."

A soft smile formed on Leslie's face. "Brigid may just be keyed up about the show." Leslie wanted her theory to be correct. She fished for some proof. "Are you having relations?" Normally so personal a question wouldn't have been considered by someone with Leslie's respect for privacy. Champagne loosens tongues as well as morals.

Star was not offended or shy about answering. "No. But, that isn't uncommon. When Brigid is totally absorbed in her art she's been known to forget to eat and sleep. I don't mind—it seldom goes for long."

"Your loss is the artworld's gain." Leslie decided her theory was as good as any, and Star seemed satisfied. "You look like the cat that swallowed the canary, Star. What are you up to?"

A lustful smile transformed Star's worried look into one of desire. "I was just thinking about our drive here tonight."

Leslie leaned closer like a conspirator. "Tell me."

"Well," Star savored, "she did break her fast tonight. Before we reached town, she pulled off the road and made love to me."

Leslie was already thoroughly aroused. Her reluctant exhibitionism had made her the object of many and frequent lewd proposals. From time to time she spied Ryan's conniving expression from across the room. It was a sexual conspiracy. Women leered, ogled and flagrantly beheld their hostess' inviting nakedness. One dance partner was bold enough to reach into the immodest front and steal a hearty squeeze of a breast few had touched, but many had coveted.

Star's confession set her afire and forced an indiscreet moan from her. Each woman gave the other a knowing look. "We do have seven extra bedrooms. Perhaps you and Brig would like to . . ." Leslie suggested.

Star winked and left Leslie's side to find and seduce her mate. Leslie followed with her eyes and watched as Star succeeded. The couple exited the ballroom in the direction of the staircase.

A soft kiss near her ear raised the hair on the back of Leslie's neck. It was a familiar kiss.

"Join me in the kitchen." The hot, alcoholic invitation seared down the length of Leslie's body and back again. She put her cigarette in an ashtray and abandoned her drink. Her reply came in the form of action as she led the way to the party's nerve center.

Inside the large, gourmet kitchen Ryan sidled her lust interest near an unoccupied counter. Several servants, some regulars, others hired only for the night, busied themselves quickly. Instantly, the sightless eyes of domestic service created an aura of anonymity for their employers.

Ryan moved her hand under the top flap of Leslie's dress and pulled away the bottom flap. Her spindly digits slid under Leslie's lace panties, seeking their polestar.

"Ryan. You know how I feel about making love in front of the staff," Leslie protested with a purposeful whisper.

The middle and most talented finger left its pleasure mission. "Are you telling me *no?*" The finger gouged Leslie's vagina cruelly to illustrate her question.

"Sssss." A trembling exhale followed. "Oonn, you know I can't," Leslie betrayed herself.

"Besides, I'll only be here a moment or so. *Won't,*" another deep thrust, "*I?*"

Leslie nodded her head greedily. She wanted the probe to return to its vocation. It did, performing its duty enthusiastically and well.

Ryan nibbled on her lover's trapezius, which never failed to raise goosebumps on Leslie's velvet skin and deepen her breathing. Each exhale pulled her excited breasts away from her dress, exposing her taut, blushing nipples. Both their owner and their possessor thrilled at the sight.

91

"You foxy wench," Ryan whispered hoarsely. "Hot bitch."

"Oh. Oh, Ryan," Leslie encouraged achingly.

The names grew less flattering and more stimulating. "Wanton harlot. You're eeeasy, aren't you, hussy?"

"Yesss," Leslie answered breathlessly.

"Whore!" The words came more urgently. "Cheap pussy!" Ryan accelerated the massage of the rigid nerve bundle at the end of her finger. Climax was imminent. "Slut! Cunt!"

If the servants couldn't make out Ryan egging Leslie on in detail, no doubt remained of the results. Leslie doubled over, moaning loudly and grasping Ryan's hand with both of hers to force it into her ache. When Leslie began to recover, Ryan injected herself between her lover's line of vision and the servants. She soothed and praised her, then escorted her discreetly back to the party. As Ryan had hoped, the guest of honor was quite under the influence and suffered no ill effects of her pornographic behavior. In fact, the opposite proved to be true.

The party plunged into another stage. Nearly half the guests had gone home, leaving behind the more inebriated, ribald party-goers, most of whom would be unearthed from various corners of McKinley long after sunrise.

Leslie continued to drink liberally. She encouraged suggestive remarks and indecent flirtations from women who were as wrecked as she was becoming.

Twice, Ryan had to intercede when flirtations began to look like assaults, but for the most part, she stood aside to indulge in voyeurism and eavesdropping. For her, champagne had cloyed and she sobered quickly.

Instead, sexual intoxication gripped her every nerve and muscle— boiled in her bloodstream. The vessels of self-knowledge contained, among their gifts, a full awareness of when she had reached her limit.

The orchestra had fulfilled their contract and had retreated. The rock band played on energetically. Ryan stubbed out her cigarette, reached to her bow tie, pulled it free and undid her collar button. A beeline across the dance floor brought her to her wife. Taking Leslie's wrist from her dance partner's shoulder, she yanked her lover away and escorted her swiftly out of the ballroom. In her condition there was no patience for helping a tipsy woman up a flight of stairs. She simply swept her wife up in her arms and ascended them steadily.

Leslie purred and hummed the whole way. Ryan closed the bedroom door behind her with her foot and crossed over to the bed where she placed Leslie gently down.

While taking the studs off her shirt she spoke. "You are *drunk,* lady."

"Hmmm. Are you going to take advantage of me?"

"I am," Ryan answered matter-of-factly. She pulled away the skirt that shimmered in the moonlight pouring through their window and spread the provocative, helpless legs apart to receive her.

It took great control to check her passion but Ryan wanted something.

Leslie wouldn't get what she wanted until Ryan did. She climbed on top of Leslie and began grinding her hips slowly and effortlessly. "You *are* an exhibitionist. Aren't you?"

Leslie nodded her head slowly. She was shy about admitting it.

"Aren't you?" Ryan asked again with narrowed, searching eyes.

"Yes," Leslie whispered.

"I can't *hear* you," Ryan insisted.

"Yes, I am," Leslie proclaimed clearly and passionately. Her head felt like it was floating.

For months, Ryan had been methodically unlocking the doors of Leslie's libido. The last door of inhibition remained locked before her and she was determined to unlock it on this night. All day the tumblers had fallen into place to open the combination and free her wife. Now excitement threatened to overcome her and shake loose the final tumbler, dangerously near dismantling her careful work. She held on and continued to press her sex into her mate's with a purposefully timed rhythm. "I saw Lonney cop a feel when you were dancing with her. You enjoyed it, didn't you?"

"I did. Ohn, Ryan. I've never been so aroused in my life," Leslie revealed frantically.

"That's because I've never made you wait so long." Ryan went silent to let her meaning sink in. Still with the aggravating pace.

Leslie pulled her knees toward Ryan's shoulders and answered the silent, endless grinding with urging of her own. To no avail. Ryan wouldn't allow herself to give in.

Then it happened. The final tumbler fell into place and the door opened. The last bastion of genteelness collapsed in the face of Leslie's need. She could no longer control herself. She wailed and pleaded, "Oh, Ryan! Fuck me! Please, fuck me!"

Ryan moaned from her guts in reply. "Yeah, baby. Like you've never been fucked before." With blinding fury, she took what she had been waiting for, what belonged to her for all time, what Leslie gave and could never take back.

Enchantment winged into their presence and lifted them away. At last, all conscious resistance faded and Ryan was free to take her mate to a place beyond the realm of angels, beyond the pleasure palaces of abandonment, beyond the inner sanctums of their inner selves. A place safe and free from Anara's relentless terrorism and mockery.

"Venadia?" Blaise called the name sovereignly. It was quiet where she stood, except for the gentle, universal hum of power and light that served as their shroud. Her red eyes contracted and focused on the image that formed before her.

They had met in this web of peace before, these lovers, many times over the eons. To recognize and welcome one another, to conjoin in harmony, to share or reassure—whatever was needed to perpetuate the union. To endure apart from time and space.

Here, their true selves could form and be recognized. When their physical, earthbound bodies happened upon one another Venadia (Leslie) saw, behind jade eyes, a pair of red ones set evenly in a pale oval, deceptively delicate face. Wine-colored lips. Smoke-grey hair that was long and full, nestled in the hood of flowing charcoal robes.

Venadia stepped forward at the sound of her name of power to inspect the jewels of her beloved, Blaise (Ryan). About Blaise's neck, hovering on a harp note, was a large ruby. Venadia smiled when she noticed the garnet ring on Blaise's finger and the necklace of flames resting on her breast. "You are whole then. Welcome, Blaise." Venadia extended her milky hands in greeting.

"My love." Blaise beheld the quintessential beauty without fear for its demise. She lifted the gauzy, ivory veil to reveal the face one-half shade lighter than the veil, polished and reflecting the light of the golden eyes and clear hair. The color of her lips was one not yet discovered on their planet: a pigment near dull yellow gold with the ability to bend light rays twice upon themselves before letting them free in a glossy hue that invited and intimidated. She was draped in layer upon layer of veils of ivory trimmed with gold threads. The black diamond scalloping on Blaise's robes reappeared on Venadia's neckline.

They kissed quietly and blissfully, renewing their oneness. After a time, Venadia spoke. "Does Anara know you have been given your name of power?"

"She has not yet learned of it, though it can't be kept from her much longer. It isn't reasonable to expect the secret to survive until I need it." Blaise was sad.

"One cannot attempt to rise to a position of power in the scheme of things without gathering enemies. Or allies. Her fear of me is perhaps our best weapon." Venadia remembered when she herself had chosen the path her mate was embarking upon and she knew of the sadness—was touched by it.

Blaise sighed and buried her face in her hands. "Venadia, must I go through with this?"

"I have served my term, Blaise," the golden beauty prompted compassionately. "The Throne of Council will be vacant soon and there are only the two of you eligible to take my place. Would you default and abandon our planet to her and her kind?" Venadia gave her lover a brief glance of what would happen if she did default, leaving the Throne to the Contender, Anara.

"She would set matters back considerably." Blaise shuddered. "Very well, I shall go on." Blaise was master of her own fear, but was prey to melancholia.

"The Goddess of Fire spoke to you about your temper?" Venadia knew why her mate had done what she had done, but she was certain that Blaise was unaware of how others viewed it.

"She did," Blaise nodded, remembering how the Goddess of Fire had given to her the necklace that brought her name of power to her. And how she had wisely counseled her about the use of her temper.

"But not of your sadness."

"It is not her domain to do so. I wish to cancel the sadness out with the temper."

Venadia nodded her head with approval. "When I first learned of your plan to return to the physical plane I didn't understand your motives. There are members of the Council who are vexed with you for doing it. They claim that it has made a mockery of the balance of my service to be forced back to the physical world also."

"Does anyone know of your whereabouts on the physical side?" Blaise queried.

"I have invoked the power of the Veil as I always do to protect my location from the idly curious. It is best that certain of the Council believe that I have gone my own way to satisfy some fancy or other. Anara has allies among us. The less they know, the better. It would not do to have her learn that I am assisting you in this struggle."

"We must return now. It is late," Venadia advised gently.

Blaise agreed and together they descended through the mists to find their bodies resting peacefully in their dark suite of passion.

# PART II

# 11

Indian summer was banished from the land—overthrown by a snow-flake coup. McKinley responded as though she had been briefed in advance by Demeter herself. A dozen massive marble fireplaces came ablaze more from instinct than from the skilled ministrations of house-maids, filling the atmosphere with scented smoke.

The Classic Revival mansion drew the fleecy blanket about her like a shroud of intimacy and drama, and withdrew into herself. If sunrises were her offering to those who inhabited her, her fellowship with winter was her gift to those who viewed her from without her solid walls. From certain angles McKinley appeared as a part of a watercolor painted by a thoughtful, patient artist of grand design. One step taken to either side and the sight would quicken with life, animated by playful contrasts of lines, part of a carefully planned marriage of nature and architecture.

Of all the contributions made to McKinley by previous owners in return for the privilege of dwelling there, none was more insightful than Leslie's. It was already beginning to be said among the elite that it seemed McKin-ley had been waiting too steadfastly, over the decades: for her. One cannot be impatient for the likes of Leslie. She would arrive in her own sweet time, and McKinley knew of this—warmly and wisely.

From the first, the day Ryan had brought her to see the proud resi-dence, there was a joyful recognition. The structures and grounds almost sighed visibly when the couple passed through the electric gates that parted the monstrous walls surrounding Leslie's first and last real home.

McKinley recognized immediately, as Ryan had, that Leslie was what could be termed "true aristocracy." Her inborn sense of style and design, her solemn dignity and her native calm commingled with that of the great home, and all was well. In four short months the business of bringing the quiet reflective order McKinley deserved came to a close. The last worker had driven away, the last plan was drawn, all that remained was the seasonal advancement of the gardens and the acquisition of art. The latter was progressing nicely, to Leslie's great satisfaction. The much-awaited telephone call had come at last and Leslie was eager to share the good news with her mate.

She found Ryan standing before the many-paned window of her study, a contemplative stance that suggested a monarch posing for a sculpture.

A door had been opened the night of Leslie's birthday. She awakened the next morning to find that her imagined division between herself and Ryan was a thing of the past. She could, then, approach her mate with ease and without the tickling in her stomach that had plagued her before. Neither of them tried to explain the change; it was just accepted—quietly.

Leslie glided into the den. "We won the bid for 'Jeune Fille'," she informed Ryan with confident energy.

The outdoor crystalline playground had been the hiding place for Ryan's thought for nearly an hour. She joined the present and smiled serenely. The Renoir had long been a favorite of hers, and when she learned the gallery in Rome had released it, she phoned her agent immediately. The crayon rendering would be the first of many major art purchases to find a final resting place upon the willing walls of McKinley.

The smile of acknowledgment was too brief, and too quickly replaced by vacant pondering. Even this good news didn't salve the inflammation reddening Ryan's nervous system. Something was eating at her, and Leslie knew what it was. The strain was beginning to show permanently; thus she resolved to do something about it.

Chess never failed to bring Ryan out of her silent preoccupation, and this time was no different. Leslie sat down at the table then entered her golden pawn onto the field of play. The set had been commissioned by Patrick O'Donnell in Italy when Ryan was five years old. The board was green and black jade. One set of pieces was gold with diamond eyes while the other was sterling silver with emeralds for eyes. It was prophetic at the very least— Leslie's metal was gold and her stone: diamond.

Ryan joined her silently, commencing with an innocuous-looking comeback. The game proceeded without verbal exchange well into the middle game; then, Ryan's inattention returned.

After a serious pause on Leslie's part, "My love, you've resigned masters, so there will be no pretending that *I'm* giving you fits." She received an empty stare in reply. "You've been contemplating your next move for ten minutes."

"Have I?" Ryan asked with genuine surprise.

Another sober interlude transpired before Leslie continued. "You couldn't think about her more if she were living here, Ryan."

Ryan shifted in her chair uncomfortably. An unconscious brush of her fingers through her hair heralded a disgusted sigh. She didn't want to talk about it.

Which was of no concern to Leslie. This time, she was going to get *her* way. "You can't go on avoiding Sanji. She calls three or four times a day and you refuse to speak to her. A letter arrives daily from her that you won't read. She's turned away at the door every morning and evening."

"I can go on refusing to see her, and I will," Ryan pronounced.

"That's going to be a little hard to do now," Leslie countered nonchalantly as she moved her remaining knight to capture one of Ryan's pawns.

Ryan knit her brow and visually pressed her lover to explain herself, then made a surprise move with her bishop.

Leslie remained firm. "Because I've hired a moving company to go after her possessions this afternoon. She is to be installed in the bedroom next to Corelle's old one by this evening."

Ryan was floored and speechless. Leslie felt just a little smug about the whole thing. "I've decided that my original plan really was the best one. I need that woman where I can keep an eye on her—here." Compassionately, she added, "There is nothing to be ashamed of, Ryan. You need a sex-slave. It's part of who you are now and denying it will not make it go away."

Then very seriously, "Sanji's unrequited love is turning into an obsession with her. The harder you shun her the harder she's going to try to get you back. I'm putting a stop to it—today.

"My secretary has called her and informed her that she is to become a member of our household, in *service* to you."

Ryan was thoughtful and receptive, but still a little surprised by her lover's reversal in attitude.

"I know you don't love her and you never will. She can't interfere with our relationship, but this damned obsession that's building can. She'll have to settle for what she can get from you, and I trust you to be reasonable about how much of you she does get." Leslie moved her queen. "Check," she announced, and smiled sweetly.

Ryan nodded her head approvingly. "Well, you sly fox." She picked up her silver sovereign; she wasn't so shocked that she stopped doing what came as natural to her as breathing. "All right, lady," the king parachuted onto the appropriate square, revealing the slanted attack of her own bishop, "you've got yourself a deal. Checkmate." And she winked.

The stunned silence was opened with laughter which relieved some of the tension and almost upset the remaining pieces, making them laugh all the more.

Leslie pushed the button of the tape recorder to 'on', then settled herself into a comfortable chair pulling a heavy quilt around her to keep out the chill of her darkened office. A tiny lamp gave off its meager glow from the far corner of the room giving only such light as was needed for Leslie to see what she was doing.

She had learned that she could concentrate better on what was being said on these stolen tapes if she minimized any distractions from the outside world. She felt she could hear easier in a tenebrous atmosphere.

It was cold. And Leslie knew it would get colder as the next hour progressed. Just thinking about it made her reach for the hot tea in the large mug on the table next to her and take a swallow to reassure herself.

It had become clear early in the process of listening to these tapes of David Martin interviewing Ryan's late friend Rags that Mr. Martin saw fit to turn on his recorder the moment Rags entered his office for her regular parole reports. It had been a wise plan—at times Rags was most revealing when she was the least wary: before she sat down. Leslie listened carefully for any unexpected candor but could only hear the shuffling of feet and— to the trained ear—a telling silence between Rags and her parole officer.

Leslie could imagine the visual staredown between the two somber, tough . . . friends. For Rags and David were friends in a sort of haphazard way. There was an informality between them that allowed for quick tempers and equally quick forgiveness. Somewhat like gentle sparring matches: each measuring the other's cunning and reach.

Sounds that told Leslie Rags was seating her square, indestructible frame into the ancient chair opposite David's desk galvanized her attention. She knew the general history of what had transpired prior to this meeting and it was easy for her to guess that Rags was angry, felt cornered. She was not surprised that David was the one to speak first.

"I called the hospital today. Ryan is *still* on the critical list. It's been two weeks."

Silence.

"She had better not die, buddy. I called in every marker I've got to keep you from being sent back to prison for this one. But murder, Rags . . . I can't help you there." David's voice sounded reproachful, even threatening.

"She won't die." Rags' voice was tight. Leslie knew her eyes were narrowed and her breathing shallow.

Leslie shifted in her seat as she knew David Martin had to have when he heard the cold, unfeeling surety in Rags' reply. Rags had beaten Ryan to within a centimeter of her life in an attempt to break Ryan's will. Unsuccessful, Rags had been the one who had taken Ryan to the hospital herself, literally placing herself at the mercy of the authorities. Ryan had been taken to emergency surgery, Rags to City Jail. Well acquainted with the justice system, Leslie hadn't been at all surprised when she'd learned that Rags had been walking free an hour later.

"You had better pray she doesn't. Well, let's get to it." David's reply was a blend of detachment from a situation too volatile for him to want to tackle, and excitement. Rags was finally in a compromised position. He finally had the upper hand and Rags had no choice but to submit to hypnotism. Leslie remembered clearly the look on his face when, before Rags' death, he had told her about how he had blackmailed Rags into going under hypnosis to allow him to seek the answers to her riddles. It was a look just short of gleeful.

Leslie was one of the few people who knew that prison was the one thing in the physical world that had ever gotten the better of Rags. And prison was winning again. Her near pathological dread of being locked up again far outweighed her reluctance to have David pry into her past, such as it was, and her reason for being. With what sounded to Leslie like a defeated sigh, Rags had replied, "Yeah, christ," and had risen from her seat. The crackling of leather could be heard as Rags took her place on David's couch.

Leslie was tempted to listen to David's process, but she thought better of it. There was always the danger of becoming hypnotized herself. She advanced the tape in short stutters until she bypassed that part and began to listen as David tried to regress his parolee into her childhood. She knew he wouldn't succeed. Rags had not had a childhood, never been born or had parents. Her coming into being was as calculated as it was incredible. She simply was. In the right time and place to begin nearly two decades of reprisal and terrorism against a select group of individuals who had lived as the constituency of a clan of Pagans three thousand years past.

This vicious scheme of vengeance would unfold before David as he would progress through numerous sessions in the months that followed this first one that Leslie was now only listening to with fragmented interest.

It was getting colder again. Leslie shivered. Her tea was no longer warm, the quilt no longer enough to keep out the chill. For some unexplained reason, her thoughts began to wander. Without knowing why, she called up the image in her mind of someone she would rather not see just now: flowing royal purple robes, expanses of black streaming hair, alluring salmon-colored lips and unsafe, silvery-white eyes. A beautiful woman, a dangerous enemy, Anara was intangible but her presence was felt everywhere one cared to take notice. Leslie shivered again. She didn't want to think about Anara.

But Anara wanted her to.

Slinking back into her carved amethyst demi-throne, Anara felt a spasm of pleasure overtake her. She could never grow tired of needling her way into the consciousness of this little wench. From her gleaming, haunting chamber in the other world, she watched Leslie squirm in her seat, fidgeting to get warm, to shake loose her presence.

At least the other wench, the dark one, has the good sense to be frightened of me, she thought to herself. This one, with her ridiculous curiosity, is a fool.

"Ah, but I do love tormenting fools," Anara purred. Then she laughed out loud, a bone-chilling laugh, when at last Leslie could take no more of it.

Leslie turned off the tape machine and left the room hurriedly in search of Ryan's comfort and the warmth of a welcoming evening fire in a homey fireplace.

. . . . . . . The deadly, bloodshot stare in the tigress' eyes locked her in a trance, robbing her of her ability to react to the danger. Her body did not move toward the wall, did not scale the vines, did not hurl her over the wall to safety. She couldn't outrun the great cat, nor could she scream for help.

For a horrifying instant they were at a stalemate. In the next shocking breath the tigress leapt upon Korian's frail, helpless body and they both came to the ground in mindless battle.

Korian shrieked as her clothing and flesh were ripped and torn from her. Her powers failed her, leaving her helpless—completely and utterly helpless against the overpowering weight and force of Anara's agent of revenge. Time stood still. Nothing existed—only the sharp spears of teeth. Korian heard her own skull crack and all was darkness . . . . . . .

"NO!" Ryan awoke suddenly from her night terror. She was sweating and shaking. Panic constricted her breathing. The bridge between nightmare and reality had not yet been crossed. She fought and fought to free herself of death but her muscles wouldn't move nor would her voice cooperate. Frozen.

Slowly, the morning light filtered through the hallucination to free her of her imagined trap.

Leslie sat up, fully awake. She was not going to allow another terror-filled morning to become a frustration-filled day. For as urgent as Ryan's departure from bed was, Leslie's was equally so.

In her boudoir she took a quick sponge bath then used the phone on her dressing table to call downstairs. She asked Bonnie to have someone warm up her Mercedes and advised her that breakfast would be late, if at all.

Extreme nervousness was not a condition that Leslie was accustomed to, but it was one with her now. She didn't relish following Ryan to the firing range. Guns frightened her. Afraid and turbulent was not the way to approach her new Rolls. She needed a vehicle that would respond quickly to her mood without being insulted by it. Her sporty 450SL would speed her swiftly through the frigid morning air like a chariot in hot pursuit.

Her new personal servant stood by helplessly. Leslie dressed with such dispatch as to avoid any solicitous attention that might soothe her nerves or give her time to reconsider her mission.

Mantled in cool greys: mink, wool, silk and leather, she braved the breathless morning air on her way to the garages that had once been proud stables. In the distance she could hear the muted roar of her beloved's motorcycle. The sound filled her with a new surge of determination.

Leslie thanked the servant for making ready her car and dashed out of the drive and down the quarter-mile lane to the main road adjacent to their property. The distance to the firing range was just short enough to keep her courage engaged. She came to a dangerous, skidding halt on the gravel parking lot. Without realizing it, she had become caught up in Ryan's angry emotions. The sheer act of following her mate on this destructive chore had made her a party to it.

She opened the heavy metal door to the stark building and half expected a guard to be in the hallway who would require her to check her reason and sanity at some small booth in exchange for a little numbered tag. Instead, only a long empty corridor painted mint green, a color she would never be able to look at again without becoming nauseous, reflected a dirty light from the ceiling.

What sounded like tiny muffled explosions showed her the way, and she walked stiffly toward it. She rounded a corner then entered through another metal door. The sounds became loud cracks puncturing her resolve.

Leslie had to ignore the attention she had drawn to herself when she entered the glass protected room above and to the side of the firing alleys. The two men in the room with her whispered among themselves. She didn't hear them, she only saw what went on below.

"Who's the dame?" A wiry man in battle fatigues leaned over to ask the resident marksmanship instructor.

The instructor, a lively, spicy individual, smiled and concluded, "It sure as hell isn't Bart's old lady. My guess is that's Ryan's latest."

"She sure can pick 'em."

Momentarily both men brought their attention around to who everyone was now staring at with varying degrees of fascination.

Ryan.

A monolith of intensity and rage, Ryan only moved to put a new magazine in her weapon. Shells flew about like agitated grasshoppers; she ignored them. The sound in her alley was continuous, for which she wore a protective headset. She continued to aim with fearsome deadliness at what was left of her limp target. Agonizing jets of pain seared through her arms with each thrusting flurry of bullets, serving to focus her seemingly hopeless attempt to obliterate the real target. Not the silhouette of a human form. Ryan didn't see that. As real as life, squarely in her sights, was the massive round head of a white tigress. A three thousand year old tigress to be precise, come to remind her of how she had died in her last lifetime. Vengeance indeed.

"What does she see down there?" the instructor wondered. "Have you ever seen that look on someone's face before?"

"Yeah," replied his companion. "In Nam, on guys that had lost it."

For some unknown reason the instructor looked Leslie's way and commented, "Where have you seen *that* look before?"

The other man shivered. Never in his memory, horrible or otherwise, had he seen such an unearthly expression on man or woman.

"Lady, are you okay?"

Leslie hugged herself and tried to get warm. She was cold. Mercilessly cold. She shook; the blood began to leave her head slowly. Replacing it was Ryan's undiluted hatred. Her active intent to understand what Ryan was feeling had unwittingly produced a keyhole in her defenses. Through that opening flooded Ryan's deranged aggression.

Leslie fainted.

Suddenly, Ryan felt her maniacal energies drain out of her. Slowly, painfully, she put her gun on the ledge before her, along with her headset, and turned toward the observation booth. The instructor's voice came over the loud speaker. "Ryan! Come here, quick!"

In what seemed like the next breath Ryan ascended the stairs and burst into the room. She gasped, "What happened?" and fell to her knees beside her wife.

The other man had been trying to revive the gentle woman, which Ryan resented. She abducted the frail body from his arms and began to rock her quietly. "Leave us," Ryan commanded sternly.

When the men hung about, unsure, they were warned by a look they could not mistake. Ryan knew what she was about and didn't really need them to tell her what she had done. They left the couple to a degree of privacy, but would not go far, if for no other reason than that they were curious and concerned.

Ryan cursed herself for not seeing it coming before. Anyone who had the slightest acquaintance with Leslie knew that she had a most inquiring mind and would not be denied answers to her questions.

"Stubborn fool," she chastised herself. "Why didn't you just tell her what was wrong? She didn't need to find out like this."

Leslie's spirit had begun to revive itself the instant it sensed Ryan's familiar presence. Revival of the body was close at hand.

"Ryan?" The sweet, plaintive voice tore at Ryan's heartstrings.

"Yes, angel. I'm here."

"May we get out of this place?" Leslie begged.

"Of course. This instant," Ryan assured her while helping her to her feet and out of the too-small room.

"Are you all right, miss?" The instructor was worried.

"Yes, yes. I'm fine now, thank you," Leslie replied weakly.

After receiving Ryan's loving assistance into the passenger seat of her car, Leslie stopped Ryan before she could walk around to the driver's seat. "Who were you trying to kill back there? Who could you possibly hate that much?"

Ryan squatted beside her wife and quietly explained about the great cat, the dream that was not a dream but a reliving of death. She apologized for all she was worth for not having shared it with her before and for allowing the dream to assume such grave proportions. They vowed together to take the terror head on and jointly, knowing all the while that two could fight better than one.

Once again Ryan marvelled at Leslie's great determination and courage. Once again Anara's attempt to separate them produced the opposite effect.

## 12

"Have you seen Oregano?" Star asked, mildly concerned. The aging calico cat was seldom out of sight of either Brigid or herself for any length of time.

Brigid looked up from the paper shredder, her face impassive, trying to envision the last time and place she had seen the eldest of her three cats. Perplexed, she shook her head. "Now that you ask, I don't recall seeing her at all today."

Star was picking up armsful of shredded newspaper, then packing it into open crates that lined the west wall of their too chilly barn. She looked about the work area as she did, and was surprised by Minerva jumping indignantly out of the once empty crate she was napping in. Brigid laughed at the Lilac Point Siamese and her haughty antics.

"She doesn't want to be shipped off to California, Star," Brigid teased.

"No sense of humor," Star pretended to grumble. "It's time for Oregano's medicine. I'd better find her." She didn't break stride on her way out of the barn, uninterrupted by the familiar love pat on her plentiful backside. Brigid returned to her chore of making packing material to envelop her art and protect it on its journey to the galleries in California.

"Oregano?" Star called out to the lost feline. She began opening cupboards in Brigid's ceramics shop, speaking inviting terms of endearment to entice the calico from its hiding place. Just when she was sure the cat had at last shown its first sign of senility, a muffled plea reassured her.

The unhappy meow was traced to some canvases leaning against a seldom used bench. Star crouched beside the paintings and nudged them aside. "Come here, baby. You're safe now," Star spoke soothingly to Oregano. Finally the cat crawled to freedom and a comforting hug.

Something of the crisp color showing on the corner of one of the canvases caught Star's eye. The idea of giving the cat her medicine was shelved in favor of her curiosity. The error in reasoning that had brought the cat great discomfort lay in wait to ambush any other victim that happened upon that dark corner's secret. Star wondered why this one work was framed when the others in front of it were raw. It slid out easily to destroy nearly eight years of married life in one swift blow.

Star would never be alone in her unabashed, trancelike response to Dana's intimidating beauty, captured with such precision, such lasting admiration, that it made Star immediately afraid. Afraid, because before her was truth. Burning, scathing truth.

It was several minutes before the inevitable anger made its way into her now purged heart. Star didn't, indeed couldn't, love Brigid at that moment. She couldn't even cry. All she could do was stoke the fire, fuel the intense emotions that were electrifying her even as she continued to stare at Dana's exceptional beauty.

She felt rejected, surely. How clear it was that Brigid had fallen in love with the haunting, ethereal "Whore," Star breathed. The spell was broken. Star picked up the picture and followed her tracks through the light film of snow that was covering the walk she had so recently shoveled. It was betrayal, and all the hatred that stampedes over rationality like so much cattle, that motivated her every action. From slamming the shop door to nearly ripping open the barn door, to yanking the plug of the shredder from the socket, Star was consumed with a whirl of malice.

She had gotten Brigid's attention, as she had meant to, but for some reason it was not enough. With sheer, mindless loathing she hurled the painting at its author with all her might.

Brigid's bulky sheepskin coat protected her from harm from the air-borne painting, but no amount of clothing could shield her from Star's wrath.

"How could you?" Star shouted. "You low-life cunt! I trusted you. When I asked you where you'd been, you told me 'out'! Why didn't you just tell me the fucking truth? Just say it. I *dare* you. Say, 'Well, Star. I don't *really* love you anymore. I'm just keeping you around for good company, good food, and an occasional screw. I get what I really want and need down the road a ways'." Star's bitter remarks progressively became more sarcastic and self-effacing as she went on. "You couldn't just tell me that I wasn't pretty enough for you any longer, not sexy enough. You had to sleep where every other low-life before you has slept! I'm so horrible that even a slut was an improvement?"

Brigid broke in. "Star, settle down! It wasn't like that at all."

Star pointed her finger at Brigid angrily. "Sure. Then why did you fall in love with her? You fucking fell in love with that bitch. I can't believe this is happening to me. How *could* you fall in love with her?"

This was it. The duel that had been brewing for years. The saved and unspoken irritations, suspicions, injustices and general complaints that had been buried in the name of peace, had surfaced.

Brigid was determined to maintain her grasp on her churning, wrenching emotions. She had never seen Star act so cruelly or heard her speak to her in such a manner. Being caught off-guard was understating her situation. Other people's affairs of the heart appeared simple to solve. Her own were normally simple and uncomplicated. She realized now why she had wanted to keep it that way and had for all her life—until now.

Pleading, but calmer, "Star, baby, it had nothing to do with you. I swear it."

"Of course not. You didn't think of me for one minute! Not once did it occur to you how hurt I would be. The woman I've loved for all these years has been lying to me. Cheating on me. Betraying me!" Star spat. She was beginning to detest Brigid more by the second.

The words stabbed Brigid clear through her heart. Star was right. She hadn't considered the consequences. She just that instant realized, not only Star's undeserved pain, but that she was indeed, hopelessly in love with Dana. Somehow she had expected Star to understand that—tolerate it even.

But she loved Star, too, with a deep lasting kind of love that went beyond the ecstasy and thrill of being with Dana. A love and support she depended upon—the balance, harmony and stability she counted on as a backdrop for her artwork. And sex was good with Star. It was truly lovemaking. Intimate, real and theirs alone. She had to save their love—at all costs.

Unwanted and unhindered, tears formed in Brigid's eyes. Because of Brigid's calm, solid demeanor, few people ever realized that they had never seen her cry. Once before, when her loyalty to her cousin had forced Star and her to separate, she had come very near breaking down. Brigid was more like her cousin than she knew.

The thought of losing Star again was more than she could bear. "Star, don't do this to me. I can't . . . I can't take it." Brigid shifted her crutches and began to walk toward Star. She was ready to beg for forgiveness— what ever was necessary to get rid of the panic that was overcoming her.

But Star wouldn't have it. *"You* can't take it! You selfish pig. Who the fuck cares whether or not you can take it? This whole thing is your fault!" She was no longer blaming herself for Brigid's emotional and physical infidelity. She was fast coming around to placing the blame where it properly belonged. And she was going to make the participants pay, and pay dearly.

Brigid had stepped nearer, reaching out for her. Star's fury studded her words with barbed wire, which she flung at the broad-shouldered adultress. "Don't touch me."

"Ooun. Star, please. Don't," Brigid sobbed openly.

Star had always feared for the day when she would see this passionate Irishwoman cry. She hadn't wanted to know what horror would come to pass that would finally puncture the dike that held back those tears. She never thought she would live to see the day when she would be the cause, much less that she would enjoy it. But she was enjoying it.

"And don't think for a minute that I'm going to let your pretty little girlfriend get away with this," Star threatened.

As suddenly and unexpectedly as the tears came, they disappeared. Brigid's eyes went flint hard, colder than the air swirling about them. Dangerously, she fought back with a threat of her own. *"Don't you dare."*

Star went silent for a moment—studying the artist. Then she nodded her head knowingly. "I thought so."

Star couldn't do very many things better than Brigid, but she could outrun her.

"Star! Come back here." Brigid gave chase. Outside, her words were bombarded by pelting, stinging snowflakes. Star had already taken her flight through the back door of the house, toward the front door.

Brigid grabbed the keys to her Bronco from the entryway table and dodged a worried yellow dog to get out the front door. In the distance, Star's Subaru rounded the first curve down the mountain.

There aren't many first-hand accounts of high-speed chases down snowy mountain roads because not many people live to tell about them. The last thing in Brigid's mind was the idea of living. How could she if Star left her? Such was her unreason, her panic.

Throughout the perilous course Brigid tried numerous times to run Star off the road. The Subaru was too nimble and goatlike to be bullied by the less stable Bronco, so Star made a successful trip down—ten miles—in what was to become the first major blizzard of the season.

Del and Dana's western style home showed all the signs of being occupied as it normally would be on an inclement Saturday in late October.

Star bypassed Del at the front door and headed straight for Dana. She stopped short of going for the jugular. Star was not normally a violent person, but she had a tongue as sharp as any scorned female.

While Star lit into the unruffled seductress, firing at will, Del had to pull herself together to answer the door, just moments after her greeting to Star had been ignored. One look into Brigid's maniacal eyes and she didn't even want to ask what was going on.

Del hated scenes. She normally left when they began in other people's homes. But this one was in full bloom in her own living room and there was no place to go. Star was railing at her wife with words she hadn't thought Star knew, and she was positive Dana hadn't heard before. Brigid was frantic and unsuccessful in getting her to stop. Dana was quiet and undemonstrative. Del thought, just for a brief second, that she'd seen a look of satisfaction on Dana's face. There was no way out—only one way to go and that was in. Del hadn't been a criminal lawyer for fifteen years for nothing. She seized control of the situation with ease.

"Star, shut up and sit down," Del commanded as she put a heavy hand on Brigid's shoulder and squeezed. She transmitted her sensibleness to Brigid, which brought about the calm she sought.

"Brigid, what is going on here?" Del asked firmly.

Brigid turned to answer her friend. Their eyes met briefly, then she looked away, shaking her head. Mute.

"Dana?"

No answer was forthcoming from her either. Just a noncommittal look of surprise.

"Star?" Del asked reluctantly. Before Star could begin she cautioned her, "Quietly."

As instructed, Star revealed the truth. "Brigid and Dana have been sleeping together and . . ."

"What?!" Del ripped her hand from Brigid's shoulder, jerking the taller woman around to meet her stunned, hurt eyes. At that moment Brigid envied bears their hibernation. Couldn't she just crawl into a den somewhere and wait for all this to blow over? She didn't want to have to go through with the inevitable. She closed her eyes and nodded her head solemnly, confirming both the truth and her complete mortification.

"My god." Del was possessed of an athletic body that didn't stumble easily. She took two awkward steps to the side—overcome with shock.

"And," Star continued, savoring the deliciousness of it, "she's in love with Dana."

This time, Del's visual appeal was directed toward her lover. Dana shrugged her shoulders with a "first I've heard of it" look pulled neatly over her laughing eyes. Between Star's utter contempt, Brigid's look of surprised betrayal and Del seating herself soundly in her favorite chair, Dana was in She-devil heaven.

Del had always known Dana was unfaithful—that was how she had gotten her away from Ryan. Up to now, Dana's game had always been single women.

By now, Brigid had lowered her defeated form onto the arm of the sofa. She crossed her arms over the tops of her crutches and put her forehead down on the resulting bridge. Star had calmed down, her work done—or so she believed.

A long pained silence ensued, broken by Del's broken voice and broken heart. She would forgive Dana—she always would, but she couldn't bring herself to forgive Brigid. All present knew just how long Del could hold a grudge where Dana was concerned. She and Ryan hadn't been civil to one another for several years.

"How long?" she inquired.

Brigid's head came up slowly and turned toward the question with one of her own on her face.

Del emphasized each word as though she were speaking to a foreigner. "How long have you been in love with my wife?"

Brigid was past crying. A numbed daze hung over her. All was lost and there was no point in holding anything back. Why bother, she wondered to herself. Her helplessness was not lost on Dana.

The only unpleasant part of Dana's mission was the very real guilt she felt when she saw just how much damage she had done to the sensitive artist. Their eyes met momentarily. Dana realized the scope of the fervent ardentness that Brigid had harbored for her for what must have seemed like a lifetime to any sane person. Many lifetimes to the intense, and now very sad, master artist.

"Ten years," Brigid provided matter-of-factly.

Star gasped. She could never have expected Brigid to make a complete travesty of their entire relationship with just two, seemingly harmless, words. "It's bad enough that you stopped loving me. Now you say you never loved me in the first place." Star couldn't stand it any more and she began to weep.

"That's not true, Star. I've always loved you. Always," Brigid contended forcefully.

"You can't love both of us," Star snapped.

"I do . . ."

Star had to hurt back, deeply and viciously. "I know what it is now. Tell me, Brig. Tell me why you slept with her? Did she make you feel like a *whole woman?* Something we all know you'll never be!"

Even Dana was shocked by Star's cruel accusation. Everyone ducked when Brigid stood suddenly. She was riding on her cousin's reputation for violence. She didn't hit Star, but only at great cost to her nerves. Her eyes were orbs of fury and disgust.

"God, I'm glad I didn't really buy that son-of-a-bitching bar. I'd hate to have my farm, the only thing I've got left, tied up to the keep the likes of you," Brigid shouted fiercely.

"No," Star breathed. She shook her head in disbelief.

"That's right, lover. Ryan still owns that hell-hole, and now I'm damn glad she does."

"Get out!! Get out of my home! I will not listen to any more of this from either of you. Brigid, I *never* want to see you again. I swear to god, if you ever come near Dana again, I'll kill you. You lying, cheating . . . you're just like your fucking cousin. Get out!" Del shouted violently.

Both the offenders had no choice but to leave quietly. Bitter silence filled the air. Brigid had done it now: betrayed her lover, thrice over, ruined a perfectly good friendship and lost the two people closest to her heart in less than an hour. Her drive home was mechanical, empty of thought, and careful to follow Star closely until they made it safely home, where their wordless suffering would continue long into the night.

—·◈❈❈◈·—

It had been barely five days since Sanji's arrival and already the unspoken animosity between Leslie and Sanji had taken on a life of its own. Their deadly visual exchanges poisoned the once harmonious atmosphere of McKinley.

Sanji continued to entertain hopes of winning Ryan's heart. She was easily misled into believing she could succeed because Ryan was spending inordinate amounts of time with her. Far too much time.

Leslie knew that a need long denied very often must be overindulged temporarily to bring about harmony. She understood that Ryan's too frequent attendance at the slave's quarters were characterized solely by sexual encounters. The romance, love and tenderness, though greatly diminished in occurrence, were still where they belonged. That knowledge made listening to Sanji's screams of ecstasy no easier. Regularly finding the habituated couple drowned together in exhausted sleep—Sanji naked and welted, Ryan damp with exertion—did little to promote understanding on Leslie's part.

A very real potential to destroy Ryan's relationships with both women was dangerously obvious, even to her. Ryan couldn't find a better way to solve the problem than to graphically illustrate to each woman exactly where she stood.

Resolved, she walked into Sanji's room with a plan. Ryan hadn't allowed Sanji to keep many of her personal belongings and none of Rags'. Plans had been laid to paint the room white, remove the carpeting and replace it with white tile. Stark white furniture and draperies had been ordered. The room was a slave quarter and Sanji was to become aware of it, and remain so every moment. For now the room was a forgotten array of left-over furniture and decorations left by the previous owner, dreary and oppressive.

Sanji put her book down and stood when Ryan entered. Silent and expectant, she waited to serve in whatever way she was called upon to do. Since being installed in the household, she had been used with such constancy that she didn't bother to wear street clothing or workout clothes. She only bothered with the soft white nightdress that buttoned from her cleavage down to the part in her legs. She wore it because Ryan enjoyed slowly unbuttoning it and watching it fall from her womanly shoulders to reveal her cocoa-colored form.

Ritual was as much a part of Ryan's sexual makeup as her need to dominate and be served. She stepped near the dark entrancing woman and unfastened the first button at the top. Sanji's breasts raised and lowered faster with each button. Working the last two brought Ryan's fingers in contact with her partner's raw, puffy, but very aroused outer sex lips. Lips that were *still* as sensitive as a virgin's. Sanji's body responded like a well-trained laboratory mouse racing down the path of its maze to its final reward.

Ryan's body wanted to follow but she wouldn't let it. The mind-muddling fragrance of Sanji's sexual lubrication pulled at her. The fire in her own bloodstream nearly sabotaged her mission, but she held on. She wanted Sanji naked and needy. Struggling, she raised her hands to the well-defined collarbone and smoothed her fingers purposefully over the tempting shoulders, taking the straps of the nightdress with them. When the garment drifted to the floor, Sanji was left unconditionally vulnerable, beseeching Ryan to take her with her eyes, body and deepest soul.

Up to now, Ryan had given no clue that she wasn't going to follow through with what she had begun. When Sanji was instructed dispassionately to kneel, she knew something was amiss. Ryan had somehow cut a hole in her net and escaped. She dropped deftly to her knees unable to hide her disappointment.

Ryan grabbed her jaw firmly and held the troubled face up to her penetrating gaze. For long moments Ryan studied her Jamaican prize.

"I defy anyone to find a more willing slave than you are and always have been," Ryan praised her confidently.

Sanji's eyes beamed and gradually her whole demeanor took on the appearance of her pride in her station.

Ryan's voice lowered somewhat. "You've served me so well in fact, that I can think of no better way to reward you than to give you more opportunity to serve. It's time you had a Mistress, slave. You need to learn a more refined form of service. Because I value you so highly I am going to give you that chance."

It was a bittersweet moment for Sanji. She had both lost and won. She had lost, forever, her chance to win Ryan's love for herself. The meaning of what was to follow was clear to her. Her role as slave was to be solidified and made everlasting. And, as any true slave would, she rejoiced. Between the sadness and the elation, she managed to reply, "I am deeply honored, Master. I shall serve in a manner that will continue to make you proud."

Ryan smoothed her cheek tenderly. "I have no doubt. Remain kneeling. I will return shortly."

Ryan left her slave to process her emotions in private to seek out her mate. She found Leslie in the sitting room staring into the gentle blaze in the fireplace. With very little effort, Ryan coaxed Leslie into a receptive mood, and Leslie agreed to join her oft-absent lover in Sanji's room. Leslie was about ready for a confrontation herself. If this was to be it, then she would go with resolution.

Leslie was shocked to find Sanji kneeling near her bed. More shocked because it aroused her. More than she could account for. Ryan had to nudge her closer and, as she did so, Leslie's determination deteriorated. There was something uniquely irresistible about Sanji—something, Leslie found, that she had a low immunity to.

There she was, standing so close to the sex-goddess that her thighs were being rubbed by hardened nipples. Sanji's full, capable mouth was inches from her navel. She was beginning to understand Ryan's weakness for her.

Sanji felt it too. She leaned into her rival ever so slightly to get more of the sensation of Leslie's coral satin lounging robe on the ends of her breasts. The thick incense of Leslie's French perfume and womanhood filled her nostrils with the essence of femininity. This was the refinement Ryan spoke of. To Sanji's amazement she found herself craving it.

Ryan smiled. This was going to be easier than she thought. These women, adversaries though they were and would most likely remain to some degree or another, wanted each other. The room was filled with their wanting.

Leslie was putty in Ryan's hands. There was no resistance at all when Ryan removed her robe, underneath which was a tan lace negligee. Sanji's response was immediate. She had always been curious about what the blonde looked like. She leaned away to see for herself and was not disappointed. Her disrespect brought about immediate results.

Ryan took her jaw and yanked Sanji's head around to face her displeasure. "I brought her here for you to serve, not gape at!"

Sanji was instantly contrite and slavelike. "I beg your forgiveness, Master. Her loveliness is such that it is difficult not to gaze upon it without utter fascination."

"That is so. Nonetheless, you will restrain yourself in the future," Ryan instructed.

"Yes, Master."

Ryan forced her slave to sit on her heels, then urged her wife to draw nearer still by straddling the black thighs beneath her. There was no longer any need to speak coherently. Once the lace skirt was gathered in Ryan's hands to reveal Leslie's sex, she guided Sanji's mouth forward to her ultimate test of servitude.

Trying to prepare someone for what it would feel like to have Sanji perform cunnilingus on them was like trying to tell a small child how a hot iron was going to feel. The only way to go about it was to do it.

It was for this reason that Ryan braced herself behind her unwarned wife. When lightning struck, Ryan was ready.

"Aahh!" Leslie exclaimed sharply as she jumped backwards suddenly when she felt the electric shock of Sanji's tongue.

Ryan caught her and calmed her. "Relax, my love. This is how it is to be served by the best. You deserve this, and I know you are able to survive her kiss."

Leslie listened intently to her lover's words. They were soothing yet designed to challenge her to rise to the occasion. Again, she was moved closer to the dark slave. The first step taken, her feet wet, she could, and did, go on. When again the service began, Leslie melted to it crying out, "Ooohh. Oh, Ry-hu-an." Her hips dipped and plunged forward then swayed back to demand more.

With Ryan for support, Leslie was able to concentrate on the feelings—all new and different—overcoming her. Sanji's soft full lips became one with her own flesh. They were like pillows that she had fallen into—deceptively receptive. In reality—traps, set out by a huntress to snare any unsuspecting creature that happened upon them.

Until now, Leslie had thought that Ryan was the most talented individual alive when it came to this act. Sanji's tongue removed all doubt that it was she whose gift for pleasing women surpassed all others. The snake

117

swirled and curled, flicked and prodded.

Unexplored conduits were electrified in Leslie's brain. Mindless. She clutched Ryan's hands and dug her nails in so hard that she broke Ryan's fragile skin—drawing tiny droplets of blood. An orgy of sensations visited themselves upon her. Uppermost were the sharp stinging jabs of unforgiving pleasure in her clitoris. The radiation of rapturous impulses flooded her pelvic floor and spilled down her legs. Her over-enthusiastic intake of oxygen lightened her head, making her float—seemingly in mid-air. Ryan's harsh, excited breath near her ear inflamed her nerves in rapid downward waves that met up with the vibrations of Sanji's urgent moans of delight. Her control was too severed even to join in with moans of her own expressions of ecstasy.

For Sanji, too, this was a new encounter with a different type of woman. She so enjoyed putting this delicate, elegant woman totally out of countenance, it was almost beyond her to comprehend how good it felt. She was doing what she had been born into this life to do: drive women wild. Any woman. Every woman. There was a subtle feeling of control—Leslie was at her mercy. The proud aristocrat was subdued by a mere slave.

Delicious though the irony was, Sanji finally came around to the truth of the situation. While Leslie had lost her physical composure, she was as cool as ever in her heart. Leslie surprised Ryan and Sanji with her endurance. Were it Ryan delighting her, she would have climaxed long ago, but she was not going to give in to Sanji until she felt that Sanji had truly and completely given in to her. Among the three women present, Leslie's will would prevail and remain forged of iron.

It wasn't long before Sanji felt the humiliation, degradation and defeat she was meant to feel. It was Leslie who Ryan loved. It was Leslie who Ryan would sleep with each night. It was Leslie who Ryan worshipped, indeed lived for, and nothing Sanji could do could change that. Sanji was Ryan's sex-slave and would never progress beyond that point. While she might gain privileges and honors in her life, the love she sought was possessed solely and completely by her adversary. An adversary with whom she was reduced to copulation. Where she had thought that she *wanted* to pleasure this woman, she was realizing that she had been forced into this act of fornication.

She was being dominated *and she didn't like it.*

This was what Ryan was waiting for. She let it sink in for a few moments then pulled Sanji away from her wife. Leslie's hemline fell atop Sanji's breasts, but Leslie didn't move away. She was shaking with delight from her first taste of overpowering another person.

Ryan lit a cigarette and squatted next to Sanji. She made her mouth into the shape of a kiss and blew the smoke into Sanji's face with something akin to contempt. "You really hate her, don't you?"

Sanji's eyes widened fearfully. An answer was required of her. One that wasn't a lie. Her trembling revealed her dilemma.

"You may answer without fear of harm," Ryan reassured her. Only the truth would serve her purpose.

Trust had always been the cornerstone of Sanji's relationship with Ryan. Without complete unbounded trust the relationship could not exist. She summoned her courage and revealed what they all knew was so. "Yes, Master I hate her with all my heart."

"Ah, but she tastes and feels finer than anyone you've ever had. Am I not right?" Ryan taunted.

"Than even your perfect self, Master," Sanji assented.

"You enjoyed serving her," came the next ridicule.

Sanji's eyes swept downward, only to be more deeply reminded of her situation when she saw the fine Irish lacework covering her breasts. "Yes, Master," she whispered.

"Pardon me?" Ryan jeered.

Closing her eyes, fighting back the tears, Sanji proclaimed clearly, "Yes, Master, I enjoyed serving my Mistress." When she opened her eyes and looked to see if more humiliation were on the horizon, she was taken aback by the look of awe on her Master's face.

Ryan was filled with wonder by her slave's loyalty, determination to please even at great personal cost, and sublime submission. It was perfection equal to any master artist, equal even to Leslie's great beauty. For such things in life, Ryan had nothing but absolute respect.

Leslie was profoundly moved by this special relationship. She hadn't known how pervasively it had spread or how dependent the principals had grown upon one another. There would be times when Sanji would be extremely irritating, but it would prove worth it to Leslie. For in tolerating this unusual symbiosis she could, at last, give Ryan something she truly needed. Something money could not afford.

Ryan whistled under the breath and shook her head. She flicked her ashes to the carpet and stood. Sanji's eyes followed her every move, sheerly devoted and ready to do anything required of her.

When Ryan looked at Leslie, calm now but still thoroughly stimulated, she wondered why her wife had remained so silent during the scene. Then it occurred to her. "You've never spoken a word to Sanji, have you?"

"Never," Leslie replied indignantly, surprised that anyone could suggest that she would do such a thing as lowly as speak directly to the rival.

"This is perfect. I love it." Ryan had wondered how to handle this part of the newly-formed relationship. But Leslie's behavior had always been disdainful toward the Jamaican, so there was only the one way to proceed.

"Before I let you finish your task, slave, I will instruct you in the proper way to behave toward and around your Mistress. From this moment hence your eyes are never to rise above the level of her magnificent breasts. Nor will you address her or be addressed by her. If, for any reason, you have a request to make of her, you must do so through someone of the proper station. As reward for your long-term faithful service to me, you will be allowed to kiss her breasts, sex and backside, but never,

*ever* her perfect mouth. Do you understand?"

"Yes, Master, completely. I am blessed to be allowed to serve my Mistress," Sanji responded humbly.

"Truly so." Ryan stubbed her cigarette out on the aged carpet then lifted the hem of the negligee again. "You may finish, slave."

Sanji did so with avarice—a greed for the riches of her Mistress' sexual favor. Finally, as Sanji knew they would, Leslie's hands found their way into her hair. As expected, Leslie was reduced—spilling forth screams of delight, forcing Sanji's mouth nearer her need than was humanly possible. Sanji gave her gift willingly and, after all was said and done, as all women before her had, Leslie burst. Waves. Contractions. Waves. "RYAN!" Leslie screamed frantically again and again. Her orgasm was ripped from her unmercifully.

Strong as she was, Ryan could barely hang on to her wife. Teeth shattering convulsions overtook the delicate woman until Ryan worried she might hurt herself. Accompanied by heaving relief, the spasms lessened, then subsided altogether.

Leslie was now in an altered state that Ryan fully intended to exploit for the rest of the night. She sent Sanji to bed and carried her collapsed spouse to their own connubial suite where she alternated passionate lovemaking with gentle, until dawn.

# 13

Ryan's study was the warmest room to be found in McKinley. With hardwoods blazing in the fireplace and a solid dose of brandy, Ryan was still cold and empty. She sat in the midnight green leather chair that her father had used for reading. If she pulled it any closer to the hearth it would have become kindling wood.

Leslie was kneeling behind her trying to massage the tension away. She was insufferably hot and more than concerned for her spouse's condition. When Ryan leaned back and sighed, she quit rubbing Ryan's stiff and achy neck. "It's not working, is it?"

"No." Ryan desperately wanted it to, but nothing seemed able to chase away the frozen numbness.

"Do you really think it's Brigid?"

"It has to be. The last time I felt close to this bad was when she lost her leg. If she would just answer the phone. Something is wrong, I know it." Ryan couldn't believe she had let it go on this long. She had enjoyed Leslie so completely for the last two days, enough to allow herself the luxury of ignoring the danger signals. She was worried now that her own selfishness hadn't caused her to be too late. "We've got to go up there, Leslie."

Leslie had anticipated the suggestion. "I thought you might want to. I asked that chains be put on the Silver Cloud. It's probably the only car we have that we can trust to make it up there in these conditions."

"You're amazing." Ryan looked at her brandy snifter and shaking hands. "Will you drive?"

121

The snow was powdery and soft. It crunched and squeaked under the massive weight of the Rolls that had once belonged to Ryan's father as it blazed a trail down the uncleared drive to Brigid's house. The Bronco was half covered by a sleek drift, and the Subaru was nowhere in sight. Nor was there any smoke coming from the fireplace or kitchen stacks. Half through a Monday morning the farm was normally alive with activity.

When Leslie turned off the engine there was deafening silence that chilled their hearts. Ryan was dressed as she always was; Leslie had come prepared in jeans, heavy boots and a down parka. They trudged through the two feet of snow to the front door. Ryan forced the storm door open; the front door was unlocked as it usually was. Leslie walked into the parlor and shivered.

The central heating was on but the genuine warmth was gone. So were many of the wall hangings and nick-nacks. They both looked about them, then at each other. "You check down here, I'll check upstairs," Ryan suggested.

She ascended the stairs quickly, knowing instinctively where to look. The bedroom door groaned when she opened it as if to say, "It's about time."

There, face down on the bed, lay Brigid. Ryan sensed that she was still alive, and when she spied the empty liquor bottles on the night stand she was positive. Unlike her own, Brigid's constitution could withstand abusive drinking. Brigid wasn't the suicidal sort.

Ryan took a step forward then froze. On the bed with her cousin were three cats, all eyeing her with great suspicion and the tiniest bit of malice. Perhaps she was imagining the malice, but her mouth went dry just the same. Her phobia quaked in her heart. Her inner demons screamed at her, "Run. Run, they're going to kill you! Run!"

Her sensible self countered, "They are just house cats. Your cousin needs you. Flesh and blood, your closest friend. Coward!"

Unexpectedly, the thought of Rags and all the hell she had experienced at her hand jarred her from her dilemma. If she could survive that, she concluded, she could face this.

She edged along sideways, keeping the cats where she could see them. After a short eon she managed to sit on the bed, cradle her cousin's leaden body in her arms and begin to breathe freer. For some reason it helped to have Brigid between her and her would-be murderers.

The unconscious redhead sighed as if she knew she was safe now and could go on. The movement distracted Ryan from her inner battle of wondering why a woman who had not had a drink in over ten years was anesthetized by and reeking of alcohol. She pulled the broadshouldered torso closer and laid back into the pillows. "Why, Brigid? Wh . . . oh, god." The portrait was resting on the dresser and took Ryan's breath away. Its hazy seductive beauty and dangerous appeal could have ambushed a stone. Ryan found herself on guard against Dana's charm as though Dana could turn from oil into flesh to bind her to some partnership of ungodly eternal lust. Surely, her chances were better with the cats.

She closed her eyes against the frightening misery. "Damn you, Dana," she breathed hatefully.

Her eyes came open when she heard Leslie coming up the stairs. Leslie stood in the doorway and gasped, "Oh, Ryan."

Ryan's hand came up to still her. "She's just drunk." Then urgently, "Will you get these cats out of here, *please?*" Her voice was tight and near panic.

"Oh, yes. I'm sorry. I forgot about them. Come here, Minerva, Oregano, Rusty. Come on, girls—out!" She gathered them up, hoisting the Lilac Point Siamese onto her shoulders and catching up the ancient calico along with the placid orange tabby. She shut them up in the sewing room and returned to help Brigid in any way she could.

Sitting on the corner of the bed, Leslie found it difficult not to cry when she relayed the findings of her tour of the lower floor and shop area. "I think Star is gone—for good. Brigid's shop is ruined." Leslie shook her head. "Everything is broken to bits, Ryan." Absurdly, as if it mattered in the midst of so much carnage, she added, "Star must have taken the dog with her; there's no sign of her."

They both grieved silently for a moment. Shaken, Leslie asked, "Why? Why? What happened?"

"Look behind you." Ryan let her eyes guide her wife to the source of the trouble.

Leslie turned cautiously toward the artwork. Her hand muffled her exclamation. "Oh, no!" Twice in her life, Leslie had come within a hair's breadth of wandering innocently into the quicksand known as Dana Shaeffer. Each time a guardian angel had snatched her away at the last moment, dragging her to safety. For a longing, impure moment Leslie wished she hadn't been so well guarded. The misty allure and divine womanhood pulled her near.

Involved in the portrait, she began to appreciate the talent and love that went into creating the dangerous mirage. This very naturally led to a re-creation of the vision that had moments before shaken her to her depths: Brigid's ravaged workshop.

"When did she leave off conquering holdouts to take up home wrecking?" Leslie inquired meanly.

"My guess is that this was her maiden voyage," Ryan speculated.

"It doesn't make sense. Brigid and Star have never hurt anyone. Why them?"

"Revenge," Ryan responded painfully.

Leslie looked away from the picture with an abrupt movement. "For *what?*"

There was no way Ryan could keep Leslie from learning the reasons behind this fiasco. She tried to approach it tenderly. "My love, if you wanted to hurt me and you couldn't get to me directly, how would you go about it?"

Leslie thought about the question. Watching Ryan gaze lovingly at her dazed cousin, the answer came to her. It was because Ryan experienced Brigid's pain that they had made the trip to the farm in the first place. "I'd hurt Brig."

And how thoroughly it had been done, too. The lovely home and its devoted occupants were torn asunder. The exquisite art, both finished and in progress, were gone forever. Her closest and dearest friend had been dashed to the ground like her ill-starred ceramics. Broken into a thousand pieces by a She-devil, a witch. Star, poor Star. Another victim. Innocent and unforgiving. Leslie didn't even know where Star was.

And Ryan. She would feel it all. She would shoulder the burden willingly, perhaps too willingly.

All this because of a brief encounter in a hotel room some months ago. She recalled what Ryan had told her about how she had humiliated and rejected Dana. That Dana had sworn she would get Ryan for it.

Virulence was dripping down Leslie's throat. The toxicant of hatred and rage burned the lining of her heart. The very mention of revenge awakened the dormant possibility that lay within her.

Ryan didn't see the steely purpose carved in the wings of the doves she called Leslie's eyes; she was looking at the portrait again.

"She isn't finished yet. Nor will she be until I come crawling to her and beg her to stop. Then she would just laugh at me and turn away. I know her type."

"Ryan, you wouldn't?" Pride had always been a hallmark in their relationship. Leslie couldn't and wouldn't imagine her sovereign mate begging for anything, least of all for clemency from the likes of Dana.

Ryan stroked Brigid's strong cheekbone and sighed. "Just this once I'm going to at least consider it." She didn't want to, but she had underestimated Dana. "She won't be able to use Brigid against me again. This sort of thing can only work once. I shudder to think what she'll try next."

"There's no point in speculating about it. Is Brigid going to be all right?" Leslie's reason had returned to her.

"In time. Before I ease her out of this I need to know how you feel about her drinking." Ryan remembered well how judgmental Leslie was capable of being on the subject of excessive drinking.

Compassion was Leslie's overriding emotion. "I've learned my lesson. She's trying to obliterate the pain, just as you were. I don't blame her."

"All right. She's going to need something. Can you see how close you can come to a Bloody Mary with what's here?"

Leslie agreed willingly and left the overbred Irishwomen alone.

Brigid's eyes opened with a flutter in response to Ryan's healing touch. With difficulty, she focused on the pale, compassionate features of her cousin's face. Being held closely by someone real and warm reminded her acutely of what she no longer had. The pain she had been trying to drown flooded back into her heart like an undertow pulling away her perseverance, leaving her heaving dry sobs on Ryan's chest.

They held each other tightly. Ryan spoke to her devastated friend with soothing reassurances until she brought about calm in her patient.

"Oh, god, Ryan. You don't know what I've done," Brigid confessed.

"You did what any self-respecting, hot-blooded dyke would have done in your position. It's a rare soul that can look into Dana's eyes and not want her. I would have finished taking her myself if I hadn't wanted to hurt her so badly."

Ryan's voice was so confident and supportive that it relaxed Brigid. She took great comfort from having someone understand what happened to a person once she fell into one of Dana's traps. Relief filled her being when she realized that she wouldn't have to explain any of the morbid details of her dishonor. The extent of her folly—her truest love for Dana and betrayal of her wife— was plain for all to see in the oil confession on the dresser.

Ryan had seen it, but so had Leslie. When she arrived with the drink and some aspirin, Brigid was shamed anew.

"Here, Brig. This will help you feel better." Leslie handed the medicine to her friend, who was touched by the tender act of forgiveness.

Brigid sat up, groaning from the discomfort of her hangover, but determined to make a show of self-sufficiency. She leaned back next to Ryan and swallowed the pills as well as half the drink. "Star took off for Connecticut to live with her sister. I don't even know if she's arrived—no one there will speak to me when I call. What am I going to do? I know she'll never come back. Not after what I've done." She sought her cousin's wisdom. "Why wouldn't she understand? Why?"

"Shhh. Brig, she just isn't put together that way. You can't blame yourself for that. It's over." Ryan knew that she sounded insensitive. Now was the time to be practical and avoid getting swept away with the torment. "You're coming home with us until you feel well enough to go on by yourself."

Brigid was instantly resistant. She sat up straighter and proclaimed, "I can take care of myself, Ryan."

Ryan hastened to put the misplaced pride to rest. "I have *never* doubted that ever. But why bother? There's nothing here but memories to haunt you and prolong the recovery process. Get away from it all and get it into perspective. Our home has always been open to you. Take advantage of it." She met Leslie's eyes, knowing in advance that Leslie would welcome Brigid with open arms.

"Brig, we can send someone up to feed the animals and put things in order. You won't have a care, except to get well," Leslie encouraged.

Brigid couldn't resist Leslie's warm invitation. She knew she had exceeded her limits and could admit that she needed help. Her heart had been broken by her two great loves at the same time. That was more than she would expect anyone else to tolerate. She ceased expecting it of herself.

—·◦◆❦ ❧◆◦·—

The new boarder was installed in the bedroom farthest away from the matrimonial sanctuary. Brigid needed privacy, but moreso, she needed not to hear Leslie and Ryan making love. For as long as Ryan was able, she took Sanji to the wine cellar for the soundproof seclusion it offered.

Paint supplies and canvases were ordered in abundance. Brigid began covering canvas after tortured canvas with violent, unholy images. Gone were the subtle pastels that characterized her ceramics. Now, bold, brilliant colors assaulted the senses of the beholders. Violence and rage were evident in everything she painted. Hideous, frightening animals and erratic carnivorous plants splayed themselves across the canvas of the artist's insanity.

Ryan's most emphatic directive to Leslie and the staff alike was that whoever was around when a painting was completed was to rescue it promptly and replace it with a blank canvas. The angry paintings were secreted away to a place where Brigid couldn't get to them to destroy them, as she had her ceramics. She was not to be allowed to sink into a destructive mood for fear no one would be able to bring her out of it again. The effusive renderings of grief were not to be obstructed.

The only request Ryan made of the artist was that she refrain from portraying human images until she could do so with proper justice. The request was honored—to everyone's great relief. The imagination was taxed to dream of what a person would have looked like if Brigid had created one in her ugly state of torment.

But for all the precautions taken, no one could have foreseen the battle that Brigid would wage within herself or its frightening effects on the entire household, most especially, Ryan.

It began slowly at first and progressed unnoticed, until it was too late. More and more food was being left on Brigid's trays each time they were carried away by a kitchen servant. The first ten pounds she shed left her looking trim, but still fit. The next five brought the problem to Bonnie's attention. Some well-placed questions put to the staff not only revealed Brigid's failing health but provided her with the first clue that Ryan's appetite had slacked off also. The matter was brought to Leslie's attention without delay, but, unhappily, the pattern had already taken hold. In the weeks to come McKinley was to become a grim place indeed.

It wasn't long before Brigid stopped being able to sleep for more than an hour at a time. Her food intake dropped off sharply till the extent of her diet consisted solely of a sporadically consumed thin broth. The madness, insomnia and stubborn refusal to eat saw thirty-five more pounds disappear—fifty in all—leaving behind an emaciated shell.

Anything and everyone was tried to break through the consuming madness. Leslie spent hours on end reading to the tormented master artist. Bonnie, always handy and motherly, continued to offer brews of hops and other nerve relaxants, palatable food and nourishing drinks, to no avail. Her suggestion that Brigid's real mother be called in to assist was violently denied. Brigid wouldn't hear of it.

126

But it was Ryan who paid the penalty. She could ill afford to lose as little as five pounds, being so slender by nature. When she realized what was happening she began to force herself to eat. It was useless. Her body's unlimited empathy for her cousin's illness forced her to disgorge everything she ate. She, alarmingly, lost thirty pounds. Before the first month of Brigid's residence elapsed Ryan had become a silent invalid.

Bonnie came naturally to nursing, it being her original vocation before becoming Ryan's caretaker in life. She was accustomed to dealing with Ryan's physical needs and found she had a willing and able pupil in Leslie. Together they massaged Ryan's shrunken body, chased away bed sores, bathed her, and dispassionately dealt with the unseemly chores of maintaining a human body.

Wordlessly, Ryan endured the indignities of an intravenous diet, being utterly helpless to heal herself or her ailing guest, her own physical powerlessness to perform even the simplest of tasks for herself, and the constant presence of a professional nurse.

When she was awake, Ryan insisted upon seeing each of Brigid's paintings; the one satisfaction left to her was that she could still diagnose the progression of her kin's journey through her hellish personal war by analyzing the revealing art.

The one impotence Ryan truly resented was her inability to dissuade her physician from introducing sleep inducers into her system. The increased vitamins in the endless stream of bottles sustaining her kept her from getting worse. But Ryan didn't want to sleep.

In sleep she was defenseless, vulnerable and exposed to the nightmares that her psychic self visited upon her, courtesy of the artist's internal grapplings—the ones no one spoke of.

Leslie worried *constantly.* She had been soundly discouraged from spending too much time with Ryan. Brigid, she was told, needed her more, for in healing Brigid she would be doing the most good for her beloved. So went the endless hours of soothing music and gentle discourses mentally caressing Brigid, seemingly ignored. In time Leslie grew accustomed to Brigid's taut lifeless face, but her heart wept each time she saw the unnatural paleness, hollow eye sockets and concave cheeks carved into her mate's once proud face.

Then, as Bonnie had feared would happen, Leslie began to lose weight herself. Troubled anxiety took its toll on her otherwise stable nervous system. The sleepless tearful nights—the fear that this might be the final battle, that all could be lost, chipped haphazardly away at her spirit like a drunken sculptor.

The dark cloud of the unknown descended upon McKinley. Suffering and desperation were everywhere like a sickening odor with no discernible source. No one knew when or how it all would end.

Just when Leslie's strength to survive without hope was played out, and her despair was at its worst, Ryan took an unexpected turn for the better. Two days later a breakthrough occurred. Like the fluid from a broken blister, Brigid's vitriolic emotions drained from her, leaving her cleansed and ready to heal over. Her madness had passed. Her rage was simply spent and could no longer fuel her self-destruction.

Brigid could, finally, look outside herself, and when she did the first thing she saw was Leslie. Peaceful, patient, understanding Leslie. Beautiful Leslie.

From her, she looked around and out the window, seeing for the first time that it was winter. The estate was awash in sparkling crisp snow. From where she was sitting she could see a small lake—frozen and quiet, impervious to the ducks skidding about on top of it. Life. It beckoned to her.

"How long have you been sitting there?" Brigid interrupted Leslie's poetry recitation abruptly.

The book came down to Leslie's lap silently. She glanced at her watch. "About an hour." When she looked up, the lifelessness in Brigid's skin was even more pronounced because there was, at long last, life in her steady grey eyes.

"No, I mean how long have you been coming in here to read to me?" Brigid demanded.

"Several weeks, Brigid," Leslie replied quietly.

"What day is this?"

"Tuesday."

"The date?"

"The seventeenth."

"Of?"

"December," Leslie provided, fascinated.

"December?" Brigid was thoroughly amazed. "Where's Star?"

"She's where you said she would be. Living with her sister."

"Have you spoken with her?"

Leslie shook her head sadly. "She won't speak to anyone, not even me."

Brigid lowered her head. She was going to say something, but suddenly her eyes grew very large as if she had seen a ghost. She pinched the limp skin on her arm then let it go. Then she picked up her crutches and walked weakly to the mirror. Her hand came up to inspect her own face as a blind person's would. "Jesus, god. Where's Ryan?"

"Brigid," Leslie cautioned.

"Where is she?"

"In bed, but . . . Brigid, don't go in there." Leslie rose to her feet, wanting to stop the redhead, but she wasn't the tough guy sort.

Exerting tremendous effort, Brigid made her way to the master bedroom. She nudged a chair over to the bed and lowered herself into it sadly. Her voice was filled with heartsickness as she addressed the wasted, sleeping form. "What have I done to you?"

"Brigid, please don't punish yourself," Leslie begged. "We've all had enough of that. She's getting better now . . ."

128

"She was *worse?*"

Leslie curled her trembling lower lip under her front teeth and nodded.

Brigid stood and fixed her jaw. "This is ridiculous. You're right—enough is enough. I'm going to have to straighten myself out—and now."

The winter holidays passed quietly and without celebration. Brigid took to painting with watercolors and her presence was welcomed in the sunroom where she began the healing process with a breathtaking landscape.

She was back on solid food well before anyone thought she would be, and gained weight quickly. Brigid was hearty, sturdy and unwilling to let life get the better of her. Steady, predictable, calm, energetic and alive—for all outward appearances, Brigid was becoming her old self again, and everyone breathed a sigh of relief.

But underneath it all something had gone awry within Brigid. The rebuilding process had left out a cornerstone of conscience, a window of sensibility, and a footer of honor. There was an underlying need to deaden her unrelenting pain. She wasn't the first person, nor would she be the last, to fall upon the solution of transferring love from one object to another.

It wasn't a conscious or willful act—Brigid would just find herself staring at Leslie. The morning sun illuminating her golden hair, creating a shimmering halo about her head. Muted bronze, perfectly smooth complexion swathed the delicate features of her face. Divine moist lips shaped an exquisite invitation. Large inquisitive eyes that were peaceful and innocent one moment, cool, distant and unapproachable the next.

Leslie was accustomed to being stared at by women and men alike. She paid Brigid no mind and went on with her recitations—pacifying and soothing Brigid's victimized spirit.

At times, Leslie would join the artist on wintry afternoon walks about the grounds, stopping to feed the ducks or study snowflakes dangling from pine needles. To Brigid, the crisp air couldn't compete with the heavenly fragrance floating about in the vicinity of Leslie. She filled her lungs to capacity with it. Her attention was called to Leslie's unique grace and inimitable style. Little things engrossed her like how well ermine, a most regal fur, suited Leslie.

Though they were never alone in the evenings Brigid wasn't aware of it. When she saw Leslie's hand lift an etched crystal wine glass to her lips she saw the hand of a goddess. When the flickering light from a fireplace played across Leslie's bodice, she saw the bosom of an angel. All this before her, day after day, was the complete woman, and Brigid loved her with all her heart and everything she had to give.

Somehow, no one was truly surprised when they realized that Ryan wasn't recovering well. Her convalescence, though deliberate, was behindhand. She had always lived hard and fast. Combined with the recent years of internalized grief, self-destruction and being mentally and physically abused by Rags, her system was no longer able to pay the heavy price exacted by her most recent illness.

Her physical strength returned, begrudgingly and only because she prized it so that she willed her muscles into obedience. Her endurance came back a little over half what it once was. She was never again to know vitality.

Leslie would have liked to have been solely sufficient to satisfy all Ryan's needs; she loved her that much. However, the true measure of her love was her ability to accept that Ryan was too complex for that to be possible. Ryan had, and always would have, needs that took her away from Leslie's side.

It was plain for all to see what was needed most to counteract the emasculating effects of Ryan's depleted body. As soon as she was able to remain awake and sitting up long enough to do so, Phil came for her to take her back to her element. Every day. At first, it was much like when she had been his bright beginning pupil. He was in heaven because Ryan needed him again. She was in hell because she couldn't handle the plane on her own.

It was grueling and exhausting, but it worked. Beginning with a little sparkle in her eye, Ryan improved steadily. Phil patiently guided her — giving her the control of the Stearman for short periods, working their way up to touch and goes, and taking her through spin after spin, building up her endurance, agility, response time and mental alertness.

The day of rejoicing finally came. When Ryan came home from her first solo flight she was grinning broadly. Pride glittered in her eyes. Her self-esteem was restored.

Brigid had a rite of passage to meet as well. Just as it was known Ryan would one day fly her Lear Jet again, Brigid would take to task a human portrait.

Leslie was to be her test flight. Leslie was flattered by the request and agreed eagerly to sit for the master. Brigid took great pains with the painting, glad she had a willing and very patient subject.

Leslie could not express her feelings when she was allowed to view the completed work. She simply stood there— characteristically—holding her hand over her mouth, saying nothing. It was truly beautiful, of that she was certain. Had she not been the subject she could have explained the humbleness she knew in the presence of such mastery. Her unlimited art appreciation left her in a complete state of awe.

Brigid, too, was quite proud of the work. Indeed, once Brigid ultimately did attain the renown she deserved, the portrait was her most sought after piece.

Ryan came late to view the work, having lost track of time during her daily flight. When she walked into the sitting room she found Brigid standing behind Leslie who was still silently admiring the canvas. She smiled at her cousin, then looked at the portrait.

The pain was not unlike someone thrusting a sword through her heart. Even learning about the death of her father hadn't seared through her very being the way the shock of seeing that picture did.

Brigid had done it again. Portrayed Leslie with the same uncanny clarity as she had Dana. The crisp, youthful, inquisitive face. The subdued royalty. The dovelike peace in the eyes. Something else radiated from the portrait. Something Brigid had painted into it that told Ryan things she had no way of preparing herself for.

She looked sharply from it to Brigid. She tried to swallow the pain—shove it back where it couldn't live. Their eyes met and revealed what neither of them would admit. For an agonizing, horrible moment they looked at one another as rivals. This was not an innocent crush that Ryan could smile about and forget. The look in Brigid's stern eyes was one of determination that knew no bounds or price too high. Eyes that read of the sacred friendship between them being freely spent—for the love of a woman.

Emotionally, Ryan knew the friendship was over between herself and Brigid but she was unwilling to accept it.

She blinked and her head came around slowly to view the art once more. Her opinion was a brief, telling remark. "It's your best work." Her voice caught in her throat. She excused herself quickly. Resolved as she was to deny the truth, she couldn't battle down the heartache.

Leslie turned to Brigid. "That was mean of her, Brig. I'm sorry. I'll get her."

"No, don't." Brigid caught Leslie's arm to stop her. "Believe me. Coming from Ryan, that's the highest possible compliment. I'm pleased." Neither was Brigid willing to believe of herself that she might forsake Ryan's friendship for this beautiful woman she held by the arm. She let go of Leslie's arm, suddenly afraid of the possibility.

Misinterpreting Brigid's worried look, Leslie reconsidered recalling her lover. Brigid still knew certain things about Ryan that she had yet to learn.

Bonnie stopped outside the door of Ryan's study—caught by a sight she had hoped she would never see again. The door was ajar and the light from the hallway outlined Ryan's unhappiness.

Her heart sank, sank back thirty-two years to the night she first witnessed this sad scene. Holding his face in his long, sensitive hands, Patrick O'Donnell fought back his tears. Succeeding in doing so, the firm hands exposed his face and grasped his upper arms tightly. For support. His proud head laid back, looking upward, searching for the reason why. Why had his mate been taken in childbed? Taken away?

Bonnie had originally been hired as a nurse, a position she was never to fulfill, and into those strained arms, she—just eighteen herself—placed a lusty newborn. The grief-stricken eyes looked for the first time upon the single issue of his love. The bond was formed and the love was transferred.

But there was no child to distract Ryan, no consolation. Bonnie watched her—so much like her father. Even the expression on her face that was just now exposed as the long, rugged fingers grabbed the slender upper arms tightly. The scene replayed itself anew as the fierce, proud head lay back—tortured, asking why.

Bonnie's heart ached. She could almost hear the rent that opened in Ryan's heart. A small one, just enough to allow a constant dripping. Now, it had begun. That large, generous heart would drip, slowly, inside itself and would not mend. Bonnie knew, for she had seen this dripping for twenty-five years draining away the life's blood of Ryan's father. A faint indelible grief would visit that pale landscape, housed there like a caged bird despairing of its freedom. No one else would probably ever notice it but Bonnie, and perhaps Ryan, herself. Now the picture was complete. Ryan's face had taken on the last nuance of her father: the O'Donnell legacy of sorrow.

At that moment, Ryan was completely alone. Alone in a Universe populated with uncountable souls. Alone. The desolation of it; the utter despair stabbed Bonnie squarely in her heart. She walked on. The moment would pass and Ryan would go on as before. But she and Bonnie would hear the dripping, the endless dripping.

That evening Bonnie paid a visit on Brigid. She entered quietly, without knocking. Brigid looked up from the book she was escaping in. "Hi, Bonnie."

Bonnie sat her indestructible frame in a chair opposite Brigid. She wasn't a domestic here, she was a friend. "Brigid, my lass. You're lookin' much better now. Do you feel it?" Bonnie searched the solid, sensitive features of Brigid's face.

"Yes, dear. I am starting to do better."

"Aye. I suspected as much. You know I have never interfered with your life. Even when you were a child I left things important and such up to your sweet mother. Bless her. And a fine job she's done, too."

Brigid knew something was coming. "What is it, Bonnie?"

Bonnie took a handkerchief from her sleeve and toyed with it. "No greater friends have I seen than the likes of you and Ryan. So close and believin' in each other completely." Bonnie fixed her blue eyes on Brigid. She was no fool and she knew what had gone on. "I know, lass, that you would never hurt Ryan."

Brigid looked away suddenly. The chord had been struck.

Bonnie continued, "I think it's time you moved on, lass."

Ryan had convinced Brigid to sell the farm and the time *had* come for her to start a new life. Brigid nodded her head sharply. "I'll be gone by month's end."

Bonnie rose and walked heavily out of the room. Brigid looked after her. They both could tell that at that very moment, Bonnie had grown old.

By the end of March, Brigid had purchased a friend's carriage house and made plans to rebuild her shop in the lower floor. The show she had postponed haunted her. She was eager to begin replacing the work she had destroyed in her anger and rage. Life called to her and she answered.

# 14

Winter had been moderately severe, but in everyone the revival of Spring was embraced with celebration. Ryan had taken Leslie to New York for a private function at the Museum of Modern Art. She had donated two cityscapes by Utrillo that her father had collected two decades earlier. Ryan confided to her mate that she was glad to be rid of them, having found them too primitive and unimaginative for her tastes.

While there, Ryan didn't even attempt to keep up with Leslie's shopping, but they did take in a Broadway show, and Leslie had to *drag* Ryan out of the Intrepid Sea-Air-Space Museum.

Upon their return they found McKinley alive and delighted to see them again. The peace gardens were the first to bloom and, as the gardener had promised, they were masterpieces. White and blue everywhere.

While they were away the gardener had cooked up a surprise in the support greenhouses. Forced Easter Lilies had been timed to coincide with Leslie's arrival. Each room greeted her with a sweet leaden aroma. She was very pleased.

The dark unhappiness of Winter gave way to lighthearted tours of the reawakened holdings surrounding the mansion, which amounted to play for Leslie. Ryan joined her often on her recreational inspections, taking pleasure in her lover's delight. April was a gift.

On one such inspection, Leslie stopped to examine the swollen buds of the juvenile Ginkgo trees she had had planted in the southern courtyard, "Because," she had said, "I remember." When she had made the cryptic statement, Ryan noticed a vague hint of gold in Leslie's eyes that made her smile knowingly.

After assuring herself that the trees had wintered well and seeing that Ryan was tiring, she serenely took a seat on the masonry bench nearby.

Ryan joined her and sighed.

"What's wrong?" Leslie asked, inviting confidence.

Ryan lit a cigarette and stared at her feet. "I was just thinking about what to do with Sanji. I'm having trouble with her."

"I can't imagine you having trouble with anyone."

"Actually, it's a common problem. It happens quite often with slaves that get used as much as she has been. Pain begins to lose its effectiveness as a tool for punishment. She's begun to enjoy it."

"Have you tried avoiding her?"

"Yes, but she's shrewd and knows me too well. She knows that when I don't visit her, I'm going without as much as she is. She's getting downright flagrant about her disobedience."

Leslie pulled her cashmere shawl closer. "I can't believe she can handle you ignoring her. I would be devastated if you did that to me."

Ryan took Leslie's hand and held it. "That's because I love you and you would think I was withholding my love. Sanji knows I don't love her. What has she got to lose?"

"She's getting pretty smug, isn't she?" Leslie observed.

Ryan replied with a "no joke" expression that exemplified her disgust with the situation.

"If I know you, you've discovered a way to put her in her place."

"If I know you, you're dying of curiosity to know what it is."

"Ryan, you know I am."

"I had to come up with a weakness of hers that I could exploit most effectively. I had the right idea with ignoring her, but I need to take it one step further. She has to know that she is being denied, but that I'm not."

Leslie guessed, "Another slave?"

"Yes."

Leslie pulled her hand away, hurt. "Ryan, I thought you said you didn't need anyone else, that Sanji was enough for you."

"Oh, she is," Ryan reassured emphatically. "Sanji has always been able to satisfy me in that area. I don't *need* another slave. What I need is a way to punish the one I have. You're the one who needs a slave."

"Me?" Leslie stood disapprovingly. "Don't be silly. I don't need a slave."

Ryan laughed soundly. "Ah, my sweet, that's part of the reason I love life with you so. Being married to you is like having two women, and I never know which one of you is going to answer me."

Leslie folded her arms sharply across her chest and looked at her mate sternly. "I'm not sure I know how to take that."

"Darling, you are two women and I love you both. One Leslie is cool, sophisticated and sensible. She's quiet, cares about justice and has an insatiable curiosity. The other Leslie is easily aroused, a bitch, and craves excitement and power. That's the Leslie that needs a slave."

"How do you know that when I don't even know it about myself?" Leslie insisted.

136

Ryan was confident. "I've seen it in your eyes, lover. Every time I take you to Sanji, you quake with desire to dominate her. It's more than just how you feel about her personally, much more. You're ripe for it.

"I don't think you would have any trouble imagining the enjoyment you would get from having your own slave instead of just sharing mine."

Leslie did imagine it, and the thought brought a coy smile to her face. Ryan had seen through her, but she didn't mind. She sat next to her lover again and admitted softly, "Yes, you're right. Although I don't think I would want to try to handle someone as wild as Sanji. I prefer the gentle sort that's eager to please."

"I thought you would. I was thinking of Corelle."

Leslie was wide-eyed and gasping.

"She's perfect, honey. She suits us both so well. She has the innocence and fragility that I crave in young girls. To have her here would answer that need for me and . . ." Ryan raised an eyebrow in Leslie's direction, "keep me out of jail. We both know she wants me and loves you. That's why she left. All she wants is permission."

With longing in her voice Leslie asked, "Do you really think she'll come back?"

"Definitely."

"I miss her," Leslie sighed. "She handles everything so beautifully and with such grace. Her touch is so soft, and she's loyal unto death. Oh, Ryan, I want her back badly."

"Call her. All she needs is our permission to love us to the extent of her desire. I guarantee you, she will do anything we ask."

—◦→⊱⊰◆◦·—

"Corelle, I want to thank you for coming to see me today. I know how difficult it is for you to be here."

Corelle's voice was softer than Leslie remembered. "Milady, I am honored to be invited. How may I serve you?"

"I want you to come back to me." Leslie stilled the young woman with a gently raised hand. "Please, don't answer me yet. I will ask you again later and if, indeed, you decide you cannot be here, then I won't bother you again. For now, I want you to come with me."

She took Corelle's tiny hand in hers. It was frightening to experience the breakability of Corelle's being. Like a frozen flower petal. The slight immigrant was so maleable that it was difficult for Leslie to keep from taking advantage of her right then and there. Instead, she led her up the stairway to Corelle's old bedroom.

Corelle's imagination was running amuck when she walked into her old quarters with her Lady. Corelle had never thought of Leslie as anything else but as her Lady. The family she was serving now were dull and lifeless, making it easy for Corelle to think about her former employers a great deal.

She was startled when she noticed Ryan sitting in a chair near the bed, nonchalantly smoking a cigarette. Silently, she curtsied and blushed. Her heart raced wildly inside her bosom.

"Call when you are ready," Leslie instructed Ryan sweetly, then disappeared.

Ryan leaned back in her chair and looked Corelle over with a practiced eye. Satisfied, she put her cigarette out and walked over to where the servant was standing and trembling. "How like a flower you are. So fragile and delicate." Ryan unpinned the full tresses of chestnut which unfurled down Corelle's back, well past her waist. Corelle shivered when Ryan arranged the hair expertly about her face and shoulders. "I had forgotten how beautiful you look. Long hair becomes you."

"You flatter me, Miss O'Donnell," Corelle said softly.

"I flatter no one. I speak the truth." Careful not to frighten the young woman, Ryan lifted Corelle's chin up slowly. "The truth about you is that you are lovely and vulnerable." Corelle's eyes were searching. "Corelle, you know I wouldn't willingly bring harm to my relationship with Miss Serle, don't you?"

Corelle knew she had to look directly at the masterful eyes; her head remained still after Ryan took her hand away to allow her to answer. "Yes, Miss O'Donnell."

"She brought you to me at my request, but she did so happily. It is with her consent that I am going to take you."

"Oonn," Corelle moaned lustily. Years of fantasies crowded into the space under her skirt. She was more ready than Ryan knew.

"Corelle, because you have always been in a subservient position to us I need to know your honest feelings about this. I will ask you this one time only. I want you to search your heart before responding. If you accept, Corelle, you will not again be released from our service. Do you want me to take you?" Ryan queried with authority.

Corelle was wearing a brown and green peasant dress. Her full breasts had been poured into the cotton top and strained against the captive fabric. By way of the answer she could not verbalize, she looked down and unbuttoned her blouse. Her breasts fell out, free and alive with desire.

Corelle's innocence made Ryan smile. Her indiscretion awakened Ryan's passion. Taking the small round face between her slender hands, Ryan kissed the maiden's lips fully, with a mounting fire.

Corelle was so pliable, so willing, ready and needy. When Ryan came away from the kiss, she knew why. It had been some time since she had felt that special need in a young woman and it shook her. Breathlessly she confirmed it, "My god, Corelle. No one has ever touched you before."

Shy, but determined, Corelle presented herself. "I wish to give my maidenhood to you, Miss O'Donnell."

Ryan's moan of pleasure was as intense as any she had ever expressed. She pulled Corelle to her and gave in to her own shattered breathing.

Corelle hadn't known how special her gift was until she felt the power of its effect on the intended recipient. From that moment forward, she was in an altered, heavenlike state. Love had at last come her way—she was ready.

Ryan undressed the servant reverently and led her to what was to be a ceremonial bed. She knew completely the significance of what she was about to receive and how important it was to make the event memorable for the donor. She had received this most special of gifts from many young ladies over the years. Her own gift had been given, in all trust, to a She-devil. It was a good memory, but that part of herself belonged to someone she hated now. She hoped Corelle would never have cause to be anything but pleased with her experience.

When it came to sex, Ryan discovered, Corelle had a mind of her own. She would have no part of being dealt with gently. It had been too long in coming, too much fuel had poured into the tank of Corelle's need. When she received Ryan's knowing tongue into her mouth it was just the spark to light her uncontainable fire.

Corelle had to learn to communicate her need physically because an unexpected twist developed when Ryan began to kiss her hotly and urgently. A twist that would become a source of embarrassment for her and amusement for Ryan and Leslie. In the throes of sexual excitement, Corelle could only *understand* English, she couldn't speak it. Instead, her screams of joy, rapture and lust were decorated with perfect Gaelic.

Ryan seemed not to notice; she was thrust into a state of emergency in response to the virgin's demanding hunger. She pinned Corelle's arms to the mattress and humped her furiously.

Corelle was the sort of woman who intuited sex. She had learned a great deal from watching Ryan take Sanji—she learned how to please Ryan and how to get *more* of what she wanted. Without arguing, she placed herself in the position of being conquered. She didn't struggle to pay attention to Ryan physically; it was pointless to expect Ryan to allow herself to be made love to. Only Leslie would know that honor. Corelle simply reveled in being taken and used for another's pleasure.

And she did it marvelously. Ryan traded fitful orgasms with the eminently teachable novice, then collapsed happily on top of her supple body.

Corelle had seen how Sanji lay perfectly still and silent until Ryan recovered and chose to go on, or not. Studied concentration along with tremendous will power paid off generously for Corelle. Ryan did slide off to one side and began kissing her neck seductively. "Sweet mother in heaven. You are *very* good, little lady," Ryan praised her.

Corelle floated and drifted under Ryan's initiating kisses. She moved into each one, moaning and tossing her head about. When Ryan buried her face in one of her generous breasts, she cried out sharply, digging her nails into Ryan's shoulders.

By the time Ryan made her way to the expectant womanhood, the servant was frantic. She teased the hair about her trophy for long minutes until Corelle was literally screaming. It didn't take an interpreter to know that the dainty maiden was out of her mind with wanting it.

Ryan spoke a quiet prayer of dedication, then ran her finger firmly over the outer lips, gathering moist assistance for her mission. It was a semilunar hymen—her preference.

"Corelle, my dear. You do know that there is no way to do this without it causing you some discomfort?" Ryan asked carefully.

The gold-tinted, misty sea-green eyes had an ethereal quality about them that told Ryan her partner had crossed over into the otherworld of abandonment that she had led so many to. Intoxicated, Corelle nodded her consent.

Ryan thanked her for it genuinely, and looked back down to where her hand was waiting to perform the act of defloration. "This just sends me every time I do it," Ryan exclaimed. She went in slowly, then, before Corelle could take the time to become anxious and tense up, she ripped the skin in one quick outward movement. "Huuooonn. Ohn," Ryan moaned. She fell in and out of mini-faints, moaning and gasping, nearly weeping with distinctively female sighs of rapture.

Corelle was supremely elated. Ryan's response to her gift went beyond her most fertile dreams. They laid together for a short while, savoring it. Corelle was quiet now and could speak. She did so humbly and hopefully. Her body craved something and she wasn't ashamed to ask for it.

"Please, I beg of you. I wish you to take me with your . . ." She faltered. It was still difficult to vocalize such a desperate need.

Ryan was nonplussed. She had no idea what Corelle wanted. Whatever it was, she wanted it badly. Their eyes met, each with a question. Ryan whispered her encouragement. "What is it that you want?"

Corelle began to pant with excitement. Her answer was moaned pleadingly. "Your fist."

Ryan was winded by the request. Her forehead came to rest on Corelle's tight abdomen while she marshalled her passion. So the precocious beginner wanted an advanced lesson. So the newly unsealed, bleeding opening wasn't satisfied. Ryan raised her head and laughed. "Well, I'll be damned. From maiden to cunt in one sitting. Is that it?"

Ryan's comment was designed to shame Corelle—it worked. Even still she was panting; her eyes beseeched the Irish tyrant fervently.

"Okay, little girl. You asked for it, and I will *not* let you out of it," Ryan promised. She pulled a cigarette from the pack in her pocket and lit it contemptuously. Corelle's legs were spread meanly, and without any preparation Ryan attacked the chestnut womanhood painfully and suddenly.

Corelle tried to pull away, gasping. She hadn't counted on it hurting so much. The fingers of Ryan's free hand bore into her hip making hot ashes fall from the coal of her cigarette to Corelle's unexpecting stomach.

"Ow!"

Ryan's eyes hardened. She didn't start things and then not finish them. She shoved her fist into the unspoiled cavern. "Shut up, CUNT!"

Instantly, Corelle knew why Sanji submitted to the pain. It was a trade-off for excitement. Every nerve in her body sizzled and thrilled in her. This was what it was to be thoroughly taken, truly used, and she liked it. More than she ever thought she would.

For the next few minutes she didn't speak in any language. She just screamed and sighed while Ryan brutalized her with a lesson she never wanted to forget.

Ryan couldn't engage in this act of viciousness without it overtaking her with ecstasy. Invariably, she bordered on darkness, skirting the edges dangerously, and she *loved* it. Many a woman had submitted to her in this fashion, but it was always the same, always had the same result. Mind-bending orgasm. The moment she felt Corelle's inner muscles contract about her fist she opened the floodgates of her own tension and let loose the waves of relief.

Rays of light flashed behind Ryan's eyes, high-pitching ringing filled her head, then, briefly: incoherence. Inhabiting a highly responsive body had its rewards. When her inarticulate moans subsided she removed her offending hand from Corelle's initiated cavity slowly and carefully to make sure Corelle realized the full effect of becoming empty. The forgotten, spent cigarette had burned to a butt, which she placed in an ashtray.

Corelle was complete and weeping joyfully. She had found more than physical love. Ryan had shown her a new religion. She had taken a vow of devotion and she would live from moment to moment until her vessel would be called upon to be used again.

After holding Corelle close and comforting her, Ryan called Leslie in. Corelle was brought to her feet and Leslie addressed her firmly. "Corelle, will you come back to me?"

"Yes, milady, if you'll have me," Corelle replied meekly.

Leslie issued her first command with authority. "Kneel, Corelle."

Corelle's naked form knelt gracefully. She was stunning in that posture.

Ryan handled the balance of the instructions. "It is our wish to train you as a sex-slave. Being a sex-slave is different from being a servant. You will continue to attend to your Mistress' hair and personal things, but you will no longer be expected to deal with any household affairs. You will be available sexually to both of us at all times from this point forward."

"Yes, Miss O'Donnell."

"You will address me as Master except in the presence of a guest. Miss Serle is your Mistress now and you shall think of her as such. You will continue to address her as My Lady. Do you understand?"

"Yes, Master."

"We do have another slave, Corelle. My slave. Your status, very naturally, will be lower than hers. She has served me long and well and has earned many privileges. You too, will gain more privileges as you serve us as well as I know you will.

"There are many rules and much protocol to learn in your new position. These things you will be taught later. Here is what you must learn now."

Ryan had Corelle's full attention.

"I am your Master. You may look at me and speak to me whenever you wish. You may *not* kiss or touch me anywhere unless I tell you to."

She brought Leslie nearer the joyful slave. "This is your Mistress." Ryan placed her hand lovingly over the area of her wife's sex. "Because of your status, you may only look as high as my hand when serving her sexually. Whenever you address her, your eyes must be focused on this point so that you remember at all times what your function in life is. When attending her in non-sexual activities, you must avoid any contact with her eyes. Your punishment will be quite distasteful, Corelle, I can assure you, should you be found doing otherwise. Do you understand?"

"Yes, Master," Corelle assented.

"You may speak to your Mistress only when spoken to. Two of the main privileges you will work for is to be allowed to touch her breasts, which my slave is already allowed to do, and kiss her sweet lips. Her sex and backside will not be denied you because you have already proven your great worth to us. I guarantee you that these privileges will be hard-earned." Ryan guided the slave's attention back to herself. "I will tell you now why we have asked you to return to our service. When *I* come to visit you, it will be for one reason and one reason only. To punish my slave."

Corelle's eyes widened with surprise, but she accepted her new position gladly. Everyone was well pleased with the new arrangement.

A turbulent thunderstorm waged on outside Dana's window. Occasionally, lightning brightened her room. The thick air and low pressure quieted her nerves, making her receptive and restful.

"Fellow seeker of Revenge."

Dana turned to the hollow voice from beyond and bowed respectfully to the image illuminated on the wall directly across from her. "Yes, my Queen," Dana acknowledged her summons clearly.

Anara hovered menacingly in the saturated atmosphere. Her image—patient pale face, eerie white eyes, volumes of long radiantly black hair mingled in folds of midnight purple robes—was frightening as usual. Her voice was completely dispassionate, cold. "Did you drug the artist?"

"I did," Dana informed her Mistress.

"And what have you learned?" Anara inquired. She used Dana as a fact-finder out of sheer distaste for her prey. To her, Ryan, the lowly earthbound creature whose soul she intended to destroy, wasn't worthy of direct contact.

"Only that the Woman of Wings has information about herself that she wishes to keep from you until it is too late for you to do anything about it." Dana provided what she had learned about Ryan from Brigid carefully, worried that her Mistress might be angry with her for not having greater success in uncovering Ryan's plans to defeat Anara.

"Have you knowledge of the nature of this information?" Anara pressed her servant patiently.

"No, my Queen. The Woman of Wings is clever and has not revealed herself completely, even to her confidant, the artist."

Anara was silent for a moment, thinking about this new development. Absently, she spoke, paying no attention to Dana. "I shall discover these things on my own, now that I know she is hiding something. She can't have kept it from me without help from someone on this side." Then directly to her servant: "Are you certain the artist will betray the Woman of Wings?"

"I believe she has begun to do so already."

Anara smiled. She had been mystified by the outcome of her previous attempts to trip Ryan up by destroying her relationship with Leslie. Leslie didn't behave as a typical woman should have. Her actions were wholly unpredictable and annoying. It bothered Anara that Leslie wasn't afraid of her—a mystery indeed. But then she left off her mental wanderings and continued to grill Dana. "The murderess. Has she been reinstated in the household of the Woman of Wings?"

"She has, my Queen," Dana relayed proudly.

"You have done well. As I promised, you will have the Revenge you seek."

Dana bowed humbly again as the image faded from view, grinning devilishly. She hadn't failed after all, and her Mistress was still pleased with her work.

—◦→⟨⟨⟩⟩◆◦—

Sanji clutched her pillow to her and wept despondently into it. Through the wall, from Corelle's bedroom, she could clearly make out her Master's cries and moans of gratification. Punishment of the highest form.

# 15

Ryan was content and relaxed. The mechanic she was helping was humming quietly to himself. Together, they were fitting an older Cessna with a Stormscope. No one had known it needed one until Ryan gave up flying commercial flights and therefore that plane. Ryan always *knew* where thunderstorms were and so never had a use for a sophisticated computer to tell her where to find them. After her departure, other pilots had been forced to use the antiquated plane and complained bitterly about how badly it needed updating.

Amidst the noise and clatter of the shop where the plane was being overhauled Ryan heaved a great sigh of relief. She hadn't experienced even the slightest pang of guilt about feeling like she had been given a stay of execution when Leslie had read David Martin's obituary to her that morning over breakfast. He had died of a heart attack, bringing to a close years of struggle: she against him. Now she had heard the last of any possible exposé that would put her on stage like a circus act for others to see and exploit. All the evidence of his life's work had been destroyed forever and Ryan was glad. The fewer people who knew about her extraordinary abilities, the better.

It was a refreshing mid-April morning, and Ryan doubted that it could be improved upon. She was tempted to join the mechanic's humming—a waltz perhaps. Instead, she chuckled privately to herself.

Phil approached her and laid a telegram on her lap. Unconcerned, he walked away. She received them on a regular basis: from art dealers, investment brokers and such. Ryan tended to be difficult to reach by phone, a symptom of her excessive privacy. Over the years people learned that she wouldn't tolerate messages left by phone and that if they wanted to reach Ryan O'Donnell for whatever reason, it was best to send a telegram to Peterson's Flight Service.

It rested there, ignored, for some time while she went about her work. When the mechanic went to get coffee, she leaned back in the cockpit and lit a cigarette. Her face lit up as she read the cable:

RYAN:
GOOD NEWS! YOU DON'T HAVE TO TESTIFY AFTER ALL. THE JUDGE DECLARED THE LATHAMS UNFIT PARENTS AND MADE CHRISTINE A WARD OF THE COURT. HE HAS AGREED TO LET YOUR FRIENDS, THE SORENSENS, BE HER LEGAL GUARDIANS—SHE'S MOVING IN WITH THEM TODAY!
BARBARA MCFARLAND

A banner day. One that saw the resolution of two very painful tests of her endurance. She smiled and slipped the dispatch into her shirt pocket.

Barbara was a mastermind at gathering evidence and damaging testimonies. Ryan was glad that she was able to afford the likes of her clever attorney.

The mechanic returned with her coffee. She left off her mental celebration until she could share it later with her wife and turned her attention to the Stormscope.

—◦•❖❀❖•◦—

Sean hated Ryan. He always had. Just a few short hours after the birth of his only child, Brigid, he had received the sad news that the only woman he had truly loved, Devnet O'Donnell, was dead of giving birth. And he blamed Ryan for it.

People seldom revealed the sordid details of their pasts to their children. Patrick O'Donnell had not been the exception. No one had ever told Ryan that Sean MacSweeney had been an ardent rival for the heart of Devnet Fitzmaurice of County Kerry, Ireland. Ryan didn't know that, at one time, Sean had hated her father for having been the one to win Devnet's heart and for marrying that angelic woman.

When Ryan reached an age when she was able to recognize strife between adults, Sean had already forgiven Patrick. Indeed the cousins had become good friends. Ryan simply believed that Sean was a natural enemy, not unlike a cat, and she had treated him accordingly.

It never occurred to her that Sean had taken Aisling O'Boyle as his wife on the rebound. A proper marriage designed to be respectable—properly populating the world with many little MacSweeneys. She had no idea that Sean had moved to America to ease the aching in his heart. His plan would have worked, too, if the following years hadn't been a succession of failed pregnancies on the part of his wife. They had all but given up, when Brigid came along. What should have been a joyous occasion instead marked the end of Sean's interest in family life, once he learned of Ryan's mother's death.

Neither his black hair and slate blue eyes or Aisling's copper hair and sky blue eyes were anywhere to be found on their robust daughter. She did have a strong resemblance to someone Sean didn't like much: his own father. Brigid was, therefore, shunned by Sean, but loved thoroughly by Aisling.

Characteristically narrowminded, he fully expected his tall, virile offspring to outgrow her tomboyish behavior and make up for his negligence by providing him with an heir. When she didn't, the blame was heaped upon Ryan like so much garbage. Sean denied that he had failed as a father and husband, and in so doing, denied Brigid her rightful place in his family.

He hated Ryan all right. Looking at Leslie's hopelessly beautiful portrait above the sitting room fireplace, he hated Ryan even more. Although he refused to acknowledge the skill with which the portrait was rendered, he couldn't obliterate the truest fact that his daughter had repeated a morbid history. Every ironic brush stroke told the story of how she suffered a grave misfortune: falling in love with a wife of an O'Donnell.

Mesmerized and hurt by the portrait, Ryan stood near it, not wanting to talk. Sean stared at her for a moment, examining her. In her stylish black silk suit, he had to admit to himself that she was handsome. A lady killer just like her father.

He knew that Ryan hadn't willingly invited Aisling and himself to dinner. It had to have been Leslie's idea. He also knew that he could spend the time, while Leslie was showing Aisling the much talked about changes made at McKinley, saying absolutely nothing to Ryan. He could go on sipping his sherry, staring at her, building tension, but he wasn't going to. They were both spoiling for a fight.

"Well, Ryan," Sean began. "I came prepared to let you have it for marrying beneath you. Strictly middle-class," he mocked.

"What does that matter?" Ryan hissed her bristled reply. She had counted on Sean to do something as underhanded as checking out Leslie's background. He was a great one for slinging mud.

Sean was feeling smug. He loved getting Ryan's goat. "But," he drew Ryan's eyes painfully toward the portrait, "I can see that I was being shortsighted. She's really quite aristocratic. I had heard that she was. Now I can *see* the rumors about her are true." Even as he paid Ryan the compliment, he had made sure it stuck in her craw. It was clear the portrait was a crooked thorn in her side—he shoved it in a little further and twisted. Only Ryan's eyes revealed how much she was smarting from the remark.

Because he couldn't use Leslie as a weapon any more effectively against his foe, Sean went for his backup ammunition.

The same friends who had agreed to keep the news of Rags' murder from the public had speculated wildly among themselves about what had really gone on. The rumor mill read from the pages of the Social Register: friends and neighbors alike. Sean was as eager to discredit his eccentric cousin as anyone, but he knew that no one would believe the truth.

He couldn't resist confronting Ryan with it. "What's this sordid business about you being involved in a killing last summer?" he asked—baiting.

Ryan was standing under the portrait, elbow leaning on the mantel, her sherry precariously in hand. Her free hand rummaged through her hair when she answered. "It's over with, Sean. Just leave it alone."

Inwardly gleeful, like a child winning a game, Sean kept up his badgering. "Damn peculiar the way that other woman just happened to drive off the road and die just minutes after shooting your friend." He alone had seen that it was more than coincidental that Rags' assailant had met with her untimely end while fleeing the scene. Ryan's dark, unsettling eyes didn't weaken his attack. He stood and accused her directly. "It was you who made that happen, I know it. I tried to warn Patrick about you, but he wouldn't listen. He wouldn't believe he was raising a sorcerer. Now it's come to this. *Murder,*" he breathed spitefully. With uncut malice he threatened Ryan, "If I could convince the authorities that it was you who killed that woman with one of your demonic curses, I would have you locked away for life."

Ryan didn't like it that someone other than herself and Leslie knew of the death curse. Sean could do nothing with his knowledge—except hurl dangerous threats at her. She was burning with anger on general principles. She was on the verge of expressing that anger when the doors of the sitting room opened to let in Leslie and Aisling, who had finished their tour.

Aisling was used to the fights between these lifelong combatants. She broke the moment by reducing it to a harmless complaint. "I knew better than to leave these two alone. They hate each other desperately, you know." Her voice was sweet, almost patronizing. Her heart was filled with the unspoken bitterness of years of family disharmony and lost love.

Leslie was shocked by the exchange. Her worried glance was met with calm. With a great deal of hard work, Ryan was learning to discipline her temper at times, although not nearly often enough.

Still, the party walked to the formal dining room in silence.

The formal dining room was the pièce de résistance of Leslie's exercises in design. She took great pleasure in combining furniture, colors and accessories from different times and places. Blue and white from France imbued the long wool rug running the length of the room and variegated the draperies and upholstery. Twelve Chippendale chairs surrounded the highly polished mahogany table. Above the table, a rare find: a Waterford chandelier. To one side of the extended table was an eight-legged serpentine sideboard, a classic fireplace on the other. Silver Georgian candelabras flanked the serving tray on the sideboard, just as palms flanked the windows.

The room had already come equipped with rich expanses of hand-carved wooden paneling and parquet flooring. Warm lighting lined the upper mouldings, drawing attention to the gilded ceiling. Every available surface hosted a hybrid orchid in a vase of carved ivory.

Sean and Aisling were impressed and had no problem saying so. Against his better judgment, Sean was finding that he liked Leslie. She was everything he had heard she was, and nothing like he had hoped she would be. He had really wanted to make Ryan uncomfortable for not marrying a woman of breeding, wealth and status. But such things were only skin deep. There was something special about Ryan's wife; he couldn't put his finger on it. Whatever it was, no amount of breeding or background could have given it to her. It was something a person was born with, like Ryan's charisma, that only got better as the years went on.

It was just like Ryan to find someone as special as her mother had been and equally as beautiful. He looked at Aisling and felt a twinge of bitterness. She was a pretty woman, very pleasant in all ways—just not exciting the way a Devnet or Leslie was. Life had passed him by and he was sour about it.

He dutifully took his seat next to Aisling; Leslie sat across from them and Ryan took the head of the table.

The Custard of Chicken soup and Salad a la Russe passed peacefully under Leslie's and Aisling's gentle guidance. Leslie had hoped that the entire dinner could be as pleasant, but what she had seen in the sitting room boded ill. She sized up her chances with Sean as she would have a new judge or cranky prosecutor. The MacSweeney line was every bit as recalcitrant as the O'Donnell. If she were to succeed in reuniting Brigid with her family, Aisling would be her best prospect.

But Sean cast a big shadow; he was an important man in Colorado. He maintained his fortunes as a hobby, regularly increasing his wealth with shrewd investments. Aisling wasn't a timid woman, but she never crossed her husband. Leslie could see how much it hurt to be separated from her only child. It was going to be an uphill battle.

When the Herb Roasted Leg of Lamb was served along with the second wine, Leslie took her usual direct approach by opening the subject calmly. "Brigid has moved to town, Aisling."

"Has she?" Aisling tried to soften her surprised question, casting a furtive look toward her husband to see how he was taking the news.

A speared square of lamb came to rest on his plate. He couldn't look crossly at Leslie—it wasn't his style. It was Ryan he looked to, expecting her to solve matters promptly. His face read to Ryan as it would have to any man. Stubborn Sean had never learned to see Ryan as a female entirely. Part of him couldn't resolve the issue, so when he was uncomfortable, he resorted to the easiest relationship. His expression said, "Your wife is out of line, man. Rein her in."

149

Ryan would have no part of Sean's primitive attitudes toward women. "Yes, she has. She sold her farm and bought the carriage house on Sage Gulch," Ryan informed them both while she dipped a piece of venison chop into some currant jelly.

The room became very hushed for a moment. Domestic servants learned to read their employers quickly and the two women in the room, sensing the inevitable quarrel, shifted their demeanor to another level of anonymity. Their movements weren't like movements at all, rather they appeared and disappeared without notice.

"If I wanted to know where that person was, I would have asked," Sean declared sarcastically.

"She's your daughter," Ryan countered.

"I don't have a daughter. *You* saw to that," came Sean's mean reply.

Ryan felt like stuffing a new potato squarely down her cousin's throat. She settled for letting the tines of her fork filet the potato, slowly and with great restraint.

"Sean," Leslie drew the fire in her direction. "It is of little consequence that you think Ryan influenced Brigid's affectional preference. It's a done thing. Can't you accept . . ."

Sean broke in forcefully. "I will not discuss this with an outsider."

Ryan responded in kind to Sean's rudeness by pointing her fork at him when she addressed him sternly. "Leslie . . . is my wife. That makes her a member of this family." Then remembering herself, she sat straighter and composed her person. "And as such, she is entitled to discuss any and all things concerning this family. Most especially Brigid, having been a close friend of hers for many years."

Looking from Ryan to Leslie and seeing a serene, but somewhat imposing gaze in Leslie's grey eyes, Sean had a slight change of heart. He felt as though he could, at least, listen to her.

Leslie doubted she would get anywhere with it, but she knew she could present her case and hope for another chance at a later date and do some actual persuading. "Brigid still needs your love and help."

Throughout the verbal sparring match, Aisling had remained hopeful that if she just ignored it, it would end reasonably. A heart of a mother beat in her chest, and it rose up in rebellion when she heard that her only child might need her. "What's wrong with my Brigid?"

Leslie fought back a smile. She had been in the company of so many natives of the Emerald Isle for so long that she had managed to forget that Aisling was Irish after all. Aisling's speech was so polished and Americanized, sounding truly brogue only when she was under stress.

"She was ill and spent the winter with us," Leslie related.

Aisling muffled her tiny cry of agony in her wine glass. After she swallowed her ache she pressed for the cause. "What was she ailing of?"

"Heartache," Leslie revealed dispassionately. "She was really quite mad, and all but refused to eat. She lost fifty pounds before she pulled herself out of it."

Aisling had always liked Ryan. She knew that Brigid and Ryan couldn't have been closer if they were twins. It was no secret to the immediate family that whenever Brigid suffered, Ryan suffered. She had thought Ryan looked different—older, and like life was finally winning. She marveled at how both Ryan and Brigid had always suffered so stoically, even as small children. She could easily imagine the scene. It saddened her. "Why wasn't I called?" she demanded.

"We wanted to. Brigid wouldn't let us. She wasn't herself and nearly impossible to reach."

Ice Pudding á la Prince Albert was being served with coffee. Everyone waited until they were again alone to go on. It was Sean who resumed the conversation, to everyone's surprise.

"There are those who say that I don't know Brigid well, but even I can venture to say that madness is an excessive response for her. I gather the young woman she was living with left her." Receiving confirmation, he continued, "I don't buy it. She's too levelheaded for that."

"Star's leaving *was* enough to cause that extreme of an emotional response from Brigid. She loved Star dearly and was very dependent on her," Leslie contended.

"I have to agree with Sean. Brigid is sensitive, but she's as strong as an ox. She would have been hurt and she would have grieved, but she wouldn't have gone mad." Aisling knew her daughter all too well and wasn't about to accept Leslie's explanation.

Sean was beginning to wonder if Leslie was the cause, not knowing she was the cure. His voice was suspicious. "What else contributed to this madness you speak of?" He was relieved that the disgraceful affliction wasn't common knowledge among his peers. He was already showing signs of denying its existence.

Aisling wasn't so willing to discount the idea. She had heard of master artists falling prey to any number of forms of insanity. Seeing Leslie's portrait and the exquisite ceramic floral arrangement served to convince her that she had begotten a genius. A genius that she loved and missed immeasurably.

Leslie couldn't serve them the truth lightly, like a condiment or spice. They wanted it as a main course. She was cruelly brief about it. "Star left Brigid because she broke faith. Brigid fell in love and was having relations with . . ." Leslie found it hard to say for some reason, "Ryan's first wife."

One of the few things Aisling and Sean agreed upon was their dislike of Dana. "The Shaeffer girl?" Sean asked rhetorically and with sheer disgust. It was more than he could bear to think of. Brigid had fallen in love with *both* of Ryan's wives. He was more certain than ever that Ryan's sole purpose in life was the corruption of others in general, his daughter in specific. His mind was consumed with loathing. He didn't hear the rest of the conversation until the subject of Brigid's upcoming show was brought up. The suggestion that he and Aisling attend shook him to his senses.

"Absolutely not!" he bellowed, ending the dinner engagement abruptly.

At the door, when Aisling was being assisted with her wrap by her husband, Leslie caught a glint in her eye that suggested that the time when Aisling might disobey her mate was at hand.

# 16

The last three days of April made a soggy leave-taking, bathing the entire metropolitan area with refreshing, life-giving rain. Ryan chose to begin her celebration of May Day in the sky. Leslie opted for sleeping in late before devoting the balance of her day to her beloved gardens.

Corelle, meanwhile, was consumed with the needs of her own flesh. She was a Pagan at heart and her inner clock longed to initiate a Rite of Spring. Tiny nymphs and faeries, invisible but there all the same, danced about her, filling her with fancy and chasing away her good sense with their spritelike laughter.

The pixie people danced ahead of her, singing, and led her into the master suite where her Mistress slept peacefully in the forbidden bed.

No longer a reasoning being, Corelle dropped her nightgown to the floor and crawled on top of Leslie, straddling her knees to either side of her Lady's hips. For support she placed her hands on the headboard and let herself give in to her body's hankering.

Leslie was lying on her back and when Corelle's full, puckered nipple grazed her lips she sighed sweetly, then very naturally began to suckle the hardened teat in her sleep.

Humming softly to herself, Corelle continued to let Leslie have her way. She was pleased that Leslie's divine lips were as gentle and silky as she thought they would be. She frequently sucked her own nipple when loving herself, but she was much more aggressive.

The contrast between her way of doing it, and Leslie's, excited her.

Before long her other nipple hungered for the sweet attention its twin was enjoying. She shifted her weight to one side, ripping the moist tip from Leslie's mouth, awakening her.

The transition from drowsy sleep to sexually aroused wakefulness was an easy one. Leslie was approached frequently by her mate while she slumbered, so it was not uncommon for her to stir, finding herself wet and receptive. Still slightly unaware, she took the new nipple into her willing mouth, appreciating it fully.

Leslie had been frightened by the intensity of her desire to make love to Corelle. She had yet to approach the youth, not knowing fully what angle to take. Part of her wanted to be tender, another part lusted to just take and take until there was nothing left to be taken.

Bold as ever, Corelle had made the decision for her. When Leslie became aware of the massive breast dangling over her, her entire self moaned fiercely. A shock of pleasure like nothing she had ever felt before scorched her every nerve. Her skin heated up, her breathing emanated from her diaphragm like a trained singer's.

For a full minute she gorged herself on her new prize before she realized that Corelle was way out of line and had no business being where she was. Reluctantly, she emptied her mouth and looked up into Corelle's eyes which were looking, illicitly, directly into hers.

Corelle had come this far; she wasn't about to turn back now. She saw the beginnings of disapproval in the grey eyes of her Mistress, threatening to undo her and her work. Quickly, she lowered both her breasts and moved them back and forth over Leslie's face. She made the action deliberate, designing it to keep a milli-second ahead of Leslie's desire.

Leslie's head began to swim. Her heart pounded and her womanhood throbbed. She had to let this insubordination go on. Ryan, she decided, could punish the transgressor later when she returned from flying. For now, there was no way she knew of to prevent her body from responding wholly and thoroughly to the womanly pillows smothering her face with delight.

"Oonn." Leslie closed her eyes, making a game of trying to recapture a nipple, to seize it and make it prisoner in her mouth. Her moans melted into muffled cries when she finally succeeded.

Corelle let out a surprised cry when she felt Leslie bite her solid nub. "Oh! Oon, aye." Then came the Irish, pleading and encouraging. The silky tongue rolled around and around and then flicked at Corelle's nipple in reply.

In her state of ecstasy, Leslie had managed to free one of her hands from the bedcovers and let it smooth its way up her servant's thigh. She was far too excited to tease the young girl; she found what she was looking for without delay.

Need flattened the thick outer lips of Corelle's sex, parting them to present her even more needful clitoris. Leslie played with it, rolling her sensitive fingertip around the dripping, creamy plaything. Corelle began to hiss and sigh but she didn't move her hips about. She, in her greediness, didn't want to lose contact for even a fraction of a moment.

Leslie had another hand. And another needy clitoris to concern herself with. She reached down, parted her own blonde fur and began to massage herself with a touch so well known to her that she didn't have to concentrate on her work under the covers.

It was then that Corelle began to speak with her body, beyond the point of coherence. She yanked her nipple from its heavenly home and moved her upper self from side to side at an increasingly more rapid pace. The effect of her efforts was to slide her breasts over the face beneath her, then back again.

"Oh, yes!" Leslie encouraged. She had given up trying to pull a nipple into her. She was free-floating in a sea of rapture. Her obsession with Corelle's generous breasts blossomed anew. Somehow, Corelle had divined this obsession and was playing upon it, manipulating it, feeding it.

Nothing existed apart from those two huge breasts and the two tiny clitorises.

Leslie moved her finger sideways and started flicking her slave's need— sharply, almost cruelly. She hadn't known what it was that she needed from Corelle, but when Corelle began to react to the insistent treatment of her clitoris, she knew it was what she had always wanted from the girl. Corelle was wailing and no longer mindful of her respectful position in life. She let her inhibitions loose and began slapping Leslie's face with her breasts.

"Oh yes, yes! Ooohh please, yes," Leslie begged for it to go on. "Ooonn." Her mind was splintered and fragmented. The heat created by the spanking warmed her face and head clear to its core.

Corelle was watching herself deliver the blows, faster and faster, reveling in the smacking sounds and womanly cries they created. Louder and harder until she was literally bludgeoning Leslie's face.

Leslie's mind was now totally empty of conscious thought. She became one with her attacker's breasts. The obsession was complete and permanent. From that point on they were an extension of her self; she owned them; they belonged to her for all time. The essence of female, the epitome of woman and goddess alike.

In the marriage of Mistress and slave, Leslie took and took. Her finger moved deftly about the pointed clitoris, receiving her slave's pledge and orgasm. Corelle gave and gave, willingly, screaming, imploring, until there was nothing left to give.

Leslie pulled her down beside her and she finished herself, then promptly passed out. Corelle stole out of the room leaving her satisfied Mistress behind, to her own room where she wept joyfully until she lapsed into deep dreamless sleep.

—••◆❀ ❀◆••—

Leslie had waited until after she shared a relaxing dinner with Ryan to apprise her of Corelle's morning misdemeanor. Ryan took the news calmly. Too calmly. Leslie began to worry for her servant's well-being when she realized that the offense had awakened a quiet sort of anger in Ryan that looked the tiniest bit unstable. There was, however, nothing Leslie could do about it. She had usurped her right to discipline the girl herself, so had to settle for the outcome of Ryan's exercise of authority.

Corelle had been asked to relinquish all rights to privacy and she had done so. Therefore, her door was never closed to anyone. She had been systematically ignored all day putting her into a state of confusion. When Ryan appeared in her doorway, she was found busying herself with mending.

Ryan's eyes looked hard and frightening. They told Corelle that her pleasure and joy were going to be expensive. She jumped when Ryan addressed her.

"Strip," Ryan demanded harshly. She was genuinely maddened by the violation of her marriage bed. It was an act she would have suspected of someone like Sanji, but never, in her wildest dreams, could she have imagined this trusted innocent to have been so disrespectful.

Ryan had held Corelle with a certain amount of high regard. She had planned to make the novice's first experience of punishment distasteful, but reasonable. Now she felt nothing but contempt for the girl and cared nothing about temperance.

Corelle stood, curtsied and quickly removed what little clothing she had on. Her hair draped about her shoulders and breasts, but didn't hide the inconsistent movement of her chest or the quickened pulse in her neck. She was afraid—it showed in her large green eyes.

Ryan didn't bother teaching her how to behave or what was expected of her when she was about to be punished. She was too angry to concentrate on details. Instead, she caught Corelle by the arm and dragged her out of the room, down the hall, and descended the wide graceful staircase to the first floor.

Corelle *did* have the good sense not to beg for mercy or whimper. It had never occurred to her that Ryan would make her pass through the entire household naked. It embarrassed her to have Bonnie see her scurrying to keep up with Ryan's brisk pace, her full breasts bouncing indecently. She didn't know that Bonnie had witnessed far worse behavior from Ryan and had built up an immunity to her abuses of various women.

Loud music could be heard from the ballroom as they neared it. Ryan slid the door fully open and threw Corelle into the room ahead of her. Corelle fell, sprawling, on her face. Her breasts broke her fall and mashed painfully against the hard polished floor. Her hair was splayed everywhere, hiding her tears.

Sanji caught sight of the event in the long mirror lining the wall she was practicing before. Responding with a blend of humor and trepidation, she straightened out of her arabesque and turned to see if she, too, were to be punished. For she knew, the instant she felt Ryan's presence, *someone* was in trouble.

Ryan walked over to the control console for the stereo system and switched off the slow jazz Sanji had been dancing to. The echoing silence the music left behind emphasized the sound of the heels of Ryan's tailored motorcycle boots as she walked over to where Sanji stood, respectful and apprehensive.

Ryan leaned against the practice bar and studied Sanji briefly. She was wearing a deeply cut leotard of peacock blue, shiny silver tights and petal pink leg warmers. Ornamenting her face, breasts and bare arms, like tiny rhinestones, were beadlets of perspiration. Ryan watched one on her chest roll down and meet with another to form a full bead, which slid down her cleavage and disappeared under her clothing.

The sight of Sanji in full glow never failed to muster twinges of appetite in Ryan's well-tuned system. Her scorn was transformed into appreciation and she pulled Sanji to her.

Sanji straddled Ryan's legs and melted into her Master's arms. Ryan guided Sanji's sumptuous mouth up to hers and plunged her tongue into it. They both began to moan rhythmically, answering the other's desire. Ryan's hands defined the outline of Sanji's curves, coming to rest on her eminently grabbable buttocks. Digging her fingertips into their ampleness, she separated them and forced Sanji into her own pelvis. Their hips rocked in unison; their noises grew louder.

Forgotten and confounded, Corelle had raised her head, pulling her hair from her face to watch Sanji become, once again, a crazed sex object.

She had only seen the horrible scars on Sanji's back a few times, but they made her squeamish every time. Looking at them now, in her condition of disfavor, she was beginning to grasp the reason why Leslie's face had gone dark and distant when she had asked her about them. Sanji had to have been punished for something terrible to acquire those scars.

Her mouth went dry and her heart beat faster. She sat up and looked about her for a weapon or anything that Ryan might try to use against her. But there was nothing, so she settled down.

She didn't know that Ryan had the instrument of her chastisement within her inflamed grasp.

Suddenly, Ryan grabbed a handful of Sanji's hair and pulled her head away. "Stop it!" she ordered. "I didn't come here for this." She pushed Sanji away and caught her breath, holding the sex goddess at bay with locked arms.

Sanji's eyes searched Ryan's while she struggled to regain her composure. Ryan's eyes went from desire to regret to resolve in one quick moment; Sanji's through surprise, disappointment and fear.

Ryan stroked her cheek with a gentle consoling gesture. "There's no need to be afraid, slave. It is not you who is in disgrace here," Ryan reassured.

Sanji was instantly relieved and relaxed. Ryan pulled her close again, turning her to face Corelle.

"No, it's *that* useless rubbish," Ryan pointed to Corelle, who was again overtaken with fear, "that needs a lesson or two this evening."

Sanji looked at Corelle and smiled wickedly. "Master, what has she done to bring shame upon herself?"

Ryan experienced a new outburst of temper as she related the sins of the subordinate slave. "She looked directly into your Mistress' eyes."

"Hhhoo!" Sanji sucked in her exclamation of surprise.

"She seduced your Mistress into copulating with her." Ryan's voice was growing darker as she went on. She was purposely emphasizing the fact that Leslie was still Sanji's Mistress, as though she were contemplating removing that privilege from Corelle altogether.

The threat was not lost on either slave. Sanji was beginning to become afraid for Corelle. She, better than anyone, knew the extent of Ryan's temper and how far it could go if not soothed by some sacrificial offering.

Corelle was pale and faint with panic.

Ryan went on. "In *my* bed."

Sanji's hand came to her mouth to muffle her tiny scream. Her eyes were large and terrified. She looked from Ryan to Corelle and back to her Master. She couldn't believe what she was hearing. She had never, in all her years of service, been allowed near Ryan's bed. It was, above all else, expressly forbidden. That was the bed of love, which had remained empty for years, until Leslie had come to fill it.

"Do you see this look of terror?" Ryan held Sanji's head so Corelle could see her own peril reflecting in those giant black eyes. "She's so afraid she can't even speak, *servant.*"

Something in the way Ryan addressed the girl by using her title rather than her name shook a piece of memory loose for Sanji. She caught a flash of how Ryan had called her "dancer" once and it had meant pain. Blinding pain.

Corelle couldn't stand the strain any longer. She began to weep and beg. "Please, Master. Please don't hurt me. Please."

Ryan let go of Sanji and walked toward the frightened slave. Sanji took her hand away from her mouth and tried to warn Corelle by mouthing the words, "No, don't," and shaking her head. It was too late.

Ryan backhanded Corelle soundly. "Don't you *dare* beg for mercy."

Corelle fell to the floor, whimpering.

"I'll give you one chance to shut up, and then I won't care if Leslie doesn't want you marked. I'll let you have it, cunt!" Ryan was *furious.*

Corelle's face was red and puffy from the flush of her crying and the terrific blow—the first anyone had ever delivered to her—that was beginning to swell her left side. Deep in her heart, she understood that she was in real danger and she fell silent.

"You're damn lucky to have an intercessor in this. If it were left up to me, you'd be close to dead right now. Even my wife doesn't fully comprehend how serious an infraction this is, or she wouldn't have let you do it. You've violated my marriage bed. Sanji knows what that means." To Sanji: "Don't you, baby?"

Trembling, Sanji replied, "Yes, Master. I'd sooner die than to presume upon your place of love." Sanji made the offering for Corelle, who was too inexperienced to see it or give it herself. Sanji's absolute devotion soothed Ryan and calmed her down.

"Do you understand now what the problem is?" Ryan asked Corelle with restraint.

Corelle hadn't seen what she had done before or realized how deeply it had hurt Ryan until it was so graphically illustrated to her. She answered sincerely, "Yes, Master. I understand, and I am truly sorry for what I have done."

"And I can see that you are, but you must be punished for it," Ryan related coldly.

Corelle bowed her head and replied, "Yes, Master. I will accept whatever is my due."

Ryan nodded her approval and walked over to Sanji. "Take your pretty clothes off," she instructed her slave smoothly.

She brought the two naked slaves together and had Corelle kneel before Sanji. "Sanji, my sweet. Do you know that I know something about our little subordinate slave that she thinks is a secret?" Ryan jeered.

"No, Master."

Ryan whispered the truth into Sanji's ear, but not so quietly that Corelle wouldn't hear. And when Corelle did hear it, her face proved Ryan right. "She *hates* people of color."

Sanji had thought that to be the case. She had seen it in the girl's eyes—a look of superiority and disdain. "This is so, Master."

"Yes." Ryan walked behind Sanji and spoke into her other ear, like a taunting demon. "She thinks of you as a second class citizen, almost subhuman. She'd never say it out loud or openly show her scorn. She's too proud for that. But it's there, in her eyes."

"I've seen it, Master."

"What do you think we ought to do about it, slave?"

"Show her she's wrong, Master."

Ryan laughed wickedly. "My very thought."

Corelle's enlarged eyes were darting back and forth from Ryan to Sanji. She didn't know how they had found out about her racial hatred; she was beginning to perspire.

Sanji's smile widened when she divined what it was Ryan was going to have her do to show Corelle how wrong she was.

"Let's," Ryan encouraged. Then to Corelle: "Little girl, I am not going to mark you physically, at my wife's request. So I'm going to take something from you instead. You have never kissed a woman's sex before, and I had planned to initiate you in a most beautiful way. In a way that you would remember for the rest of your days. But, now you don't deserve that, so I have chosen another way to introduce you to this rite. I can assure you, you will never forget it."

Ryan ignored Corelle's shocked expression, turning her attention to her slave instead. She clinically checked to see how aroused Sanji was and came away pleased. Sanji was dripping and ready to be served by the subordinate slave.

Ryan forced her finger into Corelle's mouth and made her taste Sanji's musky cream. "She doesn't like it, slave. More's the better. When you're through with her, she'll hate it."

Ryan brought Corelle's head near the black sex and spread the lips to reveal Sanji's charcoal and pink pleasure point. "Do you know what this is?" she asked the frightened girl.

"Yes, Master," Corelle revealed shakily.

"You will lick this with your tongue. Lick it and suck it and keep it wet. My slave likes it done hard and fast, so you had better please her. From time to time, you are to shove your tongue inside her cunt to eat her come."

Sanji moaned, "Oooann." She loved to hear her Master speak crudely. Without realizing it, her hips were rocking toward the horrified slave kneeling before her.

"Yes, Master," Corelle assented. She knew that she had no choice, but she dearly wished that her Mistress hadn't been so particular about her flesh and allowed Ryan to mark her instead of demean her in this most shameful of ways. Adding to her mortification was the intense feeling of loss. Ryan had taken a precious gift from her. Rightfully so, for Corelle had sinned grievously against her Master. She summoned her courage and showed Ryan that she was ready to pay the price.

Precocious as always, Corelle swallowed her disgust and picked up the rhythm of Sanji's sexual music, doing her best to please. Ryan and Sanji knew she was sincerely giving of herself, but the score had to be more than even. Ryan had come out getting more than was taken from her.

"Just remember, slave," Ryan egged Sanji on, "this is where I go when I punish you."

"Ohh. Yes," Sanji breathed. Then hatefully, "I remember, always." Sanji began to demand more from the subordinate slave. She wanted to be *served*. She wanted to prove to Corelle that she wasn't less than her, in fact she was of a higher status. She wanted the subordinate slave to know it, and remember it.

Ryan took her gold lighter out to light her cigarette. She was excited by watching Sanji taking the slave. She knew Sanji better than to think it would be enough, so she wasn't at all surprised when Sanji made her heated, breathless request.

"Master. Ooonn. Sss. Master, may I hurt her?" Sanji pleaded.

Sanji was looking at Ryan with her miraculous look of supplication, which melted Ryan to her toes. She would have agreed anyway, but enjoyed the bonus. She paused to calmly light her cigarette, then she shut the lighter with a firm metallic snap. She took the cigarette from her mouth and motioned with it in Sanji's direction. It was a gesture that said, "Be my guest."

"Oohh, yeah," Sanji wailed, and she went for it. She grabbed the subordinate slave by the hair and began to fuck the helpless face for all she was worth. She slid her open cunt over the slave's nose and eyes, back down over the mouth, screaming, "Keep licking it, bitch!" Then she went side to side over the wretched mouth that had been placed at her disposal.

Corelle was in major pain. Her neck was getting sharp jabbing pains in it that made her think it was going to break. Her hair was loosening in clumps. The cartilage in her nose felt as though it might separate. Weeping and unable to control herself, she hoped that she wouldn't get in more trouble for doing so. She honestly didn't know how much more she could stand of the brutal punishment.

Ryan could barely maintain her sanity. She hadn't known how intensely she was going to react to this scene. Sanji was delirious. Ryan had to fuck *something*. The only thing available was the subordinant slave's hand. Ryan thrust it between her legs and corrupted it cruelly.

For what seemed like forever to the subordinate slave, the Master and the slave had their way with her. A team, moaning and urging each other on.

Finally, as was the way of things, Sanji approached her summit, and began to plead and beg for permission to climax. "Master! Master, please. Ooohh."

This was no sex game to Ryan; she took it very seriously. She didn't care about making anyone wait, least of all herself. "Oh yeah. Jeeez-us. Oh, baby. Come all over her face, slave. NOW!"

Tingling and convulsing, Sanji did as she was told. She held her breath for an instant then let out a primal scream that filled the rafters with rapture. Her vaginal muscles massaged the tortured mouth that serviced her and pumped her womanly substances down the virgin throat. "Swallow it, bitch. Eat it all and remember!" Sanji demanded.

While Sanji was being obeyed, Ryan tumbled over the sexual edge, falling into an abyss of ecstasy. "Hsss, gohhhhhd." When all was said and done, she had climaxed three times. She had taken what was owed to her and was satisfied.

When Sanji let Corelle go, Corelle slumped to the floor, completely exhausted. Her mouth and neck were burning as were her eyes. Despite her physical pain and the battered state of her emotions, she had come to know a full-bodied sense of pride. She had survived her punishment admirably and passed her test of character to prove that she was still worthy of her status.

It was beyond her to understand why she was being carried up the stairs and placed in her bed by Sanji instead of being made to find her way on her own. But she sensed that she was no longer in shame, that what she had given of herself had been enough.

Sanji wasn't speaking to her meanly any more and was washing her face with a warm, wet cloth. She soaked up Sanji's tender mothering and sincere praise like a neglected child. She was beginning to realize that Sanji wasn't the selfish person she had thought her to be, but rather a loving, giving individual for whom service meant everything. Corelle could understand that, for it was a trait they had in common.

Corelle was learning to see beyond her pre-conceived ideas to the person inhabiting the supple brown skin she had been taught to hate. Corelle could see, written in Sanji's mesmerizing eyes, a woman who endured the tragedy of unrequited love day after day and persevered.

It was a brief realization, but it was enough to teach her why Ryan prized Sanji so, and why she herself was of lesser status, being far less sophisticated in her ability to serve.

Sanji was sitting on the bed with Corelle and Ryan was standing, quietly, behind Sanji. Ryan squeezed Sanji's shoulders firmly, letting her know that she was proud of the way Sanji had soothed Corelle and how she had fulfilled her role so well. Sanji melted into the touch, receptive and content. Allowing her to be served by a subordinate slave was the surest display yet of how valued she was by her Master. A newly crowned queen couldn't have felt more pride.

Corelle was so innocent; Ryan couldn't bear it. "You have a great deal of courage, Corelle. I'm certain that you have learned your lesson, although you can see that you will have to work very hard to regain the right to kiss the sex of your Mistress." For the first time in her life, Ryan had shown mercy toward a sex-slave. She had planned to take all hope of ever getting that chance from the girl, but she couldn't follow through with it. Corelle hadn't wilfully committed her crime. She didn't have a conniving bone in her body. If Corelle could prove that she was deserving, Ryan felt she should have the opportunity.

While Ryan knew that it would only be a few days before she would have cause to punish Sanji again, she suspected that it would be months before there would be any real reason to discipline Corelle.

## 17

. . . . . . . The deadly, bloodshot stare in the tigress' eyes locked her in a trance, robbing her of her ability to react to the danger. Her body did not move toward the wall to safety. She couldn't outrun the great cat, nor could she scream for help.

For a horrifying instant they were at a stalemate. In the next shocking breath the tigress leapt upon Korian's frail, helpless body and they both came to the ground in mindless battle.

Korian shrieked as her clothing and flesh were ripped and torn from her. Her powers failed her, leaving her helpless—completely and utterly helpless against the over-powering weight and force of Anara's agent of revenge. Time stood still. Nothing existed—only the sharp spears of teeth. Korian heard her own skull crack and all was dark-ness . . . . . . .

"NO!" Ryan awoke suddenly from her night terror to a new, even more frightening terror. Sitting on her chest and staring into her eyes was a *real* cat.

"Oh, god!" Ryan screamed as she grabbed the ill-begotten feline and threw it across the room before Leslie could act to save it.

Poetic justice though it was, Leslie nearly heaved when she heard the cat's skull crack when it hit the wall. Ryan had hurled it with such force that its death was instant.

Ryan followed the cat out of the bed yelling at the top of her voice, rousing the entire household. "When I find the person that let that fucking thing in here, she's lunch meat!" She stopped short of coming into contact with the limp pile of fur, afraid to actually touch it to make certain that it could not hunt her down.

Acting quickly, Leslie managed to get to Ryan and drape Ryan's robe around her before everyone arrived in the doorway and caught sight of her nakedness.

Without thinking, Ryan put the robe on. She was still under the influence of her night terror—shaking, irrational, frightened. Leslie took her eye off Ryan for a moment to caution Sanji, Corelle and Bonnie, all crowding the entrance to the master bedroom. When she looked back, Ryan had her gun poised to shoot at the already dead cat.

"Ryan, don't. You can't kill it again. Put the gun down, please," Leslie urged firmly.

"I'll kill it a thousand times if I have to *and* the cunt that let it in here," Ryan insisted.

Leslie couldn't bear the thought of a gun being fired in their lovely home. Hoping to avert the violence, she voiced her suspicion. "Ryan, no one here let that cat in. Anara *put* it there."

Ryan's eyelids blinked rapidly when she heard Anara's name and she bridged the gap between where she had been and reality. The gun lowered in her hands and she turned to look skeptically at her wife.

"Were you dreaming of the tigress again?"

Ryan could only nod.

"And that cat just happened to conveniently appear on your chest at that precise moment? Doesn't it make sense that if Anara is powerful enough to incarnate a fully grown woman that a simple alley cat would pose no problem for her at all?" Leslie made a convincing argument out of what she wished weren't true.

When Ryan considered that Anara had, indeed, made Rags come into being without the use of parents and that the cat had to have been Anara's sick idea, she uncocked her gun and set it down on the dresser. Leslie and the others let out their breath with relief.

Among the women present, Sanji had the least aversion to death and unpleasant tasks, having spent part of her childhood in the slums of Kingston. The chore of cleaning up the remains of the cat was assigned to her by Ryan who was rubbing her temples and trying to respond positively to Leslie's words of comfort.

Leslie wasn't ready to broach the subject of Anara having so blatantly defiled their home. She wanted to wait until they could deal with it calmly. She suggested that they take the Lear Jet to Aspen for the day. "Sir Richard told me that he found some Ladyslippers not far from his chalet and invited us up to see them." She deliberately took advantage of Ryan's weakness for giving her special treats, and orchids, no matter what their species, were always a treat for Leslie. When Ryan agreed, it brought no real comfort to Leslie. Winning another round in a series with Anara only made her feel uneasy and worried. The odds were stacking up against Leslie, and she knew it.

—··✦❦✦··—

In the months after Brigid had departed McKinley, she devoted her daytime hours to replacing any number of the pieces of her art that she had destroyed the previous winter. Much of the new work ended up surpassing the originals in quality, refinement and skill.

Marguarita, the art dealer who had convinced Brigid to do the show originally, dropped by Brigid's new home and shop on a regular basis to check on the progress of the art and the artist alike. She remained on constant alert against the unthinkable possibility that Brigid's show might be postponed again by another emotional upheaval. As security, she convinced the still somewhat unstable artist to release the finished pieces to her in advance for safekeeping.

Brigid wrote frequent letters to Star with the hope of bringing about some sense of closure, an ending to their many years of living and loving, that would be more satisfactory than the sudden stubborn silence that was separating them. She never received any replies, but Star did keep the two vases and the ceramic cat that Brigid had made and sent to her.

All thoughts of Dana had been pushed away entirely. In that way, Brigid was very much like her father.

It wasn't until the nighttime hours that any evidence could be seen that Brigid had radically changed her outlook. In an amazingly short period of time she had developed and encouraged a newfound reputation for being a real playboy. She had sold her practical Bronco and had a bright red, customized Aston-Martin sportscar made to drive instead. The woman-about-town for all outward appearances, she was unconsciously on the hunt for a highly specialized prey.

There was only one other person alive who could look at the list of names notched on Brigid's bedpost and see the pattern that had developed. Ryan. There was not one individual among Brigid's conquests that couldn't also be found on one of Ryan's old dancecards.

Socialites, professionals, executives, flight attendants, and bored housewives—they were beautiful, stylish and always able to find an excuse to take a nighttime tumble in the loft above the artist's studio.

Dana's prophecy fulfilled itself nightly. The weed she had planted one afternoon in her lair had grown to heroic proportions, spilling hazardously over the confines of reason, and sprouting long voracious tendrils—all headed in one direction.

The night of Brigid's opening finally arrived in early July and, as planned, took place in Marguarita's gallery situated in a converted, mid-sized home in the Cherry Creek business district. Marguarita, a light-hearted, sensual woman with easily aroused Spanish blood, spirited about her work at the gallery gracefully and with a cheerful flair. Everyone that crossed her threshold felt her warmth and was at once welcomed by it.

At Brigid's request, the affair was to be casual, summery, and light on the alcohol. Marguarita had turned the back patio and gazebo into refreshing islands of pastel luxuriance. Pale pink covered the serving tables, which offered champagne punch, fruit cups and fluffy pastries. Chicory flower blue sheers festooned the air as they dangled and swayed from the ceiling of the gazebo and the awnings above the patio. Sweetening the lazy, colored atmosphere was the too rich perfume of Russian Olive released from the flowers that surrounded everything like tiny yellow stars.

Indoors, Brigid's work was on display in expertly lighted glass cases mounted on pedestals of clear lucite making each piece appear to float in mid-air. The three landscapes painted at McKinley were spotlighted against a wall of flat grey in the flattering manner that could only be achieved by a select sect of gallery owners, of which Marguarita was a charter member. But no amount of talking on her part could persuade Ryan or Leslie to release to the show the portrait of Leslie or any of the seemingly vanished canvases of tortured art that Marguarita had learned about through her private grapevine, but had never seen.

Marguarita was heartsick about the loss until Brigid arrived an hour before the show with her date, Helen, and the last and most beautiful contribution to the collection.

"Brigid! It's exquisite!" the gallery owner exclaimed as she unearthed the masterpiece from its bed of shredded paper. She handled it deftly while she examined it for any flaws, which she knew would not be found. Few people had a sharper eye than she; Brigid was one of them.

In her precise grasp was an image of a dove. The bearing was of the quiet, mysterious repose of flight. The gentle eyes of wisdom under a veil of sadness looked at her and made her feel uncomfortable, revealed, but somehow safe and loved. Subtle greys and browns, with black and ivory accents came as near as was humanly possible to depicting the divine, to representing the sacred timelessness of perpetual peace.

Marguarita couldn't, nor would anyone else be able to, adequately express her observations verbally that evening. Still, Brigid saw the truth in Marguarita's eyes and was well pleased. But, just as revealingly, Marguarita's expression changed, and she frowned.

"What's wrong?" Brigid inquired.

Marguarita walked over to the empty case that awaited the object's presence and placed it reverently inside. "I don't know how you can do this to me, Brig."

Brigid followed the proprietress across the hardwood floor of what used to be a dining room to the central location of her most prized piece and asked, "Do what?"

The gallery owner looked up to Brigid's searching eyes then down to Helen's expectant ones and clucked. Marguarita was a shrewd woman with an eye for detail. She had been to McKinley, met Leslie, and seen the portrait. That alone wouldn't have been enough to make the association for her, except that on one such occasion she had spotted the license plate on Leslie's Rolls. It had read: DOVE.

"This would have been a perfect evening if you hadn't brought this." She pointed to the dove with her finger. "I'm going to be fielding offers for it all night. I dare say I'll get at least one five-figure bribe."

Brigid looked down and nervously shifted her weight on her crutches. Her companion was wide-eyed with amazement.

"You're right, I shouldn't have brought it," Brigid admitted sadly. She didn't know what had made her bring the work. It had seemed like the right thing to do at the time.

"Why not?" pressed Helen.

"Because, my sweet," Marguarita explained bitterly, "she won't sell it. Will you, Brig?"

Brigid sighed heavily and gazed upon her creation with resolve. "No. Never. I don't want to cause you any trouble, Marguarita. Let's just put it away."

"No. I won't have an empty display on my hands. Besides, it will drive up the price on everything else. Leave it," she instructed wisely as she strolled toward the patio thoughtfully.

--·◆❈❈◆·--

"Here." Marguarita had two tiny pills in her palm and was offering them to Brigid.

"What are those?" Brigid seemed repulsed by them.

"Valium. I keep them around for artists when they look all tied up in knots from nerves like you do right now."

For the fifteenth time in twenty minutes, Brigid looked at her watch. Two guests had already arrived and were meandering around the display area, making her all the more uptight. Something caught her eye that showed her a more effective way of releasing her tension.

Her date had been taking in the show by herself and was standing between Brigid and a well-lighted display. She was wearing a tight-waisted, short-sleeved print dress made of rayon chemise. In the sort of light that was illuminating her, the dress was completely transparent.

Brigid could make out every detail that would normally be hidden by the bright floral print: the gentle curve of Helen's inner thighs, the panty line, garter belt, stockings, absence of a bra or slip. All Brigid's anxiety heated up and transformed itself into a flaring passion. She addressed Marguarita purposefully, "I have a better idea. Give me the key to your office."

Marguarita smiled and handed the keychain to the redhead. She always believed that the couch in her office should see more use than just her occasional afternoon naps.

167

Brigid approached her blonde companion from the back and smoothed her large sensitive hand over Helen's buttocks while she whispered a lewd proposal into the ear of her fancy.

A short while later, they emerged from the office to find that the gallery was filling up with guests. Helen's expression was glazed and contented. Brigid's was triumphant and satisfied. She patted the front pocket of her trousers smugly. While Helen had been wearing panties when she went *into* the office with Brigid, when she came out of the office the only thing between her and public nudity was her sheer dress. The new arrangement proved to be a source of excitement for both women throughout the evening, and well into the night.

Helen remained close to the artist, gently clinging to her arm, basking in Brigid's spotlight. They mingled together, greeting guests, accepting praise and admiration, being photographed. Whenever Brigid found herself tensing up, usually when a guest seemed uncomfortable with her disability or with her obvious display of Lesbianism, she would touch Helen. Her caresses were discreet, but undeniably erotic. Helen saved the show with her ability to remain receptive to Brigid while ignoring the occasional cruel stare. She was proud to be seen with the master and she knew she would be richly rewarded for it afterwards.

The one thing Helen couldn't help Brigid with was the arrival of Ryan and Leslie. Ryan had insisted that Leslie downplay her beauty and femininity by wearing sportswear and no jewelry. Leslie knew what Ryan was up to and didn't complain about the loose-fitting pullover and slacks that had been laid out for her. They very seldom sought out Brigid's company anymore, since being with Ryan's cousin made Ryan uneasy and embarrassed Leslie.

Leslie could have worn a potato sack and it wouldn't have changed the way Brigid stared at her with completely unrestrained longing. At first, Leslie hadn't wanted to believe what Ryan had told her about Brigid's infatuation. As time went by she realized that it was not only apparent to her, but to anyone who cared to look.

She watched Helen get wise to it almost before the introductions were completed. As if Leslie hadn't been embarrassed enough by that, she was positively blushing when Helen extended her hand flirtatiously toward Ryan.

"Why, Ryan. How are you, dear?" Helen asked melodically.

Ryan took the hand politely and kissed it. "Quite well, Helen. Thank you," Ryan answered kindly with a deadly look in her eye.

Marguarita watched the exchange carefully. Gifted with perfect social timing, she interjected herself pleasantly at the proper moment. "Ryan, Leslie, welcome. How good of you to come." She didn't know Ryan well enough to understand the significance of her leather jacket. "You must be dying in that jacket, dear. Let me hang it up for you." She didn't skip a beat when Ryan refused the offer. "Well, then, let's get you both some champagne. Can't have anyone going thirsty, now can we?" She ushered the new arrivals quickly to the back porch, cutting a pathway that deliberately circumvented the display of the dove. "Leslie, darling. The strawberries you sent over with your gardener are such a hit!"

She served them their drinks and picked a plump strawberry for herself, then drew their attention to a stately older gentleman who had at least one building in town named after him. She kept her voice low when she uttered her confidence. "Mr. Van Clayton made an offer for Brigid's last landscape of McKinley that I simply cannot refuse."

After another five minutes of rambling on, she had thoroughly relaxed the couple. They were smiling and looking ready to socialize. She would have liked to have kept them out on the patio all night, but business was business. A prospective buyer pulled her aside and engaged her full attention, and she walked back inside with him.

After about an hour of visiting outdoors, Ryan and Leslie began edging their way through the press of people to take in the tour of art. Midway between the third and fourth display Ryan felt the gentle touch of a woman taking her arm. At that very moment, Leslie saw the woman doing it. Leslie cocked her head and looked the interloper up and down with a slightly territorial expression on her face.

Ryan took the hand lightly from her arm as though it disgusted her, then raised her arm to freedom. "Ah, Marquise." She handed the offending extremity back to its owner. "How lovely to see you again," Ryan lied sarcastically. She wondered to herself how many more of her old exploits were going to crop up at the gathering.

"Marquise Sophia Frangipani, may I present my wife, Miss Leslie Anne Serle." Ryan brought her wife around to face the lady directly. "Miss Leslie Anne Serle, I would like you to meet the Marquise Sophia Frangipani of Rome, Italy." Ryan's voice was stiff, formal and the slightest bit annoyed.

"How do you do?" Leslie greeted the stunningly sophisticated woman cooly.

"Enchanted," the noblewoman replied in kind. "Ryan! Your wife? I've been out of the country far too long. How did I *ever* let you get away from me?" she asked Ryan half-sincerely with her polished Italian accent.

"I can't imagine, Sophia. What brings you to this show?" Ryan changed the subject immediately. There had been a time when she could have become quite serious about the Marquise, but for meeting Dana.

"Why, your dear cousin invited us." Then with a lowered voice, "Brigid is taking me to the ballet tomorrow. But don't tell the Baroness that. She would make such a fuss." She turned in the direction of the Baroness, a much older woman who was very possessive, and confided, "Did you know she offered a perfectly obscene price for that dove and Marguarita turned it *down?* She said Brigid wouldn't sell it."

No longer caring about social pleasantries, Ryan walked slowly away from the Marquise toward the display of the dove. Leslie hastily covered for Ryan's behavior and was loftily excused by the Marquise.

When Leslie neared Ryan's side she could feel her spouse trembling with what she knew had to be anger. Surprisingly, Ryan reached out for Leslie and pulled her close and kissed her gently on the cheek. Lingering near the kiss, Ryan whispered to Leslie, "I don't know how much more of this I can take. When is she going to stop doing this?"

"Ryan," Leslie replied, "maybe we're just overreacting. Let's at least look at the piece. It may be nothing at all."

Having no regard for what others might think of her actions, Ryan drew her wife even nearer into a needy hug. She was finally learning to share Leslie's great inner strength and benefit from the essence of peace that was Leslie's soul. She was learning to accept love instead of deny that which she needed so desperately.

Calm and restored, Ryan walked arm and arm with Leslie to view what she *knew* was another declaration of Brigid's love for her precious wife.

When at first she did see it, she forgot entirely why Brigid had crafted the work. The art connoisseur in her was at its perfect best and, as all those like her who had been bred to recognize the elite excellence in life, she wanted to possess the dove.

Then her higher self came into play and for a brief, ecstatic moment, the dove came to life and smiled at her—expressing its eternal love, uniting with her spirit. In that moment, Ryan gazed into Leslie's knowing eyes apart from time and space—joined as one.

The encounter was interrupted abruptly by a flash from a strobe-light. A photographer in the room had been watching the exchange through the lens of his camera while he was preparing to take a picture of the dove. He had seen a faint green glow surrounding the bird, and to his astonishment, Ryan's eyes appeared red, Leslie's gold.

Ryan blinked the image of the strobe from her mind's eye and made a mental note of who the photographer was and in which of the pouches on his equipment bag he placed the roll of coveted film. Except for the lasting impression on her inner self, the moment was lost and she once again began to swell with bitterness toward her cousin.

Nearly overcome with the anguish, Ryan managed to comment on the art for its own sake. "I don't know what demi-goddess was hanging out in Brigid's shop while she made this, but it's transcendence itself. I'm glad she isn't selling it. No amount of money is equal to it."

Leslie was having difficulty dealing with the dove. Its quintessence was far too obvious for her tastes. It was hard enough for her to look at Brigid's portrait of her outer self. Now the master had captured her inner self, her soul, and placed it on display for just anyone and everyone to see. She told herself that her uneasiness was foolishness, that only the initiated could see the image and trace it to her. Even still, being loved by the artist was becoming more and more expensive by the day.

"Tell me I'm overreacting now, Leslie," Ryan murmured through her clenched teeth. She didn't want to feel this hatred for her cousin; they were best friends. Only Leslie had grown closer to her than had Brigid.

Her friendship with her Irish kin had endured for nearly three decades, since early childhood, and was extremely important to her. But, just then, what she was feeling for Brigid was, if not hatred, then its twin.

Her hot gaze bore through the glass case and the press of souls, across the room and into the back of the red head. Feeling the stare, Brigid turned around cautiously. Their eyes met and spoke their rivalry, drew their battle lines, declared their war of love.

They would have continued staring each other down had Brigid's eyes not wavered, then ballooned with surprise when a late arrival appeared to the right of her field of vision.

Briefly speechless, Brigid drank in the sight and a lump formed in her throat. When she could talk, all she could say, in a low breathless tone, was, "Mother."

The rolling hubbub of voices diminished in volume suddenly, replaced by a sizzling hiss of whispers among those who knew of the longstanding banishment of the artist from the MacSweeney household.

Aisling MacSweeney, unaccustomed to making grand entrances, made the best of the scene by smiling genuinely at everyone she knew as she traversed the gallery. She stopped to greet Ryan and Leslie who were wide-eyed and relieved to see her.

Once she made her way to her daughter, the crowd began to rumble again. No one wanted to interfere with the very private reunion.

"I've missed you," Aisling revealed.

"And I, you," Brigid assented. Brigid shifted her weight to one crutch and took her mother's hand in her own, squeezing it firmly to prove to herself that Aisling was really there. They were lost in one another's eyes.

"Let's go," Leslie urged. "It's getting insufferable in here."

Ryan stalled her wife. "In a minute. See that photographer in the blue shirt?"

Leslie looked around and spotted him. "Yes, why?"

"He has some film that we can't let him keep. Walk over there and engage him in a conversation while I come around from back and lift it."

Leslie protested with her eyes.

"Just do it. I'll explain it later." Ryan nudged her reluctant mate in the direction of the man she intended to rob. When Leslie had done as she was told, Ryan approached from the rear without being noticed. Carefully, she unfastened the buckle of the pouch and stole the little silver canister. She was certain that she had the correct one because it had a vibrancy about it that she could detect with her discerning touch. She shoved it into a pocket of her jacket and disappeared into the crowd.

Before they left the gallery, Leslie looked about for Brigid and found her—hugging her mother and very near tears. She heaved a satisfied, emotional sigh of accomplishment and turned to leave.

On the way to their car Ryan commented, half-jokingly, "Another night like this one and I'm going to take up whiskey again."

Leslie laughed at the comment, hoping Ryan wouldn't notice that the threat worried her. She moved the conversation elsewhere. "I'm just glad Brigid and Aisling are back together again."

"So am I, my darling. So am I," Ryan agreed enthusiastically. It was her hope that Aisling could finish the healing process that she and Leslie had so miserably failed to do.

# 18

Sanji took a sip of her iced tea then set the glass down to inspect the condition of her gentian-blue voile sundress. It was cool to the touch and refreshing to look at on a parched day in late July. The air-conditioner in her room was turned on high because the sun had been pounding the front range for two weeks without mercy, making everything *look* hot. Even her cool white room.

She was purging her wardrobe of any item of clothing that wasn't presentable or denied access to any possible sexual advance. Ryan had promised her that she could replace every item that was donated to charity with two others that would be more in keeping with her more stringent role of sex-slave.

Sanji had always been a sex-slave to Ryan, but in the past she had had a number of liberties that were now denied her. The Volvo Ryan had given her had been donated to a promising young artist with three children. Consequently, if Sanji ever left the grounds of McKinley, she could only do so in the company of a member of the household, someone who could account for her whereabouts at all times. The dance troupe she had worked for was forced to find a replacement for her, and her dancing was confined to the ballroom area of the mansion. Her allowance was severed entirely, although Ryan continued to send money to Sanji's family, as Sanji had done throughout her adult life.

The only freedom that Sanji knew was the internal freedom derived from the ultimate sense of being perfectly and absolutely owned by her Master and Mistress. Though not romantically so, she knew she was loved and treasured for her ability to serve and willingness to sacrifice herself to satisfy the sometimes capricious, always demanding needs of her owners.

In return for her renunciation, she was released from all responsibilities to the outside world. Every care was provided for, every protection and shelter given.

Sanji was happy. Happier than she had ever thought possible in the absence of mutual love.

The sundress passed inspection and was returned to the closet. Having completed her tour of the hanging garments, Sanji turned her attention to an old suitcase loosely packed with robes and shawls. When she placed the suitcase on her bed and opened it, her eye was caught by a white corner of fabric tangled with the frill of a shawl.

She moved the other clothes aside and uncovered the carelessly packed dress. What's this doing here, she wondered to herself.

When she freed the long, backless white gown from the other things, her brain began to buzz and her stomach tried to force her last meal up her gullet. She recognized it immediately as the dress she had worn *that* night. Milli-second flashes of memory played themselves on the backdrop of her mind like a kaleidoscope of terror. She threw the dress away from her like it was intestines from some slimy creature and backed shakily away from it toward the corner of her room.

"No," she breathed. "No, please." Sanji's speech began to build in volume as she grew more panicky with each step backward. "No, stop. You're hurting me. I didn't mean to do it. Please, stop. I can't bear the pain—it hurts too much. Ssst." Sanji sucked in her breath in surprise when she came into contact with the wall. The abrupt feeling on her back transferred the mental memories into physical remembrances and she began to wail. "No, Master. I promise, I won't do it again, I promise. Please stop!"

The pain was blasting her from every angle. Her back was burning with razor sharp slices of agony—over and over again until she screamed out loud. Terror-breathing peals of human suffering escaped the confines of her carefully suppressed memories, shooting through the calm of McKinley like fire from a flame-thrower.

Ryan was the first to arrive in Sanji's room, followed closely by Leslie, then Bonnie and Corelle. Ryan found Sanji in a fetal heap on the floor in the corner, screaming and whimpering rhythmically as though she were once again being laid open by Ryan's whip.

It was Leslie who reached the girl first. She fell to her knees next to her frightened servant and gathered Sanji into her soft arms. Surprising everyone, Leslie broke her fast of communication and spoke to Sanji. "Sanji, it's all right. You're safe now. The pain is over with. No one is hurting you; you're all right." She stroked Sanji's full hair over and over as she urged her back to reality and the present. "Shhh. Settle down. You're safe and well."

Ryan, meanwhile, was frozen. She, too, had slipped into the past. A past well beyond the year or so since she had so viciously extracted her revenge from Sanji for humiliating her in public and breaking two of her

174

ribs. Well beyond. Ryan wasn't seeing a frightened woman with black skin cowering in a corner of an early twentieth century mansion. She was seeing a teenage girl with olive skin huddling in a dark corner of a pre-Christian alleyway, fearing for her life, hiding from an angry mob that had learned of her part in the murder of their High Priestess.

"Lizack," Ryan managed to utter breathlessly.

When she heard the ancient name, Leslie whipped around to face Ryan who was still staring at Sanji, unmoving and uncertain. "Ryan?"

"It's her. She poisoned Anara," Ryan declared hypnotically.

Leslie returned her gaze to Sanji and held her away for a moment, as if to get a better look. Sanji's eyes were large, moist and wary, but she was calmer and had stopped screaming. She looked into Leslie's eyes, momentarily forgetting her station in life. She wanted to know what was going on; everything was confusing to her.

Suddenly, everyone in the room started. Sanji pulled Leslie closer and held on for all she was worth. A loud snapping sound had startled them, followed by taunting laughter. Each of them could hear it, but none of them were laughing.

Bonnie and Corelle crossed themselves with the sign of the cross. Leslie reassured Sanji and turned her stunned eyes upon Ryan. Ryan was holding her ears against the unearthly laughing and, when she could bear it no more, she began to yell louder than she had ever yelled. "Stop it! Stop it! Leave me alone! Haven't you done enough? What do you want from me?"

Not because Ryan wanted it to, the laughter ceased. Ryan knew that she had played right into Anara's hands by begging her to quit the torturous invasion of her life. She had done more than ask Anara to stop laughing; she had begged for Anara to end the inhumane retribution that was bleeding her spirit dry, but was little more than a game to Anara, although a deadly one.

Bonnie stepped forward and helped Ryan to a chair. Once, in a weak and drunken moment, Ryan had told Bonnie about Anara. Up until this time, Bonnie hadn't known what to make of the information. After hearing the wicked laughing and realizing that it had to have been Anara, she was afraid for Ryan, for Leslie, for anyone who took Ryan's part. Her saints were going to hear from her about this experience. Anara had never seemed real to Bonnie, nor had her threat to Ryan's well-being. Like a mother protecting her cub, Bonnie resolved to do what ever she was called upon to assist Ryan in her struggle. Even, she whispered a prayer for forgiveness before she thought it, if it meant consorting with demons.

Although it tore at her heart to see Ryan so near the end of her limits, Leslie could see that she was in good hands. She couldn't easily pull away from Sanji who was still very upset and needed her warm protection. Leslie knew what had gone on, but Corelle was in the dark and petrified. Her eyes searched everyone's for enlightenment but were given none. "Master, I'm afraid. Where did that horrible laughing come from? Why was Sanji screaming? What is going on?" she asked frantically.

For a long moment Ryan looked Corelle's way. Sighing painfully, she looked to the floor and collected herself. She ignored Bonnie rubbing the base of her neck and lit a cigarette. She felt defeated, vulnerable, sick. When she was able to explain, she did so in Sanji's direction, not Corelle's.

"That was Anara, whom I'll tell you of later, when I'm feeling better than I do now." Ryan searched Sanji's eyes compassionately. "Sanji was screaming because she remembered that it was me who ruined her back. She was re-living the pain that I inflicted upon her in the name of revenge."

Sanji's eyes were locked on Ryan's; she was trying desperately to understand why Ryan had hurt her so. She knew that what she had done was wrong, what she didn't know was how it was wrong enough to deserve the extreme punishment that she had received.

"Leslie was right when she told me that nothing you could have done," Ryan wasn't addressing Corelle any longer; she was making her peace with the woman she had irrationally abused and nearly killed, "would have been bad enough to warrant trying to murder you. I won't try to excuse my behavior, Sanji. It's too late to ask you for forgiveness, but at least now I understand what happened. I was doing more than retaliating for my public disgrace and personal injury; I was avenging Anara's death."

"Why? I thought you hated Anara," Sanji demanded, still forgetful of her status.

Ryan and Leslie were both overlooking the misbehavior. Sanji had the right to know what had happened to her, and she had the right to have her emotional wounds healed.

"I do," Ryan answered emphatically. "With all my heart. She *used* me, just like she used Rags—to get even with the people who betrayed her in her last lifetime. Except I didn't know it. I don't know why I didn't. You and Leslie are the only ones who have seen Anara, but I never questioned that. It never occurred to me that *you* were part of all this." As Ryan was explaining, Sanji's eyes were getting a faint, glassy look to them, like she was somewhere else.

"In your last lifetime, Sanji, you were the girl I asked to poison Anara. And now you've had to pay for it, at my hand. This is Anara's sick idea of justice, and *that* is why she was laughing."

"I did it because I loved you," Sanji replied with a hollow, distant voice.

"I know," Ryan whispered her acknowledgment of Sanji's sacrifice. She and Leslie looked at one another—relieved. They both had worried what it would be like if and when Sanji ever remembered the brutal attack.

Ryan stood and brought Sanji to her feet. "I am grateful to you for your faithful service." She kissed Sanji on the cheek and hugged her firmly. She turned to the others in the room. "To all of you, for standing by me in my time of need. I wish that I could say that you've given enough, that I don't need any more than you have given." She faltered and couldn't go on. It hurt to consider the price she might have to ask any of her loyal servants to pay.

Bonnie spoke for everyone. "We will serve you in whatever way that we can, Ryan. Never fear, you can count on us."

Ryan returned her look to Sanji, seeking verification from her.

Sanji didn't hesitate to pledge herself. "Anything, Master. Just ask and it is yours."

Ryan's eyes were coated with a thin film of tears. She looked from Sanji to Corelle and Corelle nodded her agreement.

Ryan was still too inhibited to cry in the presence of those in service to her. She took Leslie's hand and quickly left with her for the master suite where she would pour out her emotions onto her wife's willing bosom and receive the comfort she had gone without for thirty-three years.

---

Ryan had wept a small few times in her life, but she had never really cried. None of the torture and abuse she had suffered from Rags had amounted to anything so devastating as the trials of emotional upset that Anara had been inflicting upon her: the constant attempts to push Leslie away from her, the incessant nightmares of death, the ever present awareness of Anara's meddling in every aspect of her life.

Ryan knew that it was Anara who had deprived her of her father, lured Dana into the arms of another, nearly made her kill Sanji, took her friend Rags from her and placed her in a position where she was forced to commit an act of murder to avenge that death.

All these things Ryan knew, but she never saw any of them until after the fact. Somehow, Anara had manipulated events and people to keep her schemes unrevealed until they had played themselves out to their bitter ends.

The sorrow rose up and double-crossed Ryan when she could least afford to have it come. She was weaker than she or Leslie had realized. When the tears finally did spill forth, they didn't quit for several hours. The labor of grief left Ryan drained and exhausted.

It was nearly midnight before Leslie was able to get Ryan to sleep or to join her weary mate in bed. She was worried because Ryan looked so fragile and helpless, so exposed. She was doubly concerned because when stars crossed for Ryan, they crossed in batches. And when the odds stacked against Leslie, they stacked in heaps.

When she lay next to Ryan her skin tingled and her hair stood on end as though lightning were about to strike in their vicinity. The feeling persisted for several moments and Leslie knew something was seriously wrong. In the same split second that she was going to awaken Ryan to warn her, pandemonium broke loose inside her brain.

177

A deafening, resounding, primordial cry rang out throughout the galaxy. The last thing Leslie saw before she passed out was Ryan's body stiffened into a backward arch of agony.

When Anara quieted her shrill cry of outrage she had before her nearly a dozen souls who had been unwittingly called from their earthly endeavors because of their finely tuned sensitivity to the vibration of Anara's complaint. But, among them, Anara had caught the fish she was hunting for. Unconscious and crumpled in a heap of grey robes was the reason for Anara's distress. Not recognizing or needing any of the others that loitered nearby, Anara dismissed them with a curt wave of her hand and they disappeared.

"Well, Ramonye." Anara addressed the dignified, regal man standing next to her royal chair. *"This,"* Anara snarled and pointed toward the crumpled mass on the floor before her, "is what I must do battle with to ascend to the Throne of Council?" Anara asked in her most unpleasant manner.

"Yes, my Queen," Ramonye replied as he stared adoringly at the lovely Anara. Her deep majestic purple robes outlined her graceful figure in shadows and tempted him to touch her radiant person. "I have inquired about, as you commanded, and learned from more than one source that the Woman of Wings is to be your opponent when next the Throne is vacated."

Anara laughed callously. "This is too easy. That time is nearly upon us and she hasn't even been given her name of power yet."

Ramonye looked away suddenly. He was nervous and worried about making Anara upset with him. He had tried to tell her something after he had betrayed the Woman of Wings, but Anara's shriek of anger came so swiftly, there wasn't time.

Anara turned her head slowly in Ramonye's direction. He was an elegant man, dressed in forest green velvet robes. His sharp, intelligent green eyes appealed to her. She thought to herself that if she cared for men she might have been tempted to take him as a consort. "Have you failed to tell me something, Ramonye?"

He could not, indeed didn't even want to, avoid her penetrating visual inquiry. He made a point of peering directly into her magnificent white eyes and replied, "I believe that she has, my Queen."

Anara's half-smile faded into a frown. "How?" she hissed.

"Not coincidentally, the Goddess of Fire gave it to her."

"Damnation to Perdition!" Anara swore. She sat back in her high-backed chair of amethyst and tapped her long finger on the arm of it while she contemplated the reversal of events.

She stood and walked calmly to her unaware adversary and turned the limp body over with her foot. The action uncovered and revealed the fiery necklace with Blaise's name inscribed within its flaming borders. "I might have known that the one being I couldn't hide this necklace from would be Hestia." Anara disrespectfully referred to the Goddess of Fire by casually using her name of power. "She is here about, isn't she?"

"Yes, my Queen," Ramonye affirmed. "As is the One Who Seeks Knowledge and Justice," he advised carefully, knowing of Anara's fear of their observer. He could easily recognize her presence because of his frequent encounters with her in Council.

Anara whirled around to look behind her. "Where?"

Ramonye cleared his throat politely. "To your left, my Queen. Behind the curtain of silver light."

Anara turned slightly to look at the shimmering mirrored wall. "I wish to see them," she commanded.

"I have my powers and they are strong, but as you well know, males aren't allowed to see behind Veils. The One Who Seeks Knowledge and Justice has always had the power of the Veil. I, myself, have only seen her in her Veiled form. As for the Goddess of Fire, she is seen only when she chooses to be seen."

Anara shuddered and walked back to her seat. It bothered her to know that she was being observed, but she didn't let it show.

--·◆✛❦❦◆·--

Behind the incandescent barrier the One Who Seeks Knowledge and Justice was resting easily on a long comfortable couch. She was lying partially across the lap of the Goddess of Fire, Hestia, and together they were viewing the drama below them.

The Goddess of Fire ran her fiery fingers through the clear hair of her companion and friend. "Blaise has been betrayed by a member of your Council, Venadia." Besides Blaise, the Goddess of Fire was the only being who knew of her companion's name of power or was allowed to view her in an unveiled form.

"So I see, Hestia. I expected little else from Ramonye. He is as greedy for power as is Anara," Venadia replied unhappily.

"But more respectful, my dear," Hestia added. "Did Anara hurt you with her hideous shrill display of anger?" The Goddess turned Venadia to face in her direction, then searched the golden eyes and polished ivory face for any signs of distress.

Venadia returned her look of concern with one of assurance. "I am well, as is my physical body. I fear Blaise's body may have suffered some damage; it is too soon to tell." Venadia found gazing into the scintillating eyes of her Goddess friend soothing and exciting at once. They held no real color of any sort, but radiated light and heat by turns according to the mood of their owner.

Hestia's image embodied flames, taking each characteristic of fire and arranging it as she saw fit, congruent with her company or whims. On the

179

rare occasions when she kept Venadia company, she chose to personify her image and take on the more beautiful, warm aspects of her element.

The special effort did not go unnoticed by Venadia. She knew Hestia wanted more than a sisterly fellowship between them. Even though deepening the intimacy wouldn't threaten her relationship with Blaise, the idea of becoming Hestia's consort made Venadia uneasy. A stirring drew Venadia's attention in the direction of Anara's chamber below.

Anara gave a tempermental flick of her hand to summon her servant to her side. A tall, broad-shouldered woman with bronzed skin approached reverently and quickly—her eyes averted. A straw-colored lining of downy hair covered her smooth scalp. Among the many humiliations and punishments Anara had visited upon her handmaiden for failing in her earthly mission to break the will of their unwilling visitor, Blaise, Anara had had the hair of her servant ripped out by its roots. The hair was just beginning to grow back.

"Fila, my pet. We have a guest, but she is being very rude." Anara motioned toward Blaise. "Go wake her up. Perhaps she can atone for her behavior and be respectful after all," Anara instructed cattily.

"Yes, my Queen," Fila responded carefully. She was both afraid and worshipful of her Mistress and did not trust her. Fila's once graceful walk was marred by a limp, produced when her leg had been purposely twisted out of its socket and never properly replaced. She knelt beside Blaise with her back to Anara. Her heart was beating rapidly from the exhilaration of seeing the woman she had so recently learned to care for during her last stay on earth.

It was beyond Fila's station to address the guest with her name of power. She nudged the grey form and addressed her with her name of growth instead. "Woman of Wings, awaken. You are in the presence of your Queen. Awaken." Her voice commanded a certain power of its own and induced Blaise to consciousness.

Blaise moaned and shook her head to clear it of the darkness of Anara's fierce assault of temper. She focused on the heavily chiseled features of the prototypical amazon leaning over her. Naked to the waist except for a coppery metal serpent that coiled around her neck, Fila appeared to have maintained her strong physique. No outward scars showed anywhere to ruin Fila's proud looks. Blaise smiled at Fila to show that she recognized her new friend.

Fila gazed into Blaise's red eyes longingly and seemed to, fleetingly, beg for forgiveness for what she had done in the physical world as Rags. In the next instant, Fila's dark brown eyes rolled up into her head, her mouth came open and choking gasps sounded in her throat. Her large hand came up to the snake that had come alive suddenly and was tightening its coil about her neck. She grappled with her assailant and fell to the floor next to Blaise.

Blaise straightened herself, then stood cooly, with complete detachment. She knew that if she sought to aid the struggling servant, or in any way took her part, that the punishment would only intensify in its severity and duration.

Instead, she straightened her flowing charcoal robes about her form and smoothed her plentiful smokey-colored hair back into place inside the hood of her garb. She took inventory of her jewels and found all, the garnet ring, fiery necklace and her throat ruby, were in place.

Anara tired of punishing Fila. At once, the snake resumed its seemingly inanimate state, which loosened the grip of agony from about her servant's neck. She dismissed her strangled faithful and turned her thoughts to her opponent.

"Will you not bow and express your fealty?" Anara taunted.

Ramonye laughed quietly. He took great pleasure in Anara's scorn.

Blaise remained standing, proud and silent. She refused to acknowledge Anara's self-assumed title of Queen. She did not owe fealty to her persecutor; they were equals now.

Blaise and Anara stared at one another for a long time, neither of them flinching or blinking.

Finally, Anara pulled away from the visual exchange and turned to Ramonye. "Be a dear and leave us, Ramonye."

Ramonye was offended and showed it. "Yes, my Queen," he agreed sarcastically. He had been looking forward to watching Anara make her opponent uncomfortable in a myriad of ways. He felt that he deserved the chance to witness the goings on in return for the information that he had obtained for Anara. He vanished into a mist and was gone.

# 19

"It still amazes me how Anara has advanced to this stage of power," Venadia bemoaned.

"One might wonder how the Goddess of Light attained her position as well," Hestia countered. She answered the golden-eyed question formed on her friend's face calmly. "With the same ruthless tactics that Anara employs." The Goddess of Fire smiled indulgently in reply to Venadia's disapproving look. "Ah, Venadia. You still seek Justice in matters where Justice does not exist. Power makes no accounting for taste or worthiness," she explained wisely. "It simply is. It is either attained or not, used or misused, but it doesn't make judgments one way or another."

Venadia allowed herself to be gathered into a fond embrace. "I dislike it no less." Her contemptuous mood wavered when she felt a flutter of rapture course through her being as Hestia kissed her lightly on her long silky neck.

Hestia knew of her porcelain fancy's weakness for fire. It was the only weakness she had ever known Venadia to have, and she was sorely tempted to exploit it. But, she mused to herself, there is a time and place for everything, and this is neither.

"I am glad that you listened to me about not allowing anyone besides myself and Blaise to see you without your Veils or learn your name of power. Ramonye would have double-crossed you as well, Venadia, and thought nothing of it," Hestia explained.

"He still thinks Anara is going to let him under her robes, doesn't he?" The two women laughed scoffingly. "He honestly believes that if he continues to give her everything she asks for that he stands a chance of sharing in her power if she succeeds in her bid to become Queen Regent

183

of the Throne of Council. She won't give him another look," Venadia added knowingly.

"You can count on him to keep nosing around about the identities of any and every being that may have something to contribute to this struggle. Now that Anara knows it is Blaise she must do battle with," Hestia warned, "she will want to know who's taking whose part. That means she'll start looking for you. Is there any danger of her finding you?"

"There is a small one now," Venadia admitted.

The Goddess of Fire tightened warily. "How is this so?"

"In the past, I have always made a point of keeping my handmaidens separated when we visit the physical world. One has always been on an island in the Caribbean and the other on the Emerald Isle. Now, they are both with me," Venadia revealed.

"That is not wise, dear," Hestia scolded. "Anyone looking for you in the physical world would recognize your handmaidens, see them both near Blaise, and put two and two together. It wouldn't take much intelligence to surmise that you'd have to be in Veiled hiding nearby."

"It's a done thing, Hestia. Besides," Venadia contended as she drew her fiery companion's gaze to the proceedings below, "I have the feeling that I'm going to need them. I may well have to loosen my grip on my Veil to the extent that I can consciously recall my past life and use some of my powers if Blaise doesn't fare well today."

Hestia sighed, wishing she could hold off the inevitable for a while longer.

---

Anara was still quite angered by being played the fool by her adversary. Her sparkling white eyes flashed dangerously as her vexation mounted. When she finally did speak, she startled Blaise with the fierceness of her voice.

"You will *pay* for this, and pay dearly!" Anara rose from her seat as she threatened Blaise. When she observed Blaise's flinch, she halted her forward progress abruptly and reconsidered her actions. "Temper, temper, Anara," she reproached herself. "She's already afraid of you. You don't want to spoil your fun by letting her have all her punishment at once, do you?" She answered her own question in a low, mocking tone. "No, of course not. Let's draw it out, make it last, savor it."

Blaise followed Anara's actions closely with her haunting red eyes. She was certain that she wasn't afraid of her foe— dangerous and vindictive as Anara could be. But she was weak, weary and alone. Before, when her identity was still unknown to her enemy, she could maintain a balance of power between herself and Anara. Now that Anara had come by a new reason to destroy her, Blaise felt vulnerable.

She tried to maintain a calm exterior, gambling that Anara would grow bored of a one-sided encounter and release her back to the physical world until the time to engage in real combat was at hand.

The pain in her head had subsided; she looked about her surroundings to get her bearings. She smiled inwardly when she sensed the presence of her beloved behind the shimmering Veil above her and to her right. A kind of nourishment strengthened her: a gift from the knowledge of Venadia's undying love.

When she saw Anara motion to Fila, Blaise unexpectedly remembered how utterly by herself she really was in this struggle and was suffused in melancholia. Her shoulders slumped slightly from the weight of her realization, and her passionate heart wept quietly inside itself.

Despite the various horrors that had been inflicted upon her by her Mistress, Fila could still act quickly. Before Anara had fully explained her intentions, Fila saw her opportunity to carry out her first directive. An expert in subduing opponents, Fila took advantage of the split second in which Blaise had seemed to give up the struggle before it was begun.

In a blinking of an eye, Fila pounced upon Blaise and wrestled her to the floor. After a brief struggle, Fila emerged the victor. The larger warrior-woman hoisted her grey-garbed prey to her feet and stood quietly beside her—awaiting further instructions.

Blaise snapped her head upward to fling her tangled locks from her flaring eyes. The hood of her garment had fallen down her back leaving her head bare. Her hands were trussed behind her. Sullenness had undone her, and her own weakened condition had left her a captive.

"Splendid work, Fila!" Anara clapped her hands together gleefully and rose swiftly to inspect the results of the short-lived fight. Satisfied that Blaise was truly her captive, Anara stood before her and smiled broadly. "She *does* have a temper," Anara observed derisively, commenting on the enraged evidence on Blaise's exquisite face.

Blaise responded to her captor by dousing her flames of anger, bringing about, once again, the quiet, proud attitude she maintained in the presence of her enemy.

Anara experienced a vague disappointment when the fire in Blaise's eyes died down. Before her was one of the few souls who would not cower before her. She was beginning to wonder if Blaise really was afraid of her. Still there was a strange excitement simmering beneath the surface of her own calm that she was reluctant to acknowledge. She merely recognized her desire to find an opening in the calm reserve of her opponent.

"Will you not speak to me?" Anara hissed. When it was clear that she was being pointedly ignored, Anara's ire was aroused anew. She grabbed Blaise's jaw meanly and forced the red-eyed beauty to meet her menacing gaze. Her threat was deep-voiced and hollow sounding—frightening. "I will *not* release you back to the physical world until you speak civilly to me." Anara finished the threat with a drawn out pronunciation of her prisoner's name. "Blaise."

Receiving no reply, Anara yanked her hand away and commanded her handmaiden to take Blaise to a lower chamber that she used for punishment and torture. Fila handled Blaise roughly, but encountered no resistance from her.

Inside the steely cold room, Blaise was escorted to and forced to sit upon a bedlike slab that was neither hard or soft but ominous in its presence there. The room was simple and free of distractions; even still, one sensed pain and suffering all about.

Fila sat behind Blaise to guard against any attempts she might make to free herself of her steadfast bonds. Anara joined them, taking a position to the side of the two women that would guarantee her an unobstructed view of the goings-on.

Anara nodded to her devoted amazon, giving her unspoken permission to carry out her orders. Fila reached around Blaise's arms and gathered the volumes of hair that had fallen across her front to place it all neatly down her back. Blaise stared into the empty space, trying to detach herself from the unpredictable objectives of those who held her against her will.

As Fila again reached her searching hands around to the front of their proud guest, Anara warned her servant. "Be careful of her necklace, my pet. It will burn *you.*"

Taking careful notice of the warning, Fila let her large, probing hands gingerly unbutton the grey robe from the neckline to the waist, then triumphantly ripped the garment away from Blaise's stunning breasts.

Anara was thankful that the attentions of her guest and servant were diverted elsewhere. The sight of Blaise's radiant breasts made her suck in her breath with surprise. Her hand had come to her mouth to cover her sudden gasp of excitement. The action had been so deliciously disrespectful—suddenly revealing the chaste bosom to her irreverent gaze.

Blaise gritted her teeth when she felt the long bronze fingers of her assaulter pass, one by one, over her wine-colored nipples. Powerless to stop them, her tips hardened to the rough touch of Fila's massive hands.

Mustering as much patience as she could, Fila made a second pass, upward this time, and felt the knobs tickle the fleshy pads of the insides of her fingers. She hissed quietly then let out her breath passionately. Her hands were tingling and quivering impatiently.

"Touch her more completely," Anara commanded hoarsely. She hadn't expected Blaise's nipples to match her voluptuous wine-stained lips. Tiny shocks of need were beginning to make themselves known in the vicinity of her belly. Fleeting memories of a striking, provocative youth named Korian—her protege during her last visit to the physical world—forced their way into her mind and distracted her ever so briefly.

Hesitation was not Fila's way. She let her hands descend upon the vulnerable well-shaped mounds and began to maul them savagely. Her mighty fingers dug into the soft flesh, bruising the womanly orbs and in places, breaking the skin or raising tiny blood blisters. She seized the nipples between her thumbs and forefingers and rolled them cruelly. She pulled at them and stretched them out from their breasts, then rubbed the ends of her thumbs over the stimulated tips.

At last, after some time of being brutally handled, Anara saw the first indication of Blaise's downfall.

Anara watched closely as the plentiful charcoal locks began to sink further down Blaise's back seemingly from their own weight. Little by little, Blaise's long neck was beginning to arch backward. The placid expression on her oval face had yet to transform, but her chest was showing signs of heaving, and her marvelous head was relaxing back and back toward passion, toward surrender.

Anara was both thrilled and dismayed by this. The sooner that her victim succumbed, the more prowess Anara felt. Her ego was swelling, but so was her desire. Her need. Her . . . she couldn't even think it. To distract herself from the echoes of her past, she turned her attention to her handmaiden and was surprised by what she saw.

Beads of sweat shone on Fila's dark skin. Her mouth was open slightly and Anara could hear her breathing becoming more and more raspy. Her eyes were feverish and veiled with a sheen of lust. It was a look Anara knew well, and missed. It had been some time since she had inspired such a response in her virile sex object.

"Why, Fila. It has been ages since you've been so aroused. Have you grown tired of me?" Anara taunted. But she seriously wanted to know.

Fila cast her passion-filled look upon her Mistress. Without disturbing her concentrated mishandling of the prize in her heated grip, she answered sincerely, "Never, my Queen. I adore you above all others. My excitement is born of your show of kindness and of the knowledge that the Woman of Wings is powerless to prevent my touch."

Anara smiled warmly. "I see. Indeed she is at your mercy. Your work is as efficient as ever, my sweet." She blew a kiss in Fila's direction. "She weakens steadily." Anara was now confident, assured. She was certain that Fila would succeed and, by way of an early reward, she let her hand trail along Fila's muscular thigh, under the simple loose skirt downward in search of the charged, erect nub that urgently awaited her touch.

She caressed her frequent bed partner intimately with the hard circular motion Fila loved best. Fila moaned and hissed and nearly swooned from the intense power of her own excitement. She hadn't thought it was possible to be any more severe in her attack upon Blaise's breasts, but she managed to find a way.

Blaise tightened the grip of her jaws to keep from crying out from the unbearable pain and unthinkable desire her assailant was filling her with. It was useless.

Her chest was expanding to capacity, then deflating fully, then filling again. It felt as though someone had tied weight after weight to her hair. Weights that were pulling her head back irresistibly. Her lips parted slightly. Her breath began to whistle through her teeth. Her self-control was quitting her—even more suddenly so when she heard Fila's moans from behind her rising to a crescendo.

Anara was in *complete* control of every action and being there. With her unequalled ability to manipulate events, Anara increased the force of her touch, undoing her servant entirely.

Fila stiffened for an instant, then from her depths she let go a fierce, deafening, victorious war cry. When she could no longer bear the searing bliss of Anara's attentions, her body collapsed onto the bed. She slid down the other side of passion and let the electric warmth engulf her, then let it pull her into a peaceful, dark faint.

Fila's need disposed of, Anara turned her thoughts to her own. Giving no warning, Anara thrust Blaise upon the bed next to her unconscious amazon and began to kiss Blaise heatedly.

Blaise yanked her head from Anara's grasp, refusing to allow the kisses to take hold or to come into contact with her mouth. She could not bear the thought of kissing her enemy. Her pride rose up and added strength to her fight. She squirmed about, frantically, trying to wrestle free of her degrading bonds. Her thoughts were consumed with revulsion and determination to end the struggle once and for all.

—··◆❧❦❧◆··—

Hestia felt Vanadia's hand tighten around hers as they watched Anara intensify her fervent kisses and draw her body closer to her victim.

Venadia tried to laugh at Anara's antics, but she was concerned. "When I sought the Throne of Council, my opponent tried a similar approach to weaken my ability to fight. It was a miserable ordeal; she only succeeded in making a fool of herself," Venadia explained nervously.

"No small wonder," the Goddess of Fire observed. "Passion isn't exactly your strong suit, Venadia. Blaise is just beginning to teach you of it in the physical world."

"You're not worried, then?" Venadia asked anxiously.

"Very. Blaise is made of passion; she thrives on it. Anara is no fool, my dear. Something is wrong here, and I don't like it," Hestia warned.

"Nor do I." Venadia toyed with the black diamond scalloping around her neckline that symbolized her eternal love for the fiery woman in the chamber below her. She began to mouth her prayers, then to verbalize them. "Resist, my darling. Hold fast against her seductive ways. Be strong."

But as she feared, Anara finally did join her lips to those of Blaise, and Blaise's struggle slowly began to diminish. Venadia came to the edge of her couch, her eyes growing large with horror as her worst fear was becoming a reality.

Blaise's sensuous body wasn't squirming fitfully from side to side any longer. It was flowing and swaying. Anara reached around to unfasten the bonds, and Blaise's freed hands grasped the womanly body that had subdued her.

Venadia turned her harried expression on the Goddess of Fire. "Tell me this isn't so, Hestia. Tell me that Blaise is playing a trick on Anara.

This is a deception, it must be."

"I don't think so." Hestia shook her head gravely. "Something is still not right. I do not like this, Venadia."

— ◦ ◗∤ ⊱◦ —

Blaise held Anara's wonderful head tightly in her arms as Anara soothed away the bruises on her milky breasts with kisses that lingered on the verge of full-blooded passion. She barely noticed the tiny tugs on her robe as Anara finished unfastening her garment to lay open her naked need. She, too, was beginning to remember the unmatched physical chemistry that she had once shared with Anara in the physical world when she was but a young girl. How Anara had chosen her from a group of aspiring celebrants, taken her to the blessed chambers of the High Priestess, and on their first night together, how Anara had thrilled her young body in ways that had left an indelible mark upon her. A mark that pointed to glorious, unbridled desire and total lasting fulfillment.

The power and persuasion of Anara's sexual expertise proved irresistible to Blaise and she gave in to it. It was even more ecstatic in the spirit world than she had ever recalled it being in her former physical expression as Korian.

But the one need that was the most gratified by the experience was her need to rid herself of her loneliness. There was something so divinely comforting about Anara's lovemaking that Blaise found she was completely relieved of her melancholia. She wasn't alone any longer and that meant everything to her.

For as much as Anara would allow, Blaise returned the intimate caresses. Afterwards they slept for awhile. When Blaise awakened, Fila had gone and Anara was gazing into her eyes with a gentleness that she had not seen in thousands of years. Blaise mirrored their softness, and they were lost in one another's eyes for a small eternity.

The transition had not been conscious on the part of either woman. They had simply come to the same place at the same time. Enmity was a thing of the past, and forgiveness took its place. It seemed perfectly natural for each of them to speak. What they spoke, in their semi-private chamber, would shake the unshakable.

Blaise watched the words form on Anara's heavenly salmon-colored lips even as they formed on her own sensuous wine-tinted mouth. "I love you," was all each said to the other—in perfect accord.

— ◦ ◗∤ ⊱◦ —

"WHAT?!" Venadia sprang off her couch suddenly. Her surprise and anger were so complete that she nearly lost her hold on the Veil that protected them from being seen by Anara and Blaise alike.

The Goddess of Fire was so shocked that her compact form lost its shape briefly. Her visible self flared and sparkled into the incandescent, white-hot image that reflected her uncontained rage . . .

Once the initial shock wave had stormed throughout the world in which they ruled, Venadia and Hestia began to settle down and restore calm to their beings.

Hestia could see that Venadia was still shaking and in need of comfort. She approached her easily and was not rebuffed. The time when Venadia would have to return to her physical body was all too near and they were both aware of it. Hestia was going to miss Venadia, more than she had realized. Hearing Anara and Blaise proclaim their love for each other—however illegal, without precedent, or painful to Venadia—raised a genuine hope within Hestia that she might succeed in her attempt to lure her beautiful friend into a love relationship of their own. She felt certain that she could make up for Venadia's speechless tears and deep sense of loss.

Her voice was soft and tender when she bid Venadia farewell. "No matter what, my darling, I will always love you."

# EPILOGUE

As it was meant to be, Sanji was the one who discovered the out-of-body condition of her Master and Mistress. Because she had seen Ryan in that state before, she knew what to do to keep their physical bodies safe in their absence. For the two days that Ryan and Leslie appeared to be "gone," their bedroom was kept dark and quiet. No one disturbed them, but they all worried and prayed that all would be well.

Their prayers were answered and both heads of the McKinley Mansion reoccupied their bodies, safe and sound. Ryan's body had, miraculously, survived Anara's painful summons and she appeared none the worse for wear. Leslie returned to a well-rested, relaxed form.

A sort of dull ache settled into the rest of the household when, after a short time, Sanji and Corelle, as well as every member of the staff, began to realize that something or someone had come between these lovers. It was intangible at best and only vaguely noticeable. Ryan was becoming withdrawn if even slightly unreachable. Leslie seemed hurt and her peaceful nature faltered at times in favor of a grim determination, peppered occasionally with flickerings of aggressive hostilities.

Leslie had made a point of returning to the physical world with full knowledge of who she was and what she was about, including memory of *her* last lifetime along with the true identities of Sanji and Corelle as well as their significance to her.

She chose a warm, languid day at the end of the seventh month to solicit the support of the two younger women. She gathered them under the shade of her favorite linden tree and sat quietly with them for a short time before speaking. For this conversation, Leslie had found it necessary to give permission to both servants to speak freely.

"Let me tell you the story," Leslie began softly, "of how we all came to be here in this place together." She settled Corelle's head on her lap and absently unpinned her long hair. Sanji brought her attention around to her Mistress and shifted to a more comfortable position on the blanket they shared.

"It started three thousand years ago in the land now called Ireland. Your Master had another name then. She was known as Korian and was quite lovely, appealing and gifted in the areas of spiritual growth. When she was just ten years of age, she was picked by the High Priestess Anara to be Anara's apprentice. That was fine; Korian needed to learn from her. But what I could only see now is that something very unfortunate happened. They fell in love and became lovers as well as teacher and pupil." Leslie leaned against the tree trunk and sighed. It hurt her to go on, but she had to.

She soothed herself by laying Corelle's mass of hair across the distance of blanket between her leg and Sanji's arm, then ran her fingers through its chestnut fullness. "Sanji, as you have begun to recall, you were alive then and there as well. Your name was Lizack and you, too, had fallen in love with Korian." Leslie noticed Sanji's head nod her agreement.

"I was Korian's mother, and it was with my guarded approval that Korian entered into Anara's service." Neither of her servants seemed surprised by the revelation. Leslie didn't really expect them to be. "The years passed and Korian grew and learned, but one day she began to see what I had warned her about—a selfishness and cruelty in Anara that was inconsistent with how she thought a High Priestess should behave. There was a meanness about Anara and her handmaiden Fila that gave Korian pause to reconsider her love for Anara.

"As I had expected her to do, Korian began to plot and scheme with the other members of her clan to kill Anara. Lizack's aid was solicited to do the actual killing. She found a way to poison Anara and was quick and sure about the whole matter."

Corelle shifted uneasily to draw Leslie's attention to herself. "What is it, dear?" Leslie invited the participation of the young woman.

"Milady, this concerns me. Are you not worried about having someone who has murdered once before to eliminate competition for our Master's heart, living with you now? Might she try the same thing once more?" Corelle asked nervously. She wanted to express her question with her eyes directed toward her Mistress, but didn't.

Sanji sat up and hugged her knees while stealing furtive sideways glances in Leslie's direction. She was trying to judge the state of mind of her Mistress and was beginning to fear for her position.

Leslie noticed Sanji's ill-ease and reached out for her. With a gentle stroke near Sanji's elbow she transmitted that she was free of worry or animosity. Tentatively, Sanji began to relax.

"I'm not at all concerned that history might repeat itself here," Leslie reassured. "Where do you think Lizack got the poison she used for the assassination?"

Sanji and Corelle's eyes widened with astonishment. In unison they breathlessly searched for verification. "From you?!"

"Indeed. I felt that Korian was ready to serve in Anara's stead and was all for ending Anara's misguided life." For no apparent reason, Leslie was saddened and sighed deeply. She looked away from her handmaidens to the distance, seeing nothing but feeling everything.

Sanji and Corelle searched one another's eyes for comfort and found themselves forming a pact between them. They were beginning to sense that they somehow belonged together in service to their Mistress.

Corelle worked for Leslie's attention again and was allowed to voice any question she had. "I do not know why you are sharing this past with me since I was not there, nor do I understand why you are showing kindness toward Sanji after so long of hating her."

Leslie smiled a little before going on. Corelle's questions made her realize just how innocent the girl really was. "It is true that you were not nearby in the physical world when all this was taking place. Even still, you were alive and free from harm. You have always been the gentle and more innocent of my handmaidens. Your absence was by design—it was necessary that you be far away to help keep my identity from being disclosed before I was ready. I have softened my attitude toward Sanji because we have to work together now. I can't afford to have bitterness and petty squabbling among us.

"My darlings, you have been my handmaidens since before time was measured. You have always done my bidding, no matter what the situation or cost." Leslie paused momentarily in her elaboration to reflect upon the recent events that had led to her needing to change the relationship between herself and Sanji.

During that pause, Sanji and Corelle drew closer to Leslie, holding out their hands in recognition and allegiance. Leslie touched each of them gratefully before going on. "The truth is that I was mistaken in my assessment of Anara. I had no idea just how vindictive she would be. The cost to Sanji has been very dear, but moreso, it has been devastating to your Master.

"For many years she has suffered immeasurably at the hand of Anara's handmaiden, Fila." To explain for Corelle, Leslie expanded. "Corelle, you never knew her, but when Rags (Fila) was alive she devoted her life to punishing everyone who participated in Anara's murder. Except Sanji, whom you know was inadvertantly punished by your Master. And, of course, myself. Anara never knew of my part in her death, and still doesn't. I've always been very careful around her. Anara considers me a minor irritation, at best, so she doesn't pay any attention to what I'm doing, except when she wants to see how I react to her feeble attempts to come between Ryan and me.

"For the most part, I never do what she thinks I ought to do. Because she thinks of me as insignificant and doesn't consider me a threat, she hasn't given my inconsistent behavior much thought."

Absently, and somewhat worried, Leslie added quietly, "That can't last much longer."

Corelle shifted her weight uncomfortably, bringing Leslie back to the present and the heart of the matter. "As I said before, I hadn't foreseen Korian and Anara becoming lovers, nor had I considered *that* to be a threat. Alas, it has become a very big threat—to everything. While Ryan and I were "away," Anara wormed her way back into your Master's heart and, it seems, that all has been forgiven. They have fallen back in love."

"No!" Sanji exclaimed frantically. "My Master *hates* Anara. They are enemies and so they must remain." Sanji's blood-pressure rose and, in the heat, she broke out into a full sweat. The thought of all her suffering being spent trying to keep Anara and her Master apart going to waste was nearly more than she could bear.

"I, too, wish them to remain enemies, but it is not so," Leslie affirmed. "Anara does not yet know that I have learned of this, which is to our advantage." Leslie stilled Sanji's irrational reaction with a steady grasp of the black woman's hand. With her other, she took Corelle's tiny extremity and squeezed it with equal firmness. "We must remain calm about this or we will lose before we have begun. Your Master needs love, lots of it. More than most people. She is well loved in this household, but she must be made to feel moreso. I have no idea what form your Master's response to Anara's love will take, but whatever it is, we *must* be patient with her. I have the very strong feeling that it will not be easy to do and that our limits will be tested sorely.

"The three of us here, and Bonnie, have to stand by her, no matter what, or we will lose her forever. And I mean—forever," Leslie emphasized unhappily. For the first time in her life, she was afraid. Truly afraid.

Corelle voiced what none of them ever really doubted. "Milady, we will stand by you in all things. We cannot lose this battle, for life would not be worth living if we failed."

Leslie brought each of her servant's hands to her chest and sighed bravely. Their devotion was reaffirmed on that overly warm afternoon as they pledged to fight, despite their fear, until the bitter end, to save the love between their Master and their Mistress.

Leslie, herself, reaffirmed her promise to Ryan, resolving to stand firm against any and all perils, to preserve her everlasting love for her beloved.

# GLOSSARY OF NAMES

Aisling MacSweeney—Brigid MacSweeney's mother.

Anara—In past lifetime three thousand years ago she was High Priestess of a Pagan clan.

In spirit world she is a demi-goddess bent on revenge against the members of her clan who were responsible for her death. She is in contention for the title of Queen Regent of the Throne of Council. Name of growth: The Contender. Name of power: Anara

Blaise—In an earlier lifetime she was Korian, Anara's lover and apprentice to become High Priestess.

In current lifetime she is Ryan O'Donnell, Leslie's lover.

In spirit world she is Anara's opposition to the title of Queen Regent of the Throne of Council. She is Venadia's lover. Name of growth: Woman of Wings. Name of power: Blaise.

Bonnie—The woman who helped Patrick O'Donnell raise Ryan; head of Ryan's household staff.

Brigid MacSweeney—Ryan's cousin and best friend; Star's lover.

Brody Latham—Christine Latham's father.

Christine Latham—Young woman who had an illegal love affair with Ryan.

Contender—Anara's name of growth.

Corelle—Leslie's personal servant and handmaiden.

Dana Shaeffer—Ryan's ex-lover, Delores Rhinehart's current lover, Brigid's mistress.

David Martin—Rags' parole officer when she was alive.

Delores Rhinehart—Leslie's former law partner, Dana's lover.

Devnet Fitzmaurice O'Donnell—Ryan's deceased mother.

Fila—Anara's handmaiden in former life three thousand years past.
 In recent lifetime she was Rags, serving as Anara's agent of revenge.
 In spirit world she is Anara's handmaiden.

Goddess of Fire—Exists in the spirit world and is in love with Venadia. Name of power: Hestia.

Hestia—Goddess of Fire's name of power.

Korian—In lifetime three thousand years past she was Anara's lover and apprentice to become High Priestess of the Pagan clan.
 In current lifetime she is Ryan O'Donnell, Leslie's lover.
 In spirit world she is Blaise, Venadia's lover, Anara's opposition to the title of Queen Regent of the Throne of Council. Name of growth: Woman of Wings. Name of power: Blaise.

Leslie Anne Serle—Ryan's lover. Three thousand years ago, in a past life, she was Korian's mother.
 In the spirit world she is the current holder of the title of Queen Regent of the Throne of Council; Blaise's lover. Name of growth: One Who Seeks Knowledge and Justice. Name of power: Venadia.

Lizack—In her existence three thousand years ago she was in love with Korian and was the one who murdered Anara.
 In her current lifetime she is Ryan's sex-slave Sanji.

One Who Seeks Knowledge and Justice—Venadia's (Leslie's) name of growth. Current holder of the title of Queen Regent of the Throne of Council. Blaise's (Ryan's) lover.

Patrick O'Donnell—Ryan's deceased father.

Phil Peterson—Ryan's aviation mentor, business partner and father figure.

Rags—In her first former life she was Fila, Anara's handmaiden in the Pagan clan.
 In her most recent life existence (as Rags) she was Ryan's friend and persecutor. She was sent by Anara to destroy Ryan's will and failed.
 In the spirit world she is Fila, Anara's handmaiden.

Ryan O'Donnell—Central figure. Three thousand years ago she was Korian, Anara's lover and protege.
 In her current life she is Leslie's lover and Anara's enemy.
 In the spirit world she is Blaise, Venadia's (Leslie's) lover and Anara's

opposition to the title of Queen Regent of the Throne of Council. Name of growth: Woman of Wings. Name of power: Blaise.

Sanji Charles—In her former life she was Lizack who was in love with Korian and was the one who murdered Anara.

In her current lifetime she is Ryan's sex-slave and Leslie's handmaiden.

Sean MacSweeney—Brigid's father, Patrick O'Donnell's cousin, Ryan's cousin.

Star—Brigid's lover.

Susan Benson—Leslie's former law partner.

Venadia—In a former life she was Korian's mother.

In her current life she is Leslie, Ryan's lover.

In the spirit world she is the current holder of the title of Queen Regent of the Throne of Council. Name of growth: One Who Seeks Knowledge and Justice. Name of power: Venadia.

Woman of Wings—Blaise's name of growth. In the spirit world she is Blaise, Venadia's (Leslie's) lover and Anara's opposition to the title of Queen Regent of the Throne of Council.

Zina Latham—Christine Latham's mother.

# OTHER BOOKS
# OF INTEREST